The Wilby Conspiracy

The Wilby Conspiracy

by

PETER DRISCOLL

J. B. LIPPINCOTT COMPANY
Philadelphia and New York

U.S. Library of Congress Cataloging in Publication Data

Driscoll, Peter, birth date
    The Wilby conspiracy.
    I. Title.
PZ4.D7816Wi3   [PR6054.R53]   823'.9'14   72–3629
ISBN–0–397–00947–X

For my mother and father

Part I

ISLAND

1

The night was cold. The black man had not thought much about the cold, although he was chilled to the bone. He could not stop shivering, but otherwise he had kept as still as he could for two hours among the hydrangeas next to the carpentry shed, waiting for darkness.

He sat staring across the road. Beyond the high barbed-wire fence on the other side all outlines had merged—the rocks, the shore, the dark sweep of the bay. Seven miles across it stood the flat mountain, etched against the sky by a glow from the city below it. Now it was time to go, but first he waited for the car he had seen approaching to pass. The engine noise grew over the rush of the surf; then its head-lights were dancing on the blistered yellow paint of the cor-rugated-iron shed, picking out the long shimmering strands of barbed wire. The noise subsided; the tail lights dwindled towards the warders' village and the lighthouse that stood winking at the south end of the island.

The wind blowing off the sea made his nose run, cut through his thin woolen jersey and drill shorts, and searched, like the impersonal cold white fingers of a warder, in secret parts of his body. There was a hollow place in his stomach and an ache in his chest, as if his heart had been beating too fast for too long. Now he was strangely reluctant to move but he stood up, blew his nose quietly into his hand, and wiped it on the wall of the shed. He looked back once to where he had come from before moving carefully out of the shadows and across the road.

Behind him the Kliptronk, the maximum-security block where the important people were kept, stood low and white and floodlit like a monument on rising ground cleared of vegetation. Beyond that, and mostly out of sight, were the buildings that formed the New Prison, among them a place called the Knifers' Camp. About twenty minutes ago Jake should have left the Knifers' Camp in a bin full of pig food, and by now he ought to be waiting with the boat.

The man walked with a limp. The cold had made his foot hurt ever since the heel had been splintered by a bullet; it was something he was quite used to. He reached the fence and stood by one of the iron posts where there would be least play on the wire as he climbed. He felt along the strands at either side of the post, finding holds between the barbs for his hands and bare feet, and hoisted himself up. The fence was not difficult. The angled part at the top projected outwards so it was just a matter of getting balanced on the upper strands, keeping clear of the barbs, and jumping. The wind tugged at him as he went up, one strand at a time, feeling with hands and toes for the gaps between the barbs before putting his weight on them. Suddenly the rhythm of the surf, surging against rocks fifty yards away, seemed much louder, and he had a moment of excitement that turned to a monstrous uncertainty. He closed his eyes and hung on the wire for a few seconds, listening to the sea and the pounding of his heart. Then he went on climbing. It was nothing important, this fear; it was only that over the years he had lost the will to assert himself. He had sensed an erosion that began on the night he and Wilby had been flushed out of their car on the border like a pair of frightened hares. There'd been a shot and his foot had gone awkward and heavy as he ran, and his mind had been numb with the knowledge of betrayal. It had seemed to matter a lot then. Now all he wanted was to redeem some favours and find exile.

The fence wobbled slightly under his weight as he reached the top. He clung tightly to the post and worked his hands into a grip that would give him enough elevation to vault. His palms were sweating in spite of the cold. He steadied himself and jumped.

He did not quite clear the wire. He felt a barb tear at his right leg as he flung himself outward and down. But he landed lightly on his feet in the short grass and rolled to break the fall, stood up, and dabbed at the blood that began to run down his calf. Then he walked towards the sea. A few yards from the fence the grassy ground shelved away onto rocks leading down to the water. He groped his way to the edge and slithered onto the rocks. It was too dark to see far, but he knew exactly where he had thrown the oars. In a minute he had them both—eight feet long, the poles crudely turned and the chiselled blades a bit too narrow, but what more could you ask? He'd had to work quickly, right under the bulbous alcoholic nose of the supervising warder in the carpentry shed. In fact he was pleased with himself; he liked to think of them talking about him afterwards as a *slim* kaffir, one of the clever ones. He got the oars balanced on one shoulder and glanced back again. The Kliptronk stood silent and white half a mile away, and the lighthouse winked at him furtively. Nothing appeared to move. He was safe till the section head warder did his rounds in an hour's time.

The boat was just a hundred yards to the south but he had to go carefully, limping over the rocks and the slimy kelp that clung to them. His feet were as hard as oxhide; his footing was surest, like his thoughts, when he could move unhurriedly.

The boat was Jake's and the oars were his own. They were his price for a share in the boat, and he could not help feeling he had done well out of the bargain. He didn't know much about Jake: he was from Port Elizabeth and was doing the first year of a bluejacket for sticking some whore with a knife. They made it hard for his kind too. In the Knifers' Camp they broke stones most of the time, but they were also sent out on seaweed parties, carrying armfuls of stinking kelp off the rocks and beaches into the sea. That was how Jake had found the dinghy, just washed up there on the rocks where the last winter storm had left it. The fisherman who'd owned it must have taken the oars overboard with him, but he'd been decent enough to leave the rowlocks. There was life for you. You sat here twelve years, and some Xosa who hadn't even had time to sweat away his fat beery guts went and found a boat. Everybody knew it was the only way off the island. In the old days the place had been a leper colony, and there were stories about lepers who'd swum the seven miles. Maybe one out of ten had made it; the rest would have drowned or died of cold. From the north-east it was only four miles across to Bloubergstrand, but the current there was too strong and would carry you out to sea. Everybody knew that as well. Everybody had the data of escape at his fingertips but no one ever did it.

The man stopped, faintly aware that something was wrong. He was close to the water. In the dark the line of rocks sprawled confusingly together, but this was certainly the small inlet where Jake had found the boat and sunk it. And Jake was not here.

So he was late. Was he? Perhaps he himself was too early. With a slight sense of panic he wondered if he had lost track of the time, and now he was listening for the sirens as if waiting for a bullet in the back.

They couldn't have been missed because the sirens would have sounded, right? He tried to keep calm. They hadn't been stupid, he and Jake; they had thought about this. If one of them couldn't make it, the other was to take the boat and the oars. All right. But he was frozen by a thought that he scarcely dared to acknowledge, that Jake had been lying, that there was no boat. Why should he lie? No answer. He had only Jake's word for it that the boat existed, and whose word could you rely on in this place? Whose sanity, for that matter?

The terrible mistrust of himself swept through him again, this thing that white men had planted in his soul, that made him afraid to act, even afraid to be free. Suddenly he did not want the burden of freedom but knew it was too late to choose. He dropped the oars and scrambled into the water. It was shallow for a few yards out, with soft sand underfoot and kelp slithering around his ankles. The wind threw spray into his face and then a wave came in, waist high, and almost knocked him over. His shorts clung unpleasantly to his crotch as he waded through a formless maze of rocks and water, feeling his confusion grow. It must have been freezing, but he was too cold now for it to make much difference. It made the cut on his leg sting, that was all, and his foot ached even more.

He blew his nose and flicked the mucus off his palm into the sea. His shin struck something and he fell forward, raising his hands to protect himself. The fingers closed on the edge of a regular solid object a foot below the surface. Ignoring the wave that washed over him he staggered to his feet, gauging incredulously the shape of the thing in the water. Then with an excited surge of energy he seized the gunwale and heaved the dinghy onto its side.

He had dared to believe it did not exist, and still it was there. He dragged it into shallower water, stumbling and grazing himself on rocks and barnacles. The wood was soft and water-swollen but still sound. Righting it again, he began baling water furiously with his cupped hands. When there were still six inches slopping about in the bottom he stopped. That would do, that would keep him afloat. Now he could be sure Jake was not coming. So bad luck, Jake. Thanks, Jake, and bye-bye. He fetched the oars and laid them across the thwarts.

Very distinctly he heard a single rifle shot on the far side of the island. It sent a rippling echo back from the prison buildings into the wind. There was a minute of silence in which the night seemed to hold its breath, and then the first siren began its harsh wail.

His skin prickled with terror. He flung himself into the dinghy. With hands that had turned to rubber he jammed the oars into the rowlocks and pushed the boat clumsily off the rocks. He dug the blades into the water and rowed out into the heaving sea.

The noise of the sirens floated, slightly muffled, into a room below the lamp chamber of the lighthouse where three white men waited. Two of them, who wore the khaki uniform of the prisons service, had already exchanged a glance and were watching the third man.

He had done nothing. He had hardly moved for two hours except to light one cigarette after another and occasionally to use the heavy binoculars he had brought with him. Otherwise he simply stared out of the window across the bay. It was doubtful whether he had seen what he was looking for, with or without the glasses. He was small and dark and curly-haired, with a pinched face and a military sort of moustache that exaggerated the downward turn of his mouth. Every time he had visited the island he had worn the same suit, which had shiny patches at the elbows and smelt vaguely of tobacco. Marais, the younger of the two prison officers, had noticed his odd way of looking past people when he spoke to them. Marais found him very difficult to talk to. But it was time somebody spoke.

"They were on their toes," he said, and thought at once that it sounded banal.

"Good," the civilian said. He turned towards them at last. "That's very good. Just one shot, over on the airport side. You placed your men well."

"We'd better wait and see whether it worked, Mr. Horn."

"I think it will be all right. I want to say we've worked well together. I want to say that, Colonel."

The colonel shrugged. He considered his position usurped. Three phone calls to the most influential people he knew in Pretoria had failed to help him against Horn, and he had taken refuge in indifference.

Marais was the night duty officer for the New Prison. He said, "I'll be needed for the search parties." In fact he did not want to go and lingered at the window.

"I'll come with you," Horn said, "if that's all right with the colonel? I'd like to see for myself, *hoe lyk dit daar.*"

His speech had a quality common in the north, a coarseness that seemed to mock the meticulous accent of the Cape Afrikaner. Marais sensed a kind of resentment in it. They liked to think of themselves as pioneers up there, plain speakers, men of the soil even if, like Horn, they belonged to a generation of farmers' sons who had lost their birthright and been forced like bewildered peasants into the mining towns. Marais collected his torch, greatcoat, and swagger stick and led the others down the spiral staircase. At the door in the base of the lighthouse he stopped. "The one with the boat," he said. "You reckon he got away?"

"I can't be sure, of course." Horn looked at some point over Marais's shoulder.

"And if he didn't?"

"I think it will be all right," Horn said.

They drove in Marais's Volkswagen past the airport and the radar station. All the sirens were wailing now, and lights had come on in the cells and along the catwalks of the Kliptronk. Half way up the west coast the truck that carried kitchen leavings every night to the piggery had pulled awkwardly off the road. There were two other vans with their headlights blazing, and a dozen men were moving about in the glare. Two others were crouched over a shape that lay under a greatcoat in the middle of the road.

A head warder stepped up to the car and said, "We were looking for you, Lieutenant." He saw the colonel in the back seat, came to attention, and saluted. "Then you know? This one was shot jumping off the back of the pig truck. Appears he hid in one of the bins and got the others to carry him out. We checked the cells and found another one missing from A section." He consulted a notebook. "Shishak Mavela Twala. Age forty, C category, Zulu."

"Political?" said Marais.

"Assisting the aims of a banned organization. Suppression of Communism Act. Separate convictions in sixty-one, sixty-five—"

"All right," Marais said. "What about this one, is he badly wounded?"

"I couldn't say. The doctor's here. . . . Jacob Zamela," the head warder said, turning a page in his notebook. "Age thirty-two. Xosa. He's not political. Eleven to fifteen years, attempted murder. The dog teams are out already. Any special instructions?"

The colonel seemed about to say something, then changed his mind. The three of them got out of the car and approached the wounded man. "It's funny," said the head warder, coming up behind them. "He got into the pig bin and then had to sit for half an hour in that locked yard behind the kitchen. Appears somebody mixed up the drivers' rosters."

"Really," said Marais. He spotted the boy who had done the shooting. He was no more than twenty, with short fair hair set squarely on top of his head, the way his cap had moulded it. The R1 rifle looked almost too big for him to handle; he was transferring it from one hand to the other.

"Let me see that, Claassen." Marais took the rifle, unshipped the magazine, pumped a cartridge out of the breech, and began deliberately levering out and counting the live ammunition. He needed something to do. He did not think the boy had exceeded his authority.

"Lieutenant told me to expect something," Claassen said. He lapsed nervously into the childish third person.

"Lieutenant didn't tell you that. I said we'd have a detail along this road at night in future, that's all. You needn't make a special point of it in your statement."

"Yes, Lieutenant."

Marais wondered if Claassen was intelligent enough to draw any further conclusions. Probably not. He walked into the white glare of the headlights and made himself look down.

Jake lay on his back. The greatcoat had been pulled down to his waist and the drill jacket unbuttoned so that the doctor could see the wound. He was unconscious and his face, soaked in sweat, was formless like a lump of melting chocolate. The blood on his clothes was mixed with a grey slime of mealie porridge, coffee grounds, and gravy.

The doctor finished probing, looked up, and saw the colonel. "It's the lower lung mainly," he said. "Perhaps some other organic damage. Can't tell till I get an X-ray up at the hospital."

"Will he live?" the colonel asked woodenly.

The doctor hesitated. An ambulance had arrived, and he signalled irritably to the stretcher bearers. "These high-velocity bullets nowadays go straight through tissue and bone like a knife through butter. There's nothing solid enough to stop them, they hardly slow down, no cushioning effect. So while you get a nice clean wound, you'll often find that the central nervous system simply collapses under the shock."

Marais envied the doctor the honesty of his work, even its transparent euphemisms. He watched the stretcher being guided into the ambulance and the doors slam on it. The head warder, who was about to drive the colonel back to the administration block, said confidingly, "That other one, Twala. He's been working in the carpentry shed."

"Yes?"

"Potgieter down there is too lax with his prisoners. Doesn't do a proper mustering. Appears Twala didn't even come back with the team at five o'clock."

"I'll see Potgieter in the morning," Marais said.

"Drinks," said the head warder significantly. "Anyway, the little hell won't get off the island."

The vehicles began moving away. In a minute Marais found himself standing alone with Horn. "Are you satisfied?" he said.

"Reasonably." The Transvaal man sidestepped the irony. He was lighting another cigarette. "Are you sending boats out?"

"It's routine," Marais said. "You wanted everything to be routine."

"But they won't look too hard, of course."

"There must have been a different way of doing this," Marais said on an impulse.

Horn looked past him. "It was the best way. . . . I didn't say I liked it," he added after a pause.

"You liked it enough to do it."

"This kaffir knew there was a risk," Horn said imperturbably. "He was prepared to take it. People who do that class of thing to their friends always expect a stab in the back."

"I wish you'd do your own stabbing, that's all."

Marais knew he was being rash, but Horn's reaction was mild. He blew smoke from his nostrils and said, "Do you believe in this country?"

"Yes."

"Do you believe we must do things our own way, make our own future?"

"What the hell has that got to do with it?"

"It's no good having faith unless you're ready to fight for it, Marais. That means attacking sometimes, not just defending. It means dirtying your hands. I think it's a small price to pay for the sake of the future, eh? For the sake of keeping Christian, civilized men in control of our future. Our men."

Marais wondered why he had not recognized the faint glint of fanaticism in Horn's eyes before. He had really learnt only one thing about the man, and that was to distrust almost everything he said.

"Don't worry about tonight," Horn advised him. "Are you a fisherman? I've been an angler all my life. Did you ever fish at some of those Transvaal dams?"

"No."

"Listen, there are really big barbel up there. Ugly old men with long whiskers. They weigh up to a hundred pounds sometimes, and they stay right down on the bottom, in the mud. The best bait you can use is a flat frog called a *plat anna,* from the same water. Use a small hook to catch your *plat anna,* then tie him to a three-inch hook and sink him to the bottom. Make sure he stays alive, wriggling. And when you feel your barbel take the bait—no, you don't strike yet, you let him run. You let that old man turn away and run a little so that the hook will take him in the side of the mouth. The upper and lower jaws, you see, are nothing but bone and lots of little teeth, like strips of sandpaper."

Marais stared at him.

"Maybe it doesn't interest you," Horn said, unabashed.

"What I'm saying, really, is that you'll never catch your fish if you start by feeling sorry for the frog." He looked down at the place where Jake had been lying. "Or the worm," he said as an afterthought.

Marais said nothing. He was only aware, in his genteel Cape way, that the analogy was obscure and somehow vulgar.

Part II

FLIGHT

2

The city curled and bunched around the foot of the mountain and spread itself along the winding shore like a snake basking in the thin winter sunshine. From the top of the mountain the ground fell gently away before steepening into a series of bare granite cliffs slashed and shattered by ravines. Rina stood near the edge, pointing out some landmarks.

"The mountain over there is called Lion's Head and the one on the other side is Devil's Peak. Along there somewhere is the Rhodes Memorial, but I think it's hidden in the trees. The white building is the Groote Schuur Hospital where they did the heart transplants. Do you see it? Keogh, are you listening?"

"Sure," said Keogh. All he had really heard were the pleasant modulations of her voice. He'd had a good lunch with a bottle of chilled Cape Riesling, and he lay on the picnic rug soaking up the mid-afternoon sun. From the bustle of the city and the harbour only a whisper of noise floated up to the sheltered spot they had found near the top of the mountain. Keogh felt very close to total and mindless contentment.

"If you're not interested, why don't you say so?" Rina demanded.

He sat up. "I'm hanging on every word, I swear it. If I'm fascinated by you, how can I not be interested in your town, your friends? Your milieu; is that the word?"

"Don't be corny. You're the one who wanted to see it from up here." She brushed a long strand of auburn hair off her face and went on deliberately, "There's a new harbour and an old harbour. That's Parliament down there, and next door is the Anglican Cathedral."

"What's the island?" he said. It lay like a dark hump-backed creature in the mouth of the bay.

"Robben Island. It's a prison."

Keogh sat looking at the view for a minute, but he was a big restless man who could not be still for long. He began to pick up pebbles and toss them down the slope, watching them stop among the shale and scrub or roll onto the cliffs.

Rina gazed out to sea. She had one of those slim square-shouldered figures that went well with skinny sweaters and high necklines, and a hollow-backed stance that gave a provocative thrust to her small breasts. "The details always sound so puny," she said. "It's beautiful, isn't it? A beautiful, sad place. Couldn't you stay up here for hours?"

"No."

"Why not?"

"I'm not given to stirring thoughts on mountaintops."

"You're a hard-headed bastard, aren't you? Why do I always get involved with hard men?" She turned and stared at him with green eyes that had the steady, knowing quality of a cat's. "You're supposed to be Irish."

"Liverpool," he agreed. "Together with Glasgow, home of the last surviving Irishmen. Matter of geographical accident that both places are on the wrong side of the water."

"What happened to all the rest?"

"The English turned them into caricatures. Out of sheer exhaustion they gave up trying to be themselves and became all the things you want me to be."

"Romantic? Sentimental?"

"And violent and moody and drunkenly remorseful."

Rina laughed. "It sums you up pretty well. You're not pious, though."

"Where I grew up I was nearly martyred five days a week walking past a Protestant school. I feel that gave me a credit balance against later transgressions. And I believe in hell because I've been there. It's on the third level of the Bowmore copper mine."

He took a final glance out across Cape Town and then lay back, staring at the sky and suddenly thinking how far he had moved from his origins: a street of back-to-backs, long since demolished, off the Scotland Road. After the war it had been the toughest part of the Pool to grow up in, and Jim Keogh had prevailed through physical ruggedness, a measure of ambition, and an inexplicable flair for mathematics which had won him scholarships all the way through to Imperial College, London, and finally a degree in mining. Though he did not claim to be culturally Irish he had inherited a navvy's build, a broad, roughly chiselled face, very blue eyes, and a head of uncontrollably thick black curls. Among the faults he recognized in himself—Irish faults?—were stubbornness, capriciousness, and a turbulent temper. Africa had done something to smooth his edges, to give him a *savoir vivre*.

With his degree and a postgraduate diploma, two years' National Service with a sapper unit and another two in the Yorkshire pits behind him, he had gone to the Northern Rhodesian Copperbelt on a three-year contract and stayed for eight. Northern Rhodesia had become Zambia; Keogh had become a senior engineer. He liked Africa; for a bachelor in his early thirties, with interests that were not specially urbane, there could be no finer place. He had earned more in the past year than his father, a semi-literate labourer from County Cork, had in the last ten of his life; he was used to hard work, high rewards, hot climates, and open spaces, and to the small, tightly knit communities that took their pleasures seriously and sometimes harshly.

One morning last month Keogh had been underground examining a suspicious fault in an ore seam. A pressure burst in the tunnel behind him sent tons of hanging crashing down, killing two men and trapping him with five Barotse miners in a passage off the main roadway. He had set them to digging themselves out, had bullied and cursed them into working harder than they'd ever worked in their lives. They were recent recruits, tribesmen newly arrived from the bush, whose spirit would wilt rapidly in this confinement unless they were sustained by work, even by anger. One man had rebelled. Keogh had held him against the wall and slapped his face again and again until he was subdued, and his eyes in the light of the helmet lamps held only a dull gleam of hate. It was raw racial hate, not an easy look to forget. They had burrowed half way through the fallen rock when the proto team broke through from the other side after twenty hours. It did not sound long to anyone who had not been there, just two and a half shifts. Nothing was wrong with any of them but exhaustion and shock, but when he had spent three days in the mine hospital the management had insisted on flying Keogh to Cape Town for a fortnight at their expense in the Mount Nelson Hotel.

He was dismayed to learn how little there was to do in Cape Town in the winter. Apparently that had been the whole idea: he was meant to recuperate. After four days he was on the verge of returning, but suddenly he cabled to ask for an extra week's sick leave. Frankly, he was malingering. By then he had met Rina.

Across the city, two tugs were nudging a freighter out of its berth in the harbour. The afternoon was cool and bright, and the blue bay yawned in a sheen of sunlight. Rina studied him with her thoughtful cat's eyes.

"Come here," he said.

"What for?"

"Three guesses."

"Keogh, don't be ridiculous! Out here?"

"You'll have to find a pretty good reason why not."

She approached with pretended reluctance. He drew her down onto the rug and then she laughed and kissed him and took his hand, pressing it to her breasts to feel the nipples hardening. Involuntarily he glanced at her left hand: against the light tan there was still a band a few shades lighter where she had continued to wear her wedding ring until a week ago.

"I was brought up pious too," she said. "It's the seventh commandment, isn't it?"

"Purely a technical offence," said Keogh.

They made love and dozed and idled the rest of the afternoon away. Nobody disturbed them: it was midweek and well out of the tourist season. When they finally packed the picnic basket and walked back to the cable station, the sun had slipped away behind Lion's Head and there was a sharp chill in the air. They had planned to have dinner at Rina's flat, stopping on the way there to buy some wine. The bottle stores would be shut by the time they reached the city, but it was common enough for trustworthy white people to use the illegal coloured outlets. Rina was trustworthy; the place she had introduced Keogh to was called Auntie Dora's.

While they waited for the cable car he said suddenly, "You could come back with me, you know."

"Where to?"

"Zambia."

He had not really planned to say it, and she had not expected it. Her face became wary before she turned to study her nail polish. "No," she said.

"Are you worried about Paul? You've got to forget about him sometime, you know. You'll be divorced within a week."

"It's not that, it's . . . I don't know, a whole lot of things. How long have I known you? Eight days."

"You needn't come at once. And if it doesn't work out you needn't stay. I've a feeling it will work, though, haven't you? Haven't we become more than just . . . ?"

"You don't need to explain it, Keogh. When I leave this country it will be for good; that's something I've always known in my bones. It sounds corny to you, but this is my country. I feel committed to it; I feel responsible for what goes on here. I must do what I can. It's little enough."

"You're going to stay and let it eat you up?" he said.

"Maybe not. I don't know." She looked angrily confused for a moment. "Damn it, Keogh, you mean a lot to me too. You've done so much for me, I've felt more alive in the last week than I have for two years. But you want a decision that I can't take lightly."

"I still say your priorities are upside down."

"We'll stay in touch. Just don't rush me."

He left the subject there, feeling slightly alarmed at himself, not fully understanding his feelings. He knew without much conceit that women found him attractive; on the Copperbelt he could pick and choose among them. He suspected his life had become too well rounded, too complete, and suddenly Rina had made him aware of a gap which it seemed only she could fill.

They rode down the mountainside preoccupied with their own thoughts and loaded the picnic gear into her car. Keogh drove through the last of the rush-hour traffic towards Auntie Dora's shebeen in District Six.

They had met in a silly way that had a touch of Victorian melodrama about it. Bored to distraction on the dismally wet afternoon of his fourth day in Cape Town, he had joined a cinema queue and noticed her standing in front of him, and suddenly she had begun to cry. Betrayed by some scoundrel, he thought; is she wondering whether to leap off a bridge? "It can't be that bad," he had said aloud, and she'd stared at him in bewilderment, and that was how it had started. It turned out not to have been that bad, in fact: she had simply lost her umbrella. She had realized that her new umbrella had gone and suddenly in the wet everything seemed to be getting on top of her and she had burst into tears. She had been through a bad patch.

She called herself Rina van Niekerk—Fun-NEE-kairk, she made him pronounce it—though her surname as the result of her brief disastrous marriage was actually Blane. She had grown up on a farm in the Orange Free State and had the strange, prickly vulnerability of people who have turned away from their kind. An English-language university had given her liberal ideas, Johannesburg had given her some sophistication, and from Paul Blane she had acquired expensive tastes, a sky-blue Valiant, and a good measure of bitterness.

He was the spoilt son of a mining millionaire in Johannesburg, disinherited for his erratic ways and supposedly living on an allowance of twenty thousand rands a year—ten thousand pounds. By the time Rina met him he was running three years ahead of the allowance. He ran a private plane, went hunting in Mozambique and gambling in Swaziland, and threw parties in his Johannesburg flat that lasted a week. From the outside it must all have seemed very exciting; they were married within ten days of meeting. The side of Blane she had not had a chance to discover in that time was his psychosis. There was no politer term for it.

He was far from being insane; for long periods he was perfectly rational and charming, and it was during one of these that he had met Rina. Whatever his condition was his family had always chosen to ignore it, and Blane himself refused to see a psychiatrist. He certainly had a leaning towards violence. Luckily a lot of his latent aggression seemed to be used up killing animals and game fish; what was left tended to be spent on Rina.

There was an element of paranoia as well: he became passionately jealous, beating her up sometimes on the grounds of suspected—and quite unfounded—infidelities. She had held out for twenty months among the scenes, assaults, tears, and humiliation, hoping constantly that he would improve under her influence. Finally it was only her

34

private discovery that he had been unfaithful to her which pushed her into leaving.

Blane's father, who despised his son but feared a scandal, had tried to persuade her to stay. She refused, driving the Valiant to Cape Town with two suitcases in the boot. She had taken a job that allowed her to keep her own hours, doing social work among coloured people for an organization called the Race Relations Council, while she went through an emotional convalescence. That had been a year ago; the divorce proceedings were in Johannesburg next week. But still Keogh sensed in her a fretful loyalty, an inability to break free of Blane's spell, and in a curious way it was linked to her involvement in the racial dilemma of her country. Well, one way or another the convalescence must soon end.

District Six, the old coloured quarter, was a cheerful wedge of Dutch colonial and Victorian slums close to the heart of Cape Town. The Government had started knocking it down, moving people out and bulldozing the edges away, but for the moment the place remained as it had been for generations, terraces of red-brick and sun-blistered stucco houses with sagging iron roofs, wooden porches, mesh and tin fences. The narrow streets were crowded with fish carts, abandoned cars, vegetable stalls, mosques, bars, spice shops, broken glass, drunks, fishermen, barefoot children, and policemen who, at night, took care to patrol in twos. Auntie Dora's was off Reform Street.

It was a curiosity of the licensing laws that while a white person could get a drink in a good hotel at any time till two in the morning, it was impossible legally to buy a bottle of anything to take home after six o'clock. People in the know used illegal sources, of which Auntie Dora ran one of the most respectable. She was proud to number "intellectuals" among her customers; white liberals and people close to the coloured community, like Rina, were frequent visitors. In the old days of the black nationalist movements the place had apparently been known as a rendezvous for conspirators, and it was said that Auntie Dora herself had not actively discouraged them. The movements had gradually been smashed, but Auntie Dora had a knack for survival. A percentage of her profits found their way to the right quarters; apart from an occasional raid in search of petty criminals, the police left her alone.

Night had fallen by the time they arrived. Rina decided to wait in the car because Auntie Dora would keep her gossiping if she went in; Keogh parked under a lamp on the main street and walked the hundred yards to the shebeen. On a corner a gang of amber-skinned youths watched him with idle insolence; in a doorway opposite Auntie Dora's an old man sat on a chair barking like a bronchial dog, staring at a ball of handkerchief clutched in his fist. The house itself was two-storeyed like most of the others, with a jungle of potted ferns standing on the stoep. Keogh knocked and waited to be inspected through the lace curtains before the bolt was drawn back and Auntie Dora's sister let him in. She was a wrinkled yellow gnome of a woman with a photographic memory for faces, who spent all day knitting in an anteroom furnished like an English parlour and guarding the door against unwelcome visitors. On the ground floor there was only one other room, the large main one where the drinking went on. The old woman nodded at him and returned to her knitting by the electric fire. He walked through.

It was not a busy night. About twenty people were sitting at the Formica-topped tables in the centre, and a few more stood about elsewhere. In the smoky air he caught the smell of dagga, the same coarse weed that the miners used in Zambia. In one corner two black men seemed to be practising scales on a clarinet and a double bass.

Auntie Dora herself billowed up to him, an enormous woman wearing a cloth *doek* tied round her head, a flowered apron, and slippers. She clutched half a dozen dirty glasses in one hand, and with the other she reached up and pinched Keogh's cheek between two fingers that felt like a pair of blunt-nosed pliers.

"Yes, Englishman. Where's Rina?"

"She's not with me, Auntie. I've come for two bottles of red wine."

"She give you up? She show you the door? She found somebody got more of what it takes, eh?" Auntie Dora made a vulgar gesture and laughed, shaking the fat in her yellow cheeks. "She's a proper lady, that Rina. You look after her. Some people is born ladies; the rest of us have to take our chances. You want wine? It'll cost you two rands a bottle."

"It's robbery," said Keogh.

"You'll have to wait, I'll get it from the shed. All my regulars drink the hard stuff. Rina done me a favour, you know. They wanted to send my brother to a work colony; they said he was a vagrant. She got it stopped. Mind you, I've been feeding him five years, it would be a weight off my back, mind you. Come, you'll sit down and wait."

Auntie Dora had countless relatives living in degrees of dependence on her, and outside the terms of business she was known as a soft touch. Keogh let her lead him to the back of the room and seat him on an old brassbound oaken kist next to the staircase that led to the upper floor. She opened the back door and waddled down the steps to the shed.

He looked round again. Most of the customers were Cape coloureds, among them a few pretty girls and two people he had met before, a teacher and his wife whose names he could not remember. He waved to them vaguely. There was a sprinkling of Africans. He was the only white person, unless he was to count a Scandinavian seaman asleep at a corner table with his head resting on his tattooed forearms.

A coloured man came down the stairs rather unsteadily, flopped into a chair next to the kist, gave Keogh a silly grin, and began making a dagga cigarette. He took tobacco from a small linen bag, spread it on a strip of brown paper, and mixed the crushed leaf in with it. He rolled the crude cigarette, sealed it with a lick, lit it, and leaned back, absorbing the first dizzying impact.

A ripple went through the room, a murmur of collective anxiety, nothing more. Auntie Dora's sister was standing in the doorway from the anteroom clucking at somebody like an old hen. The dagga smoker looked round, stood up, and scuttled up the stairs. Keogh saw Auntie Dora appear at the back door with his two bottles of cheap cabernet and the breathless grin fall off her face like a mask, and still he did not understand until the teacher, sitting opposite, silently mouthed at him the word, "Police."

3

Auntie Dora set the wine bottles down carefully on the window sill. She moved to the foot of the stairs and stood there with her arms crossed. The music had stopped. From the front door came the sound of a bolt being drawn back and hard, confident voices.

Keogh was slightly nervous. He was sure he had committed no offence, but a foreigner found in a place like this might easily be in an awkward situation. He did not like what he had seen of South African policemen: they had the kind of arrogance that always came with too much authority. The two who came in gleamed with brass and polished leather and assurance; their eyes were shaded by the peaks of their caps from the overhead light which they had switched on. One was a sergeant, middle-aged, the other a young constable with coarse features and fleshy cheeks. Clearly they were not a raiding party, probably just one of the car crews that came from time to time in search of criminals and pass offenders. But their effect on the crowd was significant: conversation had stopped and several people involuntarily stood up.

Keogh remained sitting on the kist. The sergeant was carrying a torch and he walked to the open back door, flashing the beam around the yard, while the constable stood staring for a few seconds at everyone in turn. Only the Scandinavian, who had woken up, blinked back without averting his eyes. The sergeant closed the door and confronted Auntie Dora.

She was surprisingly nervous. Though the remarks she exchanged with him in Afrikaans seemed polite enough, she was making it obvious that she did not want him to go upstairs. It was equally clear that he intended to go. Her sister hovered about the room like a schoolmistress anxious to please the inspectors. Keogh worried about Rina waiting outside. Finally the sergeant, with an impatient gesture, shoved Auntie Dora aside and climbed up the creaking stairs. The old shebeen queen made a soft clicking noise in her throat and with her cheeks trembling looked around the room in despair.

The younger man had continued to stare accusingly at everyone. Suddenly he stretched out an arm and beckoned to a man in the corner, the African who had been playing the clarinet. The black man shuffled forward, reaching automatically for his pass, and the constable paged through the green booklet. Apparently it was in order; affecting a loss of interest he flung the pass on the floor, making the man get down on his knees to retrieve it.

Keogh sighed and stood up. There was really no reason why he should sit and watch this kind of humiliation. He went to the window sill next to the back door and picked up his bottles of wine. The constable snapped at him in Afrikaans.

"I speak English," Keogh said.

"Oh, yes? You thinking of going somewhere?"

"Out."

The policeman looked at him malevolently through close-set, rather stupid blue eyes. "You'll go when I tell you," he said softly.

"I'm not black; I don't carry a pass," Keogh said, and heard a murmur of nervous laughter behind him.

"You mix with kaffirs," the policeman said in his thick accent, "then you'll get treated like a kaffir."

His right hand moved to his black leather revolver holster, and casually he undid the press stud on the flap. The atmosphere was suddenly ugly; Keogh knew he'd have done better to keep quiet. But then a door slammed upstairs and the sergeant shouted the constable's name.

"Oosthuizen!"

He appeared on the landing with the coloured dagga smoker held in an armlock. He gave him a push and the man came reeling down the stairs. Constable Oosthuizen, with a faint smile at Keogh, turned and grabbed the prisoner, spun him robustly against the wall, and searched him. He removed the tin of dagga and stood it on the window sill. The coloured man must have been stoned out of his mind; he was turned round again and propped against the wall and began sliding down it with a benign smile on his face.

"Who's this hell?" said Oosthuizen to Keogh. "Friend of yours? Eh? Your kind of rubbish?"

Standing there with a bottle of wine in each hand and feeling helplessly angry with himself, Keogh said nothing. For a moment he had sensed the crowd expecting something of him, just a gesture, but he had hesitated and the moment was gone. Why should he fight their battles for them anyway?

The sergeant came onto the landing scuffling with another captive. This time it was an African that Keogh had not seen before, a thin man in a dirty khaki dustcoat whose limbs flailed wildly as the policeman shoved him down the stairs. He hit the bottom in a heap and Oosthuizen dragged him to his feet and searched him, removing a half-full bottle of brandy from the pocket of his dustcoat.

There was a faint stirring at the edge of the crowd, as if some of them had caught their breath in recognition. Auntie Dora stood among them, very still; was this why she'd tried to keep the sergeant downstairs? Keogh looked at the prisoner as he was turned round and pinned to the wall with Oosthuizen's hand at his throat.

The black man's head was like a skull, there was so little spare flesh on it. The peppercorn hair was cropped close to the scalp, and skin with the texture of old brown leather was drawn tight across the cheekbones. His eyes— sunk in their skull sockets, slightly bloodshot, the whites flecked with brown—caught the light with a curious animal fierceness. It was hard to tell whether he was afraid or not; he looked into the policeman's face and when a question was barked at him he did not reply.

"Wie is jy? Waar's jou pas?"

Even Keogh understood the words: Who are you? Where's your pass? The prisoner wasn't telling. Held against the wall with his limp, awkward limbs dangling, he had a curious kind of dignity. Beneath the dustcoat he wore frayed grey flannel trousers and a polo-necked sweater, both of which were too big for him. The policeman repeated the questions with more menace and then, with an exaggerated sigh, let go of the man's throat and unclipped the handcuffs from the belt of his Sam Browne.

The African said something. It was a brief remark which Keogh couldn't understand, but it was something cheeky. It sent a wave of laughter round the room, and the prisoner gave a tentative smile.

The big Afrikaner's face reddened. Keogh thought, You silly black bastard, this isn't the time for jokes, and he knew with a sinking feeling in his bowels what was going to happen.

Oosthuizen stood before his prisoner. The handcuffs were in his right hand. Carefully he slipped the two steel rings over his knuckles and punched the black man twice in the mouth.

The crowd winced. Keogh felt a flood of sick anger. The policeman jerked the prisoner's hands down from his face and snapped the cuffs tightly onto his wrists while the African stared in disbelief, mechanically spitting out a piece of tooth and a dribble of blood and saliva. Keogh remembered the Barotse miner whose face he had slapped, the generations of dull hatred in it.

Oosthuizen turned provocatively to face the room. More exactly he faced Keogh. You dumb sods, Keogh thought, as long as you stand there with that ugly, painful, cringing look on your faces he knows he can do the same to any one of you. This is your business, not mine. To the policeman he said, before he could stop himself, "You bastard."

"Say again?" Oosthuizen smiled thinly. He had sensed that if there was any defiance it would come from Keogh,

43

and his right hand went not to his holster but into his trouser pocket. The sergeant was still upstairs. Past Oosthuizen's shoulder he caught a glimpse of the black man wiping blood dismally on the sleeves of his dustcoat.

"You fat, filthy bastard," Keogh said. His anger was cold and sharp now. There had been three rules for winning a fight in the Scotland Road: hit first, hit hard, and don't use your fists if you've got something better. He saw Oosthuizen's hand leave his pocket, and a truncheon with a vicious spring-mounted steel knob at the end gleamed under the light. Keogh hit him with a wine bottle.

It all happened quite simply, almost anticlimactically. The bottle was just a heavy cosh that happened to be brittle. It broke in two with a thick crunch across the base of the policeman's skull, behind the left ear. Wine sprayed over both of them. Oosthuizen's cap flew off, the truncheon clattered on the floor. He sat down in an abrupt, untidy heap and his head jarred against the brass binding of the oak kist.

The crowd stared at Keogh in horror. He stood with the full bottle in his left hand and the neck of the other in his right; his rage, too, seemed to have snapped off at the hilt and he felt giddy with confusion. Oosthuizen's eyes were open but his face had gone very white. Around them everyone began to move at once, barging for the front door in a swelling, noisy panic. He started to go the same way, hearing the sergeant shout from upstairs. A pair of hands seized his elbow and he aimed a punch at the man by his side before recognizing the handcuffed African.

"Bugger off!"

"This way." The man was tugging his arm, turning him towards the back door. "Hey, *baas,* this way!" The man went at a hobbling trot to the back door and Keogh followed automatically, tripping over the legs of Oosthuizen, who still sat against the kist. His face didn't look good, bathed in sweat and with a bluish tone beneath the pallor.

They bounded down the steps together into the confusing shadows of the back yard. The air was cold and stunningly fresh. "Come," the African urged him; he seemed to know exactly where he was going. Next to Auntie Dora's shed stood a pile of rusting forty-four-gallon oil drums. They were stacked three high in precarious upright rows between the shed and the high iron fence. The black man, with a surprising agility, leapt to the top of one, found a toehold on the second one, and with his wrists locked together somehow managed to scramble onto the shed roof. Keogh tossed aside the bottle of wine he had been clutching and followed. He felt the stack of drums sway under his weight and flung himself onto the roof as they fell with a barrage of explosive crashes into the yard.

The two of them slid down the sloping roof and dropped eight feet into an unlit alley. Keogh took a second to work out the direction of the car and sprinted towards it. The man kept close behind with his peculiar limping run and his hands clutched to his chest.

A hundred yards down, the alley intersected another and this led out onto the main road. There were no sounds of pursuit—not yet—and Keogh peered cautiously out. He could see the Valiant, with Rina in the passenger seat, parked beneath its street lamp half a block to the right.

"Thanks," he said. "Now get lost, will you?"

Both of them were panting. "It's your car, that?" said the African, wiping his mouth on his sleeves. "How would it be if I came with you? How would that be, *baas?*"

"Don't be crazy. It's me they'll be wanting; you'll do better on your own."

"Like this?" The man held up his manacled wrists. Some way behind them they both heard the crunching of boots on the gravel of the alleyway; there was no time to argue.

"Come on then," Keogh said, and ran for the car.

4

Rina opened her mouth and then closed it abruptly as Keogh slid behind the wheel, reached back to unlock the rear door, and twisted the key in the ignition all at once. He swung the Valiant into a U turn that made the tires scream, with the black man hanging half way out of the door; he was just agile enough to hold on. Once they had straightened out he slammed the door and lay flat on the floor in the back, panting. Keogh glanced in the mirror and saw a torch beam appear at the entrance to the alley, a hundred yards back, and flicker uncertainly about. Thank Christ for that, anyway: they hadn't seen the car.

Rina took a deep breath. "What happened?"

"An encounter with the law. Not to be too delicate about it, I'm in the shit."

They were out of District Six in a couple of minutes. Cinema traffic was flowing into the city from the southern suburbs, but the road towards Rina's flat in Rondebosch was fairly clear. On De Waal Drive an ambulance went racing in the opposite direction. Oosthuizen's ambulance? He tried to avoid wondering how badly the man had been hurt and said, "Give me a cigarette." The hand that he reached out for the lighter was shaking. He told Rina in about six sentences what had happened, and she took another deep breath. Watching the road, he could not see her expression.

"If you'd sat down and thought about it for a week, Keogh, you couldn't have chosen a stupider thing to do."

"I'd worked that out already. I lost my temper, that's all."

"They're going to come to me, you realize. Does Auntie Dora know your name?"

"She knows I'm an Englishman, that's all."

"All right. And she knows you're a friend of mine. They'll be questioning her by now. It's no good hiding you at my place; you must be well out of the way before they arrive."

He glanced at her in surprise. There was nothing reproachful or even plaintive in her tone. "I don't expect you to lie to protect me," he said.

"I can't pretend not to know you; it would just sound silly. What I can do is steer them innocently in the wrong direction."

"Rina! Do you know what you're saying?"

"I can handle my end of it. The real problem will be finding you a hiding place."

Instinctively he had known that she would not let him down. And there was a core of tough capability in her that he could rely on to the last. But he had been forgetting about their passenger. He called out "Hey!" and the black man's head appeared behind the front seat. "You'd better tell me where to drop you."

The man was silent for a few seconds. "Really I don't know," he said at last.

"Then start thinking about it. I've got you out of District Six; I've repaid you a favour. Go home, get someone to use a hacksaw on those handcuffs, and forget all about us."

"Home?" The man gave an odd laugh. "I'm not from around here."

"That's hardly my problem."

"What's your name?" Rina asked. She had been studying his face in the yellow glare of fluorescent lamps flashing by.

"Jack."

"Surname?"

The man shrugged. "Just Jack; won't it do?"

"Where are you from?"

"The big town. Jo'burg. See, they said I'm illegal; they endorsed me out because I'm not born up there. I came here, thought I could find work with somebody who won't ask questions. Been staying upstairs at Auntie Dora's. It was always safe there for somebody illegal. Can you help me with a cigarette?"

She passed the packet to him. Shaking it to get one out he jerked his wrists apart and winced. She lit his cigarette and he drew on it delicately. "Why don't you have a pass?" she said.

"I threw it. Just threw it away. With that stamp saying 'endorsed out,' I'd go inside for maybe two years, first time a cop stopped me in the city. What should I do, go starve in some reserve? Used to be a man down here who could print you a new pass to order, charged a pair of hands for it." He held up both palms with the fingers spread out to indicate fives. "He's dead now. At least without one I got a chance to bluff my way."

"You've got a wife? Children?"

49

"Who hasn't? In Zululand with her mother. I think."

He had stopped addressing Keogh as *baas* the minute he knew it was safe. But there was a freakishness about him which his informality, the lack of conventional deference to white people, only partly explained. They were in Rondebosch now, Main Road, close to Rina's flat. Keogh slowed the car down and said, "You've got to get out."

"Where are you going, yourself?" said Jack.

"Nowhere that matters to you."

"I heard you talking just now. You're not from Cape Town; you got no place to hide any more than I have." He paused a moment. "You could drive me to Jo'burg."

Keogh had stopped the car. He turned in astonishment. The man's face—cropped scalp, shrewd fierce eyes, split and swelling lips—was red in the glow from his cigarette. "You're crazy," he said. "Get out."

"Let him come up," Rina said. Had she gone crazy too? He started to argue with her but she gave him a look. "Don't you see? If he gets picked up now they're that much closer to you. Perhaps we can work out something between us."

"We can go to Jo'burg, both of us," said Jack, emboldened. "There's somebody there will look after me. He could see you right as well."

"I can manage without your help."

"Look," Rina said, "it will take a couple of hours for them to trace me. Auntie Dora doesn't know where I live. The only way they can find me is through the Race Relations Council, and at night that isn't easy. Jack has given me an idea. Why don't we work things out together?" She smiled faintly. "Don't sulk, Keogh. You did turn out to be an Irishman, after all."

He slammed the car into gear and turned down the street that led to her building. The last thing he wanted was to be saddled with this weird black man, but if Rina had an idea it was more than he could say for himself. His thoughts swung inevitably back to what had happened at Auntie Dora's, and by now one fact had settled into his brain, evicting everything else: he was in the worst trouble of his life.

Rina lived in an old, rather ugly, but spacious block of flats near Rondebosch station. Keogh parked the car at the side and the three of them slipped past the cleaners' quarters, across a paved courtyard, and up the fire escape to the second floor. Nobody saw them; it was important for her safety that nobody should. Inside the flat, which had cubist prints hanging on austere wallpaper, they stood and looked at each other.

"Sit down," Rina said to Jack. "I'll try to clean up your mouth. Keogh, you're covered in wine."

"I could do with a drink now," he said.

"We haven't got any. Remember?"

Jack grinned, showing a broken front tooth. He tugged awkwardly at the pocket of his dustcoat and brought out the half-full bottle of brandy from Auntie Dora's. Somehow he had salvaged it in the confusion.

"I even brought you some white liquor," he said.

Keogh grinned back. Jack grew more and more interesting. He fetched three glasses and poured big tots, downing his own in a swallow and pouring another. His thoughts became more ordered. "My money and passport are in the hotel safe deposit. I must get them out before they trace me. Or do you think they'll automatically check the hotels?"

Rina was bringing a basin of warm water and a wad of cotton wool from the bathroom. "The last place they'd try would be the Mount Nelson anyway. People who stay at the Mount Nelson simply don't go round hitting policemen with bottles."

"Do I shock you?"

She considered. "Perhaps I've become immune to shock."

She concentrated on Jack, dabbing away the gore and the powdery dried blood from his mouth. She squeezed some antiseptic cream from a tube and applied it to the bruised and lacerated lips and finally stood back to inspect her work. He had sat through it with his eyes closed.

"Now," said Rina pleasantly, "tell us who you really are."

Keogh, in the middle of lighting a cigarette, stopped with the burning match between his fingers. The black man opened his eyes, blinked at her a couple of times, and remained expressionless.

"It can't do you any harm," she prompted. "Since we're all in the same boat I thought we should know each other's circumstances. That's why I wanted you up here."

He tried clumsily to massage his wrists where the handcuffs were biting into them. Finally he looked at Keogh. "You helped me. I can see you right. One hand washes another. Isn't it enough?"

The match burned Keogh's fingers. He dropped it and stood up slowly, with menace.

"Listen," the man said desperately. "You got to leave the country, you know that? It's the only way you'll be safe. Me too. A man in Jo'burg can do it for me; I'll take you to him. You push me round, it won't help anybody."

"What's he trying to hide?" Keogh said.

"I knew right away there was something odd about

52

him, about the things he told us. Then when he used the phrase 'white liquor' I understood what it was. That's what they used to call it before it became legal for blacks to drink. In nineteen-sixty-three, Keogh, as long ago as that. It's taken for granted now. It's the kind of thing no one would think of mentioning to him while he was hiding at Auntie Dora's. He's been out of circulation for a long time, and he's not had a chance to catch up yet. He's living in the past. Where do you think he got his head shaved?"

The man looked fiercely from one to the other like a trapped animal. Then he made an irritated gesture. "All right," he said. "All right, I'm from jail."

"In fact he escaped," Rina said. "He escaped from Robben Island, about ten days ago, was it? It was in the papers. The only man to get away for years and years. He fits the description they gave. Somebody who tried to leave with him was shot. He's a political prisoner from the old Congress days, and his name isn't Jack either."

"Shack," the man said sullenly. "Shack Twala."

"Shack?" Keogh repeated. He was still slightly bewildered. "What sort of name is that?"

"Short for Shishak. Two Chronicles, Chapter Twelve."

They stared at him and a twinkle came into his eyes. " 'So Shishak King of Egypt came up against Jerusalem,' " he quoted, " 'and took away the treasures of the house of the Lord, and the treasures of the king's house.' I'm the only man in the world who ever heard of Shishak. Should have been Solomon. See, my old man was a Bible puncher, gave all his children names from the Old Testament. But he was very old and he could hardly read, and when he went to get me registered he pointed at the wrong page in his Bible. Shishak, huh!"

He gave a weird cackle of a laugh, bending over double as if the thought were funny enough to hurt his insides. Keogh, in a moment of fury, seized him round his scrawny neck and banged his head against the back of the armchair. "Son of a bitch! Full of jokes, are you? You said you'd got no pass, and you'd have let us go on believing that was all, wouldn't you? If I'd known I was helping an escaped con. . . ."

Shack Twala subsided into the chair, wiping his mouth. "You made it bleed again," he said. "I didn't tell you to play Sir Galahad. I didn't tell you to smash that Boer with a bottle."

"He's right," Rina said sharply, stepping between them.

Keogh turned away, uncertain where to let his rage settle. He felt like the victim of an artless confidence trick. Finally he poured an enormous brandy and drank it. "Kick him out," he said. "Get him out of my hair."

"Keogh, will you get this into your thick skull: we're all stuck with each other!" Her eyes blazed at him angrily for a moment. "How long do you think he'll stay free on the streets, looking like that? And when they've got him, what does he owe you? Or me? He can make it easier for himself by leading them to you, and that brings me into it. I'm entitled to ask you to use your common sense."

She stopped, looking slightly surprised at her own vehemence. Shack Twala nodded glumly at Keogh. "They'll get you for heavy assault; it could be worth a few years. The lady would go up for assisting escape and harbouring."

"Why don't you shut up?" Keogh suggested.

"All I'm saying, all I want to say, if they get me or if they don't get me, they going to throw the whole book at you. They don't like people who hurt cops. It makes sense. And don't fool yourself, that fat Boer is hurt pretty bad. He could die."

He was the first who had dared put the suggestion into words, though secretly Keogh had been aware of it all along.

Shack Twala, sensing that he had acquired a certain authority, stood up. He took a sip of brandy and winced as it passed over his cut lips. "If he dies you'll go one way, you know that?"

"He'd have done the same to me, with that steel knob on his truncheon."

"You going to prove that? Where's your witnesses? No, you got a good chance of going all up the line to the death block at Pretoria Central. And if you don't, the *ore* will make you wish you had."

"Who?"

"The ears. The jacks. The *tokoloshes*. The police," Shack explained patiently. "They'll make you sorry in their own way, down in the cells at Roeland Street. You want to wait for that to happen?"

Through his hostility Keogh recognized a coarse realism about the black man. It was what you learned in prison, he supposed, along with the things that became second nature, like opportunism and lying.

"So? You going to wait? Listen, this town is too small to hide up in. I found that out tonight, didn't I? Get out while you still got time. Drive me to Jo'burg. You got to leave the country sooner or later; you got to go that way as it is. From Jo'burg you cross the border into Botswana, then through to Zambia. It's the old Congress escape route. A man is waiting for me in the big town."

"That's nine hundred miles," Keogh said, "and we only need to be stopped once. Anyway, it's not my car. I haven't got a car."

Rina still stood in the middle of the room holding the basin of water stained with Shack's blood. "Take the Valiant," she said quickly.

"It'll involve you up to your eyes."

"No. It's not my car either; it's always been registered in Paul's name. Officially there's no reason anyone should even know I've had a car down here. Shack is right, Keogh; you've got to leave Cape Town. If you get out quickly enough the trail will stop here."

In spite of himself he had to agree. With the police still one jump behind him, this might be the only chance he would get. There was a conspiracy of circumstances. Still, at the best of times he did not like depending on other people. His instinct was to act alone.

"Who's this man in Johannesburg?" he said.

"Old Congress man. Reliable."

"His name?"

"What's the odds? You wouldn't know him."

"Damn you, tell me who he is!"

"All right, all right. Hassim Mayat. He's a jeweller. Runs a small shop in Market Street. We used to have a business arrangement, him and me, running Congress people in and out of the country. That's what I was doing when they got me. We can go the same way: stay with Hassim until he can arrange a safe time and place to cross."

"He's an Indian?"

"Part Malay as well, I think. He and his brother Yusuf are both old Congress men. Yusuf is in Botswana now; we'll need his help too."

"Have you spoken to them?"

"There's no need. They'll be expecting me."

"And me?" Keogh demanded. "How do I know they'll be willing to help me?"

"They can be persuaded. Money will make things easier for you."

"The Congress: is that the same one that operates in exile up in Zambia?"

Rina interrupted them. "The Congress was declared an illegal organization after the Sharpeville shootings in nineteen-sixty. At the time it was a peaceful African nationalist movement; now its aim is to overthrow white rule by force. And you're both wasting time asking and answering questions." She went through to the bathroom, emptied the bloody water and the cotton wool into the lavatory, and flushed it.

Shack said, "We'd better go. See, by travelling together we make each other respectable. I'm with a white man, nobody asks me for my pass. You're with a black man, they think I work for you, you must be on lawful business. You'll see plenty salesman and their 'boys' on the road." He gave the word a sarcastic twist. "Take the back roads, we can be in Jo'burg before dark tomorrow. Then we get rid of these bracelets—"

"I didn't say I was going," Keogh reminded him crossly. "I didn't ask for your advice. I didn't even say I believed anything you've told me." He paused. "How did you get off Robben Island anyway?"

"There was a boat. It got washed up on the rocks. The one who found it was meant to come with me, Jake, but they shot him. I rowed to Green Point and went straight to Auntie Dora's. She couldn't refuse an old Congress man.

57

Lucky those ears tonight didn't recognize me, but it wouldn't have taken them long. Why should I do their work for them? I hope it goes all right for Auntie Dora, that's all."

Rina returned to the room, looking businesslike. "Wherever you're going, you've got to get out. We've been here arguing for twenty minutes. Keogh, will you bring the glasses through for me? I don't want them to see I've had visitors. Shack, you'd better put the top back on that brandy bottle and take it with you."

Keogh followed her to the kitchen, carrying the glasses. He was confused, perhaps more uncertain of himself than he had ever been. Suddenly Rina was dangling a bunch of keys in front of his face. "Keep your voice down," she said. "These will get you into Paul's flat in Johannesburg. It's in a suburb called Killarney; the address is on the tag."

"Why would I want . . . ?"

"It'll give you a hiding place of your own, an ace up your sleeve. You don't realize how lucky you are to have an escape route open to you."

"But I don't like it, Rina. I don't like relying on these people. The political background worries me."

"Exactly. Outside this country the Congress is powerful. What's left of its members here I've no idea, but they're bound to be weak and disorganized. Perhaps untrustworthy too. Use them for what they can give you, but don't put yourself entirely in their hands. Paul is away on a hunting trip; I know because I tried to phone him yesterday. He'll be gone about a week."

"I still don't know if I should go."

"You haven't a chance in hell if you don't, Keogh."

He felt weary. He took the keys and put them in his pocket. "Then I suppose it's settled," he said; it seemed to have been settling itself ever since his path and Shack's had crossed. "What about you? What will you tell the police?"

"I'll manage. I'll throw them off the scent. By the way, park the car in the basement garage; it'll be a safe hiding place. I'll phone you at the flat tomorrow night."

Shack stood waiting for them in the living room. There was something absurd, Keogh thought, about entrusting your safety to a man in handcuffs wearing a dirty dustcoat with a brandy bottle sticking out of the pocket.

Keogh kissed Rina. "I love you," he said. He had never actually said it before. She just nodded absently and bit her lip, and there seemed no point in talking about when they would see each other again.

5

The lobby of the Mount Nelson Hotel was almost deserted. The girl at the reception desk looked at Keogh curiously as he passed her the safe-deposit slip, and he remembered that his clothes were stained with red wine. She would remember it too, of course, when the police questioned her. By then it would hardly matter. He told her he was moving out, and while she made out his bill he went swiftly upstairs, changed his shirt and jacket, and bundled everything that came to hand into his single lightweight suitcase.

He had taken an enormous risk in coming here, in driving back towards the city and close to District Six where the police search would be concentrated. He had only allowed himself to enter the hotel after a painfully thorough reconnaissance from the gardens at the front. His money was vitally important—for travelling expenses and for buying secrecy. In two minutes he was back in the lobby trying not to look hurried as he checked the contents of the sealed envelope. It was all there: British passport, six hundred dollars in American Express cheques, and two hundred rands in cash. He used one of the cheques to pay the bill and as an afterthought cashed another hundred dollars' worth; he would need as much cash as he could get. He picked up the suitcase and someone touched his arm.

"It is Mr. Keogh, isn't it?"

It was the hall porter, holding out an orange envelope. Keogh's insides had turned to jelly. Numbly he took the envelope and ripped it open while the porter stared. It was a telegram from the manager of the Bowmore mine. His extra week's sick leave had been approved, but it would be appreciated if he could make sure of returning by the thirty-first. They were going to give him a medal.

"Thanks," he said. He left the hotel on shaking legs and walked two hundred yards to where the Valiant was parked, with Shack huddled behind its front seat.

The Divisional Commissioner of Police for the Western Cape had been disturbed at a *braaivleis* party, and he entered his office wearing a golf club blazer and corduroy trousers, smelling faintly of woodsmoke and more than ready to be disagreeable. Horn sat facing him in the swivel chair, his feet in a pair of dirty suede shoes resting among the papers on the desk. The room was hazy with tobacco smoke. The Divisional Commissioner could barely hide his distaste for the man, let alone his helpless annoyance.

"So you made yourself at home," he said brusquely.

"Your staff captain kindly let me in. You shouldn't have troubled yourself, Brigadier."

"Let me be clear, Mr. Horn. I am in charge of this division. A matter like this comes under my personal control."

"Of course, Brigadier."

"There's been a serious offence and you want me to

countermand standing orders for investigating it. I insist on a full explanation."

Horn cocked an eyebrow. "My request was passed through to the Commissioner. It must have come back to you as an order. You spoke to the Commissioner, didn't you?"

"He agreed that I had every right to ask you for further details. Would you mind taking your feet off my desk?"

Horn complied but took his time over it. He fully reciprocated the brigadier's dislike, regarding him as one of the old dominion establishment, a stuffed-shirt Afrikaner full of correctness and self-importance. Besides, among the ribbons on the blue tunic that hung behind the office door was one with a brass figure eight superimposed on it. The brigadier had fought with the British Eighth Army. Horn's repugnance was complete. He himself came from rebel republican stock and a peasant class that had once been called "poor white." Professionally, what he lacked in polish and education was more than made up by hard work, a seedy urban intelligence, and a fervid belief in what he was doing. His rise through the ranks—first of the Security Police and then within the new Bureau into which he had been absorbed—had been spectacular.

Now he enjoyed a pause before answering. His eyes appeared to focus on something behind the Divisional Commissioner's head. "Yes, Brigadier. You have every right to ask for details. You have no right to be given any, Brigadier."

The brigadier was too astonished to be angry for a moment. "Nobody's trying to interfere with your work, Horn. We're both on the same side."

"The Bureau doesn't give you a high enough clearance, Brigadier. It's not my doing."

"Damn you and your clearances!"

"It's a matter of great delicacy, Brigadier."

"What does my constable care for that? The one who was injured tonight. Do you know how badly he was hurt?"

"Oosthuizen? The fucker was asking for it, I reckon."

The Divisional Commissioner stared at him, drawing as much contempt as he could into the look. Horn lit a cigarette. There was a tap on the door and Van Heerden came in, carrying a slim brown file cover which he handed to Horn. Van Heerden was a young man built like a barrel whom they'd sent from Pretoria to help him. He hardly ever talked, which suited Horn well; in any case, he had not been supplied for his conversational value.

Horn glanced at the five-digit number stencilled in black ink on the file cover and looked up at the brigadier.

"I mean that. You were told a week ago to get your men to go easy on random pass checks. Those two idiots should never have gone up there tonight."

"These orders just filter down from Pretoria," the brigadier said defensively, "with no explanations, no guidance about their intentions."

"It could be very inconvenient for me. It could be very awkward for you, Brigadier. The truncheon that fool was carrying: unorthodox, eh?"

"There was a mistake, and I admit it. I have trespassed on the sacred ground of the Bureau. But why should I hand the case over to you? I know what that means; it's happened before. It means I'll never hear another word about it. It means it will die a natural death rotting in a file in your archives. My man Oosthuizen is seriously ill because an Englishman assaulted him. I want that Englishman, Horn. What possible interest can you have?"

"You may find that justice follows its natural course anyway," said Horn thoughtfully, letting a blob of ash fall to the carpet.

"Who is the Englishman?"

"I expect to know that soon."

"And you expect me to stop what's been started? Just like that?"

"No, Brigadier, you won't need to do that." Horn smiled pleasantly and stood up. "I've taken the liberty of doing it myself. Through your staff captain, of course; must use the proper channels, *ne*? Bright man, that captain. Flexible mind. Transvaal man. Well"—he held up the file cover— "I've got what I've been waiting for. Shall we go, Van? Told you you shouldn't have bothered, Brigadier."

Again the Divisional Commissioner's rising anger was stifled, this time by the certain knowledge that it was not only futile but dangerous to argue. He was too near retirement to go deliberately courting trouble. Mechanically he ran a hand through his iron-grey hair and then called to the men as they went to the door.

"You're power-mad, you people! You've got too much of it for anybody's good—the country's or your own!"

"We'll see," said Horn, and left the room. Van Heerden, with a tight, muscular walk, fell into step beside him down the corridor and gave him a slow grin.

"You got an admission from Auntie Dora then," Horn said.

"She couldn't wait to talk."

Horn opened the file and glanced at the three or four photographs that had been tucked into a pocket inside the back cover. He made a lewd face.

64

"Van, maybe it was a bit of luck for us tonight after all!"

On the inside front cover were printed, as usual, the words GEHEIM/SECRET, and beneath them was a cautionary extract from Section 3 of the Act as amended by another section of yet another Act. The name neatly stencilled in black ink beneath all this was BLANE, IRINA MARIE (NÉE VAN NIEKERK).

The Valiant was out of Cape Town, its speed settled at seventy, the beams of its lights lancing far ahead along the straight open highway, and Keogh could hardly believe his luck.

A few minutes earlier, at nine o'clock, there had been a news bulletin sandwiched between the advertising jingles on the car radio. There were just three items; the one about Oosthuizen was the last and sent a quiver up his spine. It had an official, unfamiliar ring, so that he wondered for a second if they were talking about the same incident. Oosthuizen was in the Groote Schuur Hospital with a fractured skull after being attacked by a white thug at a house in District Six. His condition was serious, and police were searching for his assailant. They were also looking for a Bantu man who had been arrested and who escaped in the confusion.

"White thug," said Shack from the back seat. "You ever been called that before, Jimmy?"

"He's not dead, anyway."

"Don't let it get on your conscience. Then you really *will* be in trouble."

"I don't understand this," Keogh said. "It's serious.

They sound serious about it, yet they haven't set up a single roadblock."

"Don't wish it on yourself."

"What's the matter, are they just inefficient?"

The black man laughed and said nothing. It had been all very well for him to talk about taking the back roads. Cape Town was on a peninsula, and the only practical way off that tongue of land was on the motorway system east of the city in the bottleneck of flat ground between the mountains and the sea. There were places where a single roadblock could have stopped every vehicle entering or leaving. But there had been no roadblocks. Just once, near the airport, he had seen a police Studebaker cruising slowly ahead of them and had kept well behind until it picked up speed and turned off the road with its aerial whipping.

Both of them could feel the tension beginning to drain. Shack clumsily climbed over into the front seat and pulled out the brandy bottle, holding it between his manacled hands. "Bastard things," he said.

"Are they hurting?"

"He made them too tight on purpose. The wrists are swelling. Drink?"

"Not now. There's nothing we can do about the handcuffs till morning. I need a hacksaw." They were one more problem he did not care to think about before he had to. "Tell me about the Congress. What it is. What it wants."

Shack looked at him resignedly. "You say you live in Zambia. You never heard of a man called Wilby Xaba?"

Yes, he knew the name. It was one that carried a lot of weight up there.

"Wilby Xaba, President of the Congress in Exile," Shack said importantly.

"I'd forgotten his title."

"He's a bright boy, a *slim* kaffir. I was the one who got him out of the country; you could say I gave him his big chance. He's the only one the Boers are really scared of, you know that? We used to say he's the only black man who can think like a white man."

In fact he had more claims to distinction than that. Keogh had been in Africa long enough to appreciate the scarcity value of a leader who could create unity out of the tribal and factional conflicts of black politics. There were a dozen or more organizations of exiles in Lusaka and Dar es Salaam calling themselves liberation groups. Loosely composed of Marxists and Maoists, Zulus and Shonas, idealists, charlatans, opportunists, and plain spies, they had tended until recently to spend most of their time squabbling among themselves. As Keogh saw it, this gave them an excuse for deferring the really awesome task of overthrowing white rule in the south. From among all this Wilby Xaba and his movement had emerged in the last year or two as the one truly effective and disciplined force. Like the rest it was short money, but its prestige and membership grew at the expense of the others. Wilby Xaba had managed to make secondary issues of both ideology and tribalism. The Russians and Chinese wooed him with weapons and training for his guerillas, though politically he remained independent of both; Zambia provided him with a base from which, sometime in the foreseeable future, he should be able to launch and sustain a major offensive across the Zambezi and the Limpopo. Wilby Xaba was the leader of the nearest thing there had yet been to a black army of liberation.

The car had begun to climb away from the coastal plain; Africa is really one enormous ancient plateau separated by mountain ranges from the narrow strip of low ground along its seaboards. The headlight beams bounced off granite cliff faces, picking out tiny waterfalls that stabbed like silver needles into crevices full of ferns and evergreens. Keogh left the main road as soon as he could, cutting through two small towns called Paarl and Wellington that were already half asleep, and picking up a provincial road that wound up into the Matroosberg range.

"You know Wilby Xaba well?" he asked. He did not try to imitate the deep-throated click with which Shack pronounced the surname.

"Not well. It just happened I was taking him across the border into British Bechuanaland when I got shot—that's Botswana now; it's the same way we'll be going, only if we're lucky we won't run into any ears. I was getting him out of their way, just after the Sharpeville shootings in nineteen-sixty. They shot me on the foot. Wilby got across, and they didn't like that because he was the one they really wanted. They took it out on me. When my foot healed they sent me to the Island for four years for assisting the aims. Just before I should have come out they took me across the bay and tried me under Suppression of Communism. That was five more years, and later another five. I mean, they just call it a new name every time and it can go on for as long as they want it to." He drank what was left of the brandy, rolled down his window, and flung the bottle carelessly out. It shattered on the road behind them. "They'd leave me there till they were sure the fight was gone. See, I'm nobody that matters. I don't get English politicians visiting me to ask what I had for breakfast and whether I got fleas in my blankets. No nice liberals wonder what became of Shack Twala. I'm real, I'm not an idea in somebody's head. Out in the townships they know that, even if they never heard of me. The Boers aren't just showing me that it didn't work once, they're showing all those kaffirs that it never will work. Ever." He glanced at Keogh. "You believe me?"

"Why shouldn't I?"

"White people don't like hearing this stuff, that's all."

"Maybe I'm different."

"Yeah," Shack conceded. "You're different, Jimmy."

"I don't give much of a damn for politics. I'm not nice enough to be a liberal. It wasn't out of any noble motives that I smashed Oosthuizen, you know, it was because for a moment I hated him. You can't get any less noble than that. I wanted him to learn. I wanted to smack the ignorance and arrogance off his fat face. Of course it never works."

"I felt like that often," Shack said, "but I haven't got your size. And your temper. You're a doer, not a talker. I liked what you did there—boom! I liked that very much."

They rode on for a while in silence, and finally Shack fell into an uneasy spluttering sleep. The country changed again as they crossed the escarpment onto the edge of the great African plateau. This was the Great Karroo, a wind-swept semi-desert, rolling slopes and flat-topped hills patched with scrub and meagre grass. The silhouette of a steel wind pump rose against the moonlit sky here and there, sometimes with a flock of sheep huddled round it, backs to the wind. The traffic thinned out and finally the Valiant seemed quite alone in the middle of the great black waste-land. It would be easy enough out here to relax a bit and let his mind drift away from his predicament, except that it in-sisted on drifting back to Rina. They must have found her and questioned her by now; what had she told them? A plausible story, no doubt, as long as they were ready to listen to it. The two of them, for want of a better word, were *involved*. People who were involved could be expected to shield each other. If they were suspicious, if they sniffed around and learned that she had been using a car and found out the number—well, he would rather avoid thinking about that.

By now the police must surely have identified the African who'd been hiding in Auntie Dora's. They might easily conclude that he and Keogh had joined up and were travelling together; they might start checking up on Shack's old connections. None of it sounded as easy as it had a couple of hours ago in Rina's flat.

Soon after one o'clock Keogh stopped in a village with a ramshackle petrol station, which was open. He wakened Shack, slipped off his own jacket, and draped it across the handcuffed wrists before driving in. While the old coloured attendant filled the tank, Keogh bought two plastic cups of coffee from a vending machine, passing one through the passenger's window onto the sill in front of Shack. They were both hungry but knew there was no chance of buying food before morning. A freezing wind blew from the Karroo down the dusty main street.

"My hands," the black man whispered. He was staring down at them. "I can't feel anything in my hands."

Keogh took a surreptitious look. The handcuffs were nickel-plated steel, with each of the U-shaped pieces locking into a hollow bar on a ratchet to make them adjustable for size. They had been clamped onto Shack's skinny wrists as tightly as they would go, and the flesh above them had already swollen half an inch or more.

"Jesus," Keogh murmured. He turned to pay the atten-

70

dant and asked, as casually as he could, whether he could buy or borrow a hacksaw from the garage. The answer was no; the workshop was locked up. He crushed the plastic cup, threw it into the gutter, and slid behind the wheel. "You'll have to stick it out, that's all. Exercise your hands, keep the circulation going."

"It'll be bad by the morning," Shack said. Once the car had started and the attendant was waving them a perfunctory good-bye, he added, "You shouldn't have asked him. He'll remember you."

6

The Karroo reached away endlessly around them. Once every forty miles or so they drove through a sleeping dorp. Between these towns the white gravel road ran almost dead straight, unfurling itself three and five miles at a time from the crest of one hill to the crest of the next. There was no traffic, but still it was a difficult, exhausting road to travel. He had to keep his speed down. It was too easy to let the needle creep up from fifty to sixty to seventy and then to hit a bad bump or misjudge a bend, slither across the sand and off the road. He kept Shack awake, forcing him to talk, fighting away his own tiredness with the effort of listening.

"I knew Wilby, not well, at Fort Hare College. Yes, I was at college—you wouldn't think so—just for a year. I couldn't afford to keep myself there, and anyway I lost interest. You've either got a head for that stuff or you haven't. I would have become a teacher, I guess; what else does a black man do with that piece of paper? I went into trade-union work. It didn't pay peanuts and I ran a pirate taxi on the side. Wilby was different. Even then they used to say there was a big future for him, and the ears had a file on him that thick before he even left Fort Hare. That's where all the good politicians started, and most of them ended on Robben Island too. Anyway, he went on to take a law degree but he didn't practise law for long. I joined the Congress about fifty-five. By then I'd done a bit of this and a bit of that and got married and had a couple of kids. He was already the President. He'd turned it into a full-time job and he'd even made it pay. That was Wilby."

"And then?" said Keogh.

"What do you want to hear, my life story?"

"I want to know more about the Congress."

"It'll cost you a cigarette, Jimmy." He took one from the packet that Keogh passed him and lit it, spreading a red glow across his gaunt features. He drew on it deeply, luxuriantly, the prisoner's way. "We were never as big or as powerful as the two big movements, the ANC and the PAC. But we were well organized, see; we did good work together. Wilby had a head for all that. Make money before you make speeches, he used to say. He got teams of collectors organized to bring in the monthly dues instead of waiting for people to send them in when they felt like it, which would have been never. He was always writing and sending brochures and stuff to sympathizers overseas, and a lot of money came in that way. It was all legal then, of course. Our aims were peaceful: equal pay, better housing, more representation, and maybe one day we'd even get the vote. We had stars in our eyes, I guess.

"But things seemed to be getting done—you know, we thought we were making progress. There were meetings in the townships every weekend, marches and rallies and boy-cotts, stuff like that. People were restless; there was change in the air. And then Sharpeville happened—boom!"

"When was that?"

"The twenty-first of March, nineteen-sixty. A Monday. See, it's one day nobody in the Congress can forget."

The name was already enshrined, of course, in the mythology of the racial struggle. To those exiles up in Lusaka and Dar es Salaam it stood for the callousness and oppression of the system they wished to destroy. It was a self-evident symbol; it was their Bloody Sunday.

That day was chosen as the start of a national campaign among Africans against the pass system. It had been orga-nized mainly by the Pan-Africanist Congress, one of the two biggest black political movements, but smaller groups such as Wilby's Congress had agreed to take part. People were advised (in some cases, no doubt, with the help of threats) to stay away from work, to destroy the pass books which the law required them to carry, and to present themselves at police stations demanding to be arrested.

The response was good. As Shack had said, people were confident, buoyed up by a sense of impending change. The power of the African political movements and the prestige of their leaders had been growing. Could it be this campaign that would finally wring some concessions from the Govern-ment, force whites to take notice? All morning hundreds queued up at police stations to be arrested. The cells filled up, and still hundreds more stood outside. Both sides waited to see which would tire first; there were sporadic incidents but in general the mood seemed good. In the township of Sharpeville in the southern Transvaal that mood was sud-denly shattered.

The police station and its compound there were surrounded by a barbed-wire fence. During the morning a crowd gathered outside it and grew to several thousand; undoubtedly most of them, having stayed off work, were there as idle onlookers, but the sight of the besieged police growing steadily more nervous must have been exhilarating. Some stones were thrown. Reinforcements with armoured vehicles were called in; someone was witless enough to order jet fighters to fly low over the crowd, as if believing these sceptical townspeople would scatter like savages. It only made them more defiant. More stones were thrown, but even at this point the crowd could be called no more than latently hostile.

Someone's nerve must have cracked. Exactly what happened was never established. Without warning the police unleashed a devastating hail of fire through the fence. Sixty-nine people were killed and many more wounded; most were hit from the rear as they tried to run away.

There had been similar incidents before. This one happened to come at a time when feelings were already at their boiling point. There were more strikes, more rioting, more shootings; people made bonfires of their passes in the streets. In the next ten days the Government people were nearer than they had ever been to losing control of the townships. To ease the tension they suspended the pass laws. Africans were wildly jubilant: had the log jam at last begun to shift?

Wilby was one man who did not share in the euphoria. He could see that after wavering between concession and repression, the Government must finally plump for repression. The political movements had become too strong to control; they would be crushed and their leaders arrested. Wilby hastily made plans to go underground, to keep the leadership of the Congress intact but move it somewhere safe. To many people this would seem like quitting in the middle of a winning run. He knew that in the long term there was more to gain from leaving the country than from staying.

Shack had smoked his cigarette to within a quarter inch of the end. He dropped it on the floor of the car and ground it out with his sandal. "So I was the one who took him out. Of course I was only a small cog in the Congress. The day of Sharpeville I'd been driving my old Chev taxi round the townships handing out pamphlets; that's the kind of stuff I did. The Friday after that, Hassim Mayat came to me, said he wanted me to make two trips to the border that night. I'd done it a few times before. Even in the legal days it wasn't easy for Congress people to get in and out the country. North of Mafeking there are little farm roads that run close to the border. I'd just drop them at a spot I knew and they'd walk right across into Bechuanaland. It was dangerous; not many people would do it."

"You must have been paid for it then," Keogh said.

"Hassim used to give me twenty pounds a trip, in advance. They must have given him something for finding me; I don't know. He's not the kind to confide that sort of thing."

"Couldn't he have kept the twenty and driven them himself?"

"You need a good man at the wheel. He couldn't drive so good. Getting old, and anyway he only had a car with those special controls for cripples."

Keogh was taken aback.

Shack said, "Didn't I tell you? He's a bit crippled."

"You certainly didn't."

"Gets about on crutches. Something with his knees."

Keogh found this disturbing without finding any specific objection. Shack went on.

"It's safer to arrange these things through a third person like Hassim. He was like me, nothing important in the Congress, but he was closer to the leadership through his brother Yusuf, who was the treasurer. This time Hassim gave me a hundred pounds, so I knew somebody big was involved. The ears were already looking for Wilby and he'd gone into hiding. Hassim just gave me directions to a place on the Far West Rand, a little store right out in the veld, told me get there at eleven o'clock. When I arrived Hassim was waiting with Wilby and Yusuf. I had to take them separately—Wilby first, then come back for Yusuf—to cut down the risk of them both getting caught."

"Instead you got caught yourself," said Keogh.

"I told you about that. They were waiting on the same little track I always used, a carload of ears. But they cocked it up; I saw a reflector glinting in my headlights fifty yards ahead and stopped the car and we just ran. They got me in the foot with a lucky shot, smashed the bones. Wilby made it across the border. So that's the story."

The fine white dust of the road had been seeping invisibly into the car. Keogh could taste it on his lips. "Who told them?" he said.

"The jacks? Jimmy, I don't know. They never gave anything away. At first I used to break my skull wondering about it. Later I decided it happened by chance—yeah, things do happen by chance. I'd used that track too often, some white farmer had seen me and reported me. Or they'd caught one of the people I took across earlier and he'd blabbed. Only four people knew I'd be using that route on that night—the two Mayat brothers, Wilby, and me. None of us stood to gain, as far as I know."

"What happened to the Mayats?"

"In the prison hospital I heard on the grapevine that Yusuf had got across the border the next night on a different route. But then the British wouldn't let him through into Northern Rhodesia. He's been there in Lobatsi ever since; Wilby gave him a job as the local representative of the Congress. Hassim, he just never got involved."

"You mean you kept him out of it?"

"They had me in a place called the Truth Room, but I managed not to tell them too much. Hassim owes me that favour. That's why I know he expects me."

Keogh drove on in silence. He was more uneasy than ever about the idea of depending on Shack's friends in the Congress. A man in prison is in an emotional vacuum; he cannot comprehend how relationships and loyalties outside are shifting and being rearranged, and he comes out expecting to find them much as they were. The Congress itself, like everything else, had changed. The years before Sharpeville and the attempts to fight apartheid on its own terms, constitutionally, had led finally to despair. Men like Wilby Xaba were as committed now to a violent solution as they had once been to peace. In a way you couldn't blame them, Keogh thought. And you couldn't blame them either if they distrusted a strange white man who'd done nothing more sympathetic than knock a policeman down with a bottle. Still, he had money, and that might well be more use than political credentials.

He had studied a map that he'd found in the glove box and decided to pick up the tarred road again at Victoria West.

It was riskier, no doubt, but it would save a further detour of about a hundred miles between there and Kimberley. Speed was important, and since there had been no roadblocks in the obvious places, the chances of meeting one now seemed negligible. Once on the tar he let the needle drift up to eighty and finally ninety; in that vast empty country there was hardly a sense of speed at all.

The night dragged itself off the Karroo like a wounded beast. Soon after sunrise they crossed the Orange River at Hopetown. Shack had not spoken for a couple of hours, and when Keogh stopped to examine his wrists again he understood why. The flesh was puffed up in great livid bands around the handcuffs. Soon the swellings would surround the steel and make it impossible to get at. In the light the black man's face was a mess as well. He was sweating. His lips had been bleeding again, and when he managed to smile he showed his broken front tooth. Keogh discovered a grudging affinity for him, a feeling compounded of liking and vague pity. He no longer cared so much what he had done to Oosthuizen.

"You are going to fix these soon, Jimmy?"

"As soon as I can. How do they feel?"

"The hands feel of nothing. The wrists ache a bit."

"You don't have to be a goddamned hero."

"All right," Shack said. "They hurt like hell, all right?"

An hour later they were in Kimberley, driving past the edge of the old open mine called the Big Hole. During the diamond fever of the last century, thousands of men working their claims had dug deeper and deeper until they were crawling about like maggots in a hole two-thirds of a mile deep. Nowadays it was all done more methodically on the other side of town, where De Beers mined the diamonds and

79

regulated their flow onto the market at the right level to keep the prices buoyant.

Past Market Square Keogh stopped at a small garage for petrol. The shops were just opening. It was a cool bright morning, and people walked to work looking well-rested and clean-shaven. He felt dirty; his mouth was like a sewer. With the tank filled he moved the car away from the pumps and parked it at the front of the forecourt. Shack stayed in his seat with Keogh's raincoat spread across his arms, and Keogh went shopping.

He ordered six hamburgers from a Greek café, and while they were being prepared he visited a hardware shop, a chemist, and a bottle store. He bought a hacksaw and a dozen blades, the best file he could find, and a five-gallon plastic jerrycan. There was nothing unusual about these purchases so it must have been his appearance, unshaven and grubby-collared, that drew an odd look from the assistant. As an afterthought he took a small enamel washbasin and hurried on to the chemist: a couple of packets of gauze bandages, some lint and cotton wool, a tin of antiseptic ointment, Dettol, and a bottle of the strongest pain-killers he could buy without a prescription. Finally he picked up a bottle of vodka, collected his hamburgers, bought that morning's *Diamond Fields Advertiser*, and glanced through it on his way back to the garage. The world that its headlines were talking about seemed a very distant place. In the stop press column he found a small item on Oosthuizen, the same version as the radio had given with no new details.

His shopping had taken twenty minutes. Shack was sitting staring straight ahead when Keogh opened the door and dumped the things he had bought on the back seat.

"Two Boers are watching me," the black man said quietly.

"Where?"

"In a black car behind the petrol pumps. They been watching me ten minutes."

From where Keogh stood he could see only the rear end of a big car stained with Karroo dust. "Everybody seemed to be staring at me too," he said.

"I'm not imagining it, Jimmy. First they drove past, then they came back and bought petrol. Now they're just sitting."

"It needn't mean anything," Keogh said, but he felt something go tight in his stomach. He realized that Shack's face was gleaming with sweat.

"Let's get out," the black man said hoarsely, still not looking at him.

"Wait." He still thought Shack was wrong, but either way it was no good panicking. He took the jerrycan to a tap at the end of the row of petrol pumps and began to fill it, glancing up at the black car that was now facing him. It was a Buick Electra with a green-tinted windscreen and a short radio pylon on the roof. The two men in the front appeared, indeed, to be doing absolutely nothing. Through the green glass he could not see their faces clearly.

He went on running water into the can. It seemed to take a long time. Then as he turned off the tap and screwed the cap down he heard one of the Buick's doors opening and someone getting out. Without taking his eyes off the tap he knew the man was coming towards him, stopping in front of him. His skin crawled. He could hardly find the courage to look up but finally he did, from a pair of battered suede shoes to a nondescript dark suit creased and rumpled from travelling to sallow cheeks, a curly moustache, and a wide mouth. The features all seemed to be bunched around the filter-tipped end of a long unlit cigarette which at that moment dominated the face.

"Trouble you for a light?" said the man.

Keogh stared at him stupidly for a few seconds before taking out his lighter and holding it to the cigarette. The man drew on it gratefully and sent a stream of blue smoke out against the morning sunlight.

"Car lighter conked out," he said. "The little things always go first on these big jobs, isn't it? On your way to Jo'burg?"

Keogh was bewildered again until he remembered that the Valiant was registered in Johannesburg. The fact was clear from the TJ number-plates.

"That's right," he said. He wanted to get away. He picked up the heavy can of water and carried it to the Valiant, but the man strolled conversationally beside him. He was small, barely reaching Keogh's shoulder.

"Suppose I shouldn't smoke next to the pumps. I see you've been through the Karroo as well." He was looking at the dust on the side of the car. "I usually go through Bloemfontein. Thought this time we'd try the Kimberley way. There seems to be less traffic."

"I've never been the other way," said Keogh.

"No? Either way you can't avoid the Karroo. My brother-in-law and I go to the Cape on holiday every year. Every year I say to him, Van, I say, never again. Not through the Karroo again. And every year we find ourselves doing it." He gave a laugh that turned into a fit of coughing.

He had one of a dozen typical Afrikaans faces that

Keogh had learned to recognize among miners on the Copperbelt: wide square cheeks shelving down to a narrow jaw, bony forehead, and prominent brows. Specifically his own were the moustache, the rather bitter mouth, the sallow skin, as well as the flat-bridged nose and the particular kind of crinkly brown hair that suggested a touch of colour a long way back in his ancestry. Such people were often the most dedicated racialists of all. The eyes were dark too, and Keogh suddenly realized why he had an impulse to turn his head whenever the small man spoke. He never looked at Keogh directly; he seemed to be addressing someone else beyond his shoulder.

"These cancer sticks," he said, recovering from his coughing fit. "My gravestone is chiselled already, you know: 'Died serving the tobacco industry.'" He laughed again and took a packet of fifty from his pocket. "Sorry, I didn't offer you one."

"Not for me," Keogh said. "I've got to go."

The packet fell open as he replaced it, spilling a dozen cigarettes on the ground. While Keogh seethed with impatience the Afrikaner got down on his hands and knees and groped carefully beneath the rear mudguard of the car until he had recovered every one.

Keogh humped the jerrycan onto the back seat. "You must excuse me."

"Am I keeping you? We must go too, get back to the farm and see what the kaffirs have been up to." Shack still sat woodenly in the car a couple of feet away, but the small man spoke as if he were not there. "You know what it's like with these people, they won't work unless you're there to chase them. We grow citrus, not far from Pretoria. You should drop in one day; we'll give you a bag of oranges."

Keogh said nothing. The man, seeming to sense finally that he was unwelcome, squinted into the sun and gave a mock salute with his cigarette. "Thanks. Maybe we'll see you on the way."

He walked back to the Buick. The other man—Van, the brother-in-law, presumably—glanced up. Keogh saw only a round pale face and a pair of cheap dark glasses.

He slid behind the wheel, started the Valiant, and swung out onto the Transvaal road. Shack flung the raincoat into the back and wiped sweat from his face. "Jesus," he muttered.

"You heard it all?" said Keogh.

"What did he want?"

"A light."

"You believe that crap? Listen, you didn't see how they sat and watched me. Just sat looking me all over for ten minutes."

"What's your theory then?"

"I only know one kind of person looks at you like that. Ears."

"It's your nerves," said Keogh, without quite believing himself. He glanced at the mirror, half expecting to see the Buick slide onto the road behind them. "If they were the police why didn't they pick us up?"

"I don't know." Shack was sulkily silent for a minute. "I just got a feeling about those shits, Jimmy. That's all."

Keogh kept his eye on the mirror for several miles on the way out of Kimberley. Finally convinced beyond any doubt, he said, "They didn't follow us."

"What does that prove?"

"Take some codeine tablets. You'll need them soon."

7

The morning quickly grew warmer. Soon they were out of the Karroo and just edging into the Highveld: fields of hard brown grass, the winter stubble of mealie lands, farmhouses with their wind pumps and iron outbuildings standing at the ends of long driveways lined with bluegum trees. Herds of humpbacked Afrikander cattle were being driven along by black children in the boiling red dust beside the road.

Keogh searched for a place where he could cut off Shack's handcuffs without being disturbed. It was becoming urgent: the metal would soon be embedded too deeply in the swollen flesh, and then nothing but surgery would get it out. As it was the hacksaw was going to cut into the wrists. Keogh had been trained in basic first aid for mining casualties; he did not care to wonder what he would do if the wounds turned septic, or if the diminished blood supply to the hands had caused some irreversible damage to the tissues.

Twice he turned into the veld along unsurfaced tracks, discovered that they led to farmhouses, and had to return to the main road. The third time, the Valiant clanked over a cattle grid and followed the sandy track for five hundred yards till it crossed a small ridge and petered out at the gate of an empty livestock kraal. To judge by the broken barbed wire, the powdery dung, and the old hoofprints embedded in the hard cracked earth, the place hadn't been used since at least the rainy summer season. It seemed ideal, well away from the road and out of sight. Perhaps once the handcuffs were off they'd be able to snatch a couple of hours' sleep here; Keogh had already caught himself nodding off at the wheel.

They left the car under the trees. He took the equipment out, told Shack to sit down in the sunshine, and looked at the wrists. The steel was cutting horribly into them; in places it had broken the skin and was almost buried in the swellings. The quickest place to saw through would be the toothed ends of the rings, where they were thinnest, but the swellings were enormous there and it would be far too easy for the blade to slip through the tendons or even the artery. He would have to cut through the thick crosspiece over the bony back of the wrist. He fitted a blade to the hacksaw and looked at Shack's face. The black man was running a temperature now, and the whites of his eyes were tinged with a fevered yellow.

"It's going to hurt." He supposed he spoke with the indecent detachment of a dentist, but he could not think what else to say.

Shack nodded. "Give me a cigarette, Jimmy." He sat cross-legged on the ground, the cigarette between his lips, laid his hands out on a flat stone, and closed his eyes. Keogh squatted in front of him and began to saw.

It took an hour, an agonizing and bloody hour. The

blades slipped on the smooth nickelled surface and broke, three of them in quick succession, and Keogh began to panic. It could be that the steel would prove too tough. He tried giving the saw a start by cutting a notch with the edge of the file. It was slow, but it worked: the fourth blade bit through the hollow bar on the right wrist. Inevitably it cut Shack as well; he sat with his teeth gritted and his eyes closed, pouring with sweat. The hand and steel became slippery with blood. When Keogh finally cut through the last sliver of steel and eased the handcuff away and blood rushed through the released artery into his hand, Shack gave a snarl of pain and fell back on the ground, panting.

Keogh stood up. His arm ached and there was a broken blister on his palm. He mixed Dettol with water in the enamel basin to wash the wrist, which had now swollen up like a great brown balloon. He spread antiseptic ointment on the lint, placed it over the wounds, and wrapped a length of bandage, not too tightly, around it. He could only hope to God that it wouldn't go septic.

Shack did not have the strength to sit up again. He lay on his back, just managing to smile when Keogh gave him a sip of water. Then Keogh started on the other wrist.

This time it went more quickly, but the bleeding and the cry of pain at the end were repeated. He washed and dressed the wounds and flung the handcuffs away into the grass. He fetched his coat from the car and spread it over Shack; the black man had taken about six codeine tablets before the operation, and together with plain exhaustion they were already sending him to sleep.

Keogh washed the blood off his hands, took a long swig from the vodka bottle, and sat down to smoke a cigarette. He watched a platoon of red ants dragging something that looked like an emerald over a dry tuft of grass at his feet. It was a dung beetle with bright green wings, kicking feebly against the relentless grip of the predators. There was suddenly a nightmarish sense of unreality about this place and about the reason why he was here. Cause and effect were dissociated in his mind; he could not understand that he was actually a hunted man nor what had brought him into a lonely patch of veld with a black jailbird. He'd had the same kind of feeling when he was trapped down the mine; it was light-headedness that caused it. At least here it was sunny and peaceful, and there were turtle-doves cooing in the branches of the blue gums.

He would have liked to sleep but he knew he was still too tense. Instead he went to the car, took the toilet bag out of his suitcase, filled the enamel bowl with cold water, and shaved gingerly, looking into the wing mirror of the Valiant and noticing the signs of strain—the skin pale, the blue eyes edged with red. His hand was still steady enough, anyway. He washed and changed his clothes, putting on corduroy trousers, a cashmere sweater, and a brown leather jacket, remembering to transfer his money, passport, and keys before he packed away the other clothes. He tried, with some vague idea of altering his appearance, to comb his thick thatch of hair into a different style, but soon gave it up.

Shack slept on. It was an uneasy, mumbling kind of sleep and there were beads of sweat along his upper lip. Keogh decided to leave him for at least an hour, hoping his temperature would come down. He lit a cigarette and strolled up among the blue gums to the ridge overlooking the track and the main road.

There was not much traffic. Cars went by at intervals of a couple of minutes, and an African on a donkey cart with buckled wheels came wobbling down the road towards Kimberley. Following his progress Keogh saw a point of light, the glint of something catching the sun, among the trees on this side of the road.

It was something stationary, a small shiny surface, and when he moved a couple of yards it had gone. A piece of broken glass, perhaps. But having nothing better to do than satisfy his curiosity he walked to the right along the ridge, crossing the track, until he was in line with a small gap in the double row of blue gums beside the road. There was a sort of lay-by there, a cleared space with moulded concrete tables and stools set in the grounds, where travellers could stop to picnic. And there was a car, parked off to the side in the shadow of the trees. He could not see much of it; it was only by chance that the sunshine filtering through the leaves had struck a tiny glint off the rear bumper of the black Buick.

He stood there feeling the chill of the trees' shade and the icicles forming round his heart. So they *had* followed. But how? He had been absolutely certain there was no car in sight when he turned off onto the track. It was possible— he wanted desperately to believe it was possible—that they had stopped there by chance. The little man with the eyes that never seemed to focus had said they were anxious to get back to their farm, yet they had lingered at the garage and now they were lingering here. What did they want? Perhaps they had suspected something, had followed the Valiant here, were waiting for it to leave, and would follow again. No matter how hard he tried to shake them off, he would never outrun that 7½-litre engine.

The Buick was about a quarter of a mile away. The ridge ran parallel to the main road for a couple of hundred yards and then curved in towards it, so by following it round he could get closer to the car and have a clearer view of it. He went back behind the ridge and walked until he entered the shadow of the trees close to the road. Under this cover he came stealthily onto the higher ground again and was directly behind the Buick, a hundred yards away. It was empty. There was no one in the clearing.

He looked all round him carefully, edgily. Where the hell had they got to? Maybe he should go back, collect Shack, and clear out while he could, but the car standing there unattended was far too tempting. It would take only a minute to remove the distributor head or rip out the ignition wires and leave the two Afrikaners stranded. He went forward again, moving from one tree trunk to the next, placing each foot with care among the dead leaves and bark that covered the ground. From time to time a car sped past along the road, but he knew he could not be seen in the shadows. In five minutes he stood at the edge of the clearing. Still no sign or sound of anyone. He stepped out and went back to the Buick.

It was a two-door model and both doors were locked. The bonnet, then? But the release catch was probably inside the car anyway. He picked up a chunk of concrete, the size of his fist, that had broken off one of the picnic tables and wrapped his handkerchief around it. There was no time for delicacy. He smashed the quarter-light on the passenger's side with a single muffled crack, reached through the splintered glass, and unlocked the door.

Squatting on the seat, he reached across for the bunch of leads behind the ignition lock. But his attention was caught by the equipment fitted to the shelf beneath the dashboard in front of him. On the left was a radio telephone, which explained the need for the eighteen-inch pylon on the roof. What did a farmer want with a phone in his car, anyway? Next to it was an object the size and shape of a large cigar box, with a single-band dial and a control panel at the front not unlike that of an ordinary radio receiver. But there was a green light at either side of the panel, which was curious; the light on the left was on. Perhaps the most intriguing item was another metal box with a circular dial; the indicator needle, pivoted on a knob at the centre, could be turned through 360 degrees. Keogh moved it a fraction and the green light went off.

He knew very little about radio, just enough to recognize this as highly specialized equipment of some sort. Its appearance suggested a vague familiarity of function, but he could not place it. He reached for the ignition leads again. Then he was absurdly aware that someone had tossed a handful of small pebbles through the open door into his lap.

The big man called Van had approached so silently that he had had to do something to draw Keogh's attention. He stood twenty feet away at the edge of the clearing and he was holding a gun, a heavy-calibre revolver with a long barrel, a very utilitarian-looking gun. And the way he held it was businesslike, in both hands at arm's length, standing with his knees bent in a slight crouch, sighting down the ribbed barrel with the notch of an adjustable rear sight and the ramp at the front lined up on the spot where Keogh's collarbones met. He felt a tickling sensation there as if someone were touching him with a feather.

Van jerked the revolver very slightly to indicate that he should stand up.

Keogh got out of the car and stood with his back pressed to a window. "All right," he said, hearing his voice come out in a croak. "All right, you can put it down now."

Van did not move except to thumb back the hammer slowly, cocking the revolver. His face was pale and puffy, with a slightly greasy texture, and there was no expression on it. If there was any in his eyes it was hidden by the dark glasses. He wore a blazer with green and yellow stripes and a badge with a rugby ball in the middle.

"Would you ever stop pointing that thing at me," Keogh said. His mouth had gone dry. He stared obsessively at the muzzle of the gun, as if by a concentration of willpower he could prevent its going off. But in a corner of his eye he saw the small man approaching down the track from the ridge and had a sick realization of his own stupidity. They hadn't been at their car because they had been watching him—watching him up there until he had moved, and then Van had followed him down like a big silent animal.

The little man was lighting a cigarette as he came through the trees. He stopped next to Van, narrowing his eyes against the smoke. "Well," he said. "Well. We wondered how much we'd scared you. And now we know, eh?"

"I won't run away," Keogh said. "Tell him he doesn't need to point that at me."

"It wouldn't be clever to run," the small man said agreeably. "Old Van is bloody good. Out on the farm he practises with that Python every day. I've seen him hit six mealie cobs in a row at thirty paces—knock them right off their stalks, with the wind blowing them around too."

"I thought you grew oranges," Keogh said.

"Shut up!" hissed Van with unexpected vehemence.

"Of course," said the little man, "if you *want* us to shoot you . . . I mean, the police won't make any trouble. We caught you breaking into our car, didn't we?"

Bewildered, still staring at the gun muzzle, he felt as if it were exerting some pressure on his chest, forcing him back against the side of the car. Yet he had the faintest impression that they did not quite know what to do with him, that in some way he had upset their calculations by coming down to the Buick. "Who are you?" he said. "What do you want?"

The Afrikaner looked through Keogh with his strange eyes. "Tell me what you think."

"It occurred to me that you were policemen."

An amused grunt. "Everybody looks like a policeman when you're on the run, isn't it? No, *jong*, we're just two farm boys who happen to read our papers. The minute I saw you I said to old Van here, Those are the two they want in Cape Town. They've got a hunted look about them, I said, that bloke and that kaffir. Well, we knew our duty as citizens. We thought we'd turn you in."

"Why did you wait?"

"Oh, we couldn't be sure till we watched a bit longer. We followed you, saw you cut the handcuffs off your kaffir pal. Took a bit of guts that, I will say. But then you're right; that wasn't the only reason. We thought it would be interesting. No, to say the truth, we thought there might be something in it for us. I mean, they're not offering a reward. You'd better turn round. Lay your arms out over the roof."

Keogh did as he was told, feeling his muscles grow even tenser. Quick hands searched his pockets, removing his wallet, passport, and travellers' cheques. Behind him there was a satisfied silence while the money was counted, and then the small man said, "I knew a fellow like you wouldn't travel without plenty of this. Good clothes, American car. It was worth an hour's delay."

Something was specially humiliating about this. "The police know exactly how much money I've got with me," Keogh said. "I'll tell them what happened. I won't let you get away with it."

Again he did not hear Van come up behind him. He felt something strike the back of his head just above the hairline and knew quite irrelevantly that it must be the flat butt of the Colt Python revolver. The top of his skull seemed to lift off, the space between his eyes widened, and he felt himself fall across the cool metal of the car bonnet. Within the rapidly narrowing margins of his consciousness he seemed to understand at last what had happened. His knees buckled and he fell to the ground.

When he came round he could taste sand and the seed pods of blue gums in his mouth. A turtle-dove cooed solicitously somewhere overhead. He was lying on his side among the trees fifty yards from the clearing, and he could see at once that the Buick had gone. He raised an arm to feel his head; the movement sent pain driving through it like a steel spike. There was a patch of hair matted with dry blood.

"Bastards," he said aloud, and tried to look at his watch. It had gone the same way as his money and passport. But they had folded up two ten-rand notes and tucked them into his top pocket. As an afterthought, perhaps—afraid suddenly that he would give himself up and identify them—they had left him enough cash to get to Johannesburg, together with his keys.

It was a few minutes before he gained the courage to

stand, and then he almost fainted with the dizzying pain that lanced through his head and neck. He clung to a tree trunk for support, tottered to another, and so made his way slowly towards the ridge and the old kraal. The sun seemed at its warmest; he must have been unconscious three hours or more.

The Valiant was still there anyway, and so was Shack. It took only a glance to see that the black man had grown worse, not better. Keogh could not wake him; he had thrown aside the coat that had covered him and lay muttering and thrashing about on the grass. Keogh unwrapped the bandages. The wounds should probably have been washed every hour, but it could hardly have made any difference; the wrists were still swollen, the cuts made by the handcuffs and the saw were angrily inflamed. He cleaned them as well as he could, bandaged them again, and then went to the car, helped himself to some codeine and a mouthful of vodka. He splashed Dettol on the back of his head and water on his face.

The facts, filtering slowly through his pain and confusion, were: one, that he had been robbed and was virtually penniless and would have to throw himself on the mercy of Shack's friends in the Congress, and two, that Shack's wounds had become infected and he had slipped out of sleep into a fevered delirium. He needed a warm bed, antibiotics, experienced care. . . . He needed a doctor, why not admit it? And he needed one soon.

Shakily, Keogh lit a cigarette. This black man meant nothing to him, and he could be nothing now but a grave handicap. He was one of life's forgotten people. Nobody would miss him; he could die right here without anyone ever knowing the difference, least of all himself.

But Keogh knew he would not abandon him. It was not a gesture of self-sacrifice, just a kind of mean, unreasoning defiance. They seemed to have done everything they could to Shack, short of actually killing him, and Keogh sensed a need to withhold that final satisfaction from them.

Part III

GOLD TOWN

8

They reached Johannesburg around five o'clock, and the approach roads were clotted up with rush-hour traffic. Past the craggy yellow mine dumps at the southern edge the skyscrapers loomed, throwing long, cold shadows from the lowering sun down the canyon-like streets.

Keogh had been here before, on two very brief visits to a mining machinery plant to inspect some drilling gear before it was railed to Zambia. By now he had forgotten the names of the few business acquaintances he had made; certainly he knew no one he could trust. He had heard the fables about the place even earlier, of course. What miner hadn't? The gold mines had made it what it was: big, brash, vital, rich, and ugly. The mine dumps, great mountains of pulverized rock stained by cyanide and hardened over the years, stood guard round it like sentries. It had started life as a mining camp; at times it was possible to believe it still was one. Under the glint of newness and wealth it was a raw, brittle place where violence could strike with the sudden fury of a summer rainstorm.

Shack lay on the back seat, wrapped in Keogh's coat

and dressing gown. He was peaceful now but earlier he had been shouting, flinging himself about and falling on the floor. That had been out on the open road; Keogh could only hope he would remain quiet for the next hour. Driving in fits and starts through the traffic, he became nervous and intensely self-conscious. Apart from the irrational fear that everyone who happened to glance his way was about to recognize him, the presence of an obviously sick African on the back seat was no help at all. Besides, he found himself short of breath; he'd forgotten the place was six thousand feet above sea level.

On the south-west fringe of the city, a decaying area of old mine workings, factories, and fish and chip shops, he drove up a quiet back street, stopped at a phone booth, and opened the Johannesburg directory. With intense relief he found that Hassim Mayat's name was there, his profession listed as jeweller. It had to be the right one. His home was in Crown Road, Fordsburg, and there was a business entry as well: Market Street, Newtown.

It was an awkward time of day to turn up. Mayat could be at either address or travelling between them. The geography of central Johannesburg was a simple grid system, streets running north to south, streets running east to west. Market Street happened to be one that Keogh remembered, an east-west one. He decided to try there first.

It had been a hard drive from Kimberley. His head throbbed relentlessly, and tiredness and strain were catching up on him. Much of the time he had spent in a silent fury at Van and the man who called himself his brother-in-law. Funny, he had never learnt the little man's name. They had not just robbed him of over three hundred pounds, they had stolen his freedom of action. That was what bothered Keogh.

He now had four rands and fifty cents in his pocket; all the bargaining power he'd thought he would have with Hassim Mayat had gone. Instead, he had to depend on charity and the return of an old and dubious favour.

The two Afrikaners were a curious pair. Part-time crooks, no doubt, and yet they did not fit Keogh's conception of crooks. They were confident, *too* confident, almost. They were too good to be stupid, but what they had done remained basically rash. And there was the puzzling question of how they had managed to follow the Valiant from Kimberley, to find out where it had turned off the road, without Keogh spotting them. Anyway, here he was, a penniless fugitive with a sick man on his hands. At least he had the use of Paul Blane's flat as a hideout; they had not been able to take that away.

Newtown, huddled round one end of Market Street, was part of the old Indian quarter. East of Newtown the street travelled uphill, to the City Hall and the skyscrapers of the banks and mining corporations, and became respectable. Darkness had begun to fall when they arrived, and some of the merchants were putting up the mesh burglar screens on their shop windows. Beneath the old iron roofs, along the covered sidewalks, the doorways of dingy tenements were spaced out between textile wholesalers and silk bazaars. Faintly, smells of spiced cooking hung in the air. Mayat's shop had a narrow front, a window crammed with assorted watches and rings, and a sign in flaking gilt letters that said, "H. N. MAYAT, Quality Jewellers. Prompt Repairs, Accurate Valuations." The lights were on inside. Keogh turned down a side street and parked in the darkest spot he could find. Glancing once at Shack, hoping to hell he would keep quiet, he got out, looked up and down the street, locked the car, and hurried round the corner to the shop.

The door was half open and he went in. The place was like any other small jewellery business that hadn't the capital or the clientele to be too selective, with a few quality items gathering dust and a daily turnover in junk. There was a little glass counter partitioned into displays for Rolex, Omega, and Avia watches, a couple of trays of wedding and engagement rings, and a much larger counter full of semi-precious stones in cheap settings, filigree silver, and plastic watch straps, all with printed price tags on them.

Keogh knew almost nothing about Mayat. He had imagined him to be the way jewellers usually seemed to be, old, fussy, and rather untidy men. The man who looked up from an eyeglass was a young pleasant Indian in a white coat. He'd been examining the insides of a gold Hunter under an Anglepoise lamp at a workbench.

"Yes, sir?"

"Mr. Mayat?" Keogh said suspiciously.

"One moment." The young man moved along the counter and called out into the back of the shop. Now Keogh realized there was another room there, partitioned off by a green leather curtain. In a few moments the lower half of the curtain was drawn back.

This was more like the man he had expected. He was sixty or more, with thinning grey hair, caramel-coloured skin, and a broad, gloomy, vaguely oriental face. The eyes—heavy-lidded, with pouches of loose skin under them—looked distant and thoughtful. He had been wearing glasses with thick old-fashioned frames, and now they lay in his lap as he looked up at Keogh. He sat in a wheelchair. "Yes?" he said.

"Mr. Mayat? I need to talk to you." He glanced at the young assistant. "It's something personal."

Hassim Mayat thought about that for some moments. "Personal? You'll forgive me, perhaps I ought to know you?"

"No. An old friend of yours sent me. I have a message to give you in private."

Keogh tried to sound businesslike but he felt flustered. The sight of the wheelchair had disturbed him, and Mayat's expression—puzzlement now verging on suspicion—didn't help either. Could the Indian guess why he was here? It was difficult to tell what he was thinking. "My dear sir," he said, "this is a little confusing. An old friend? Surely this isn't the time. . . ."

"It's urgent," Keogh said flatly. "And important."

"Nothing is private about this shop. Forgive me if I'm suspicious. I am never left alone here, especially with a stranger."

"Then let's go somewhere else."

Mayat thoughtfully stroked the arms of the wheelchair with his palms. "Urgent, important, you say; I distrust words like that. At my age, the things that young men find important and urgent seldom are. I must ask you to explain what you want."

Keogh sighed. He was too tired and irritable to argue without losing his temper. "I'll give you his name," he said, and looked around for something to write on. The assistant, tinkering at the workbench, gave no indication that he had been listening, but he could hardly have stopped himself. Keogh tore a scrap off a sheet of wrapping paper that lay on the counter, took out his ballpoint pen, and wrote SHACK TWALA.

He handed it to Mayat, who put on his glasses and

studied the slip of paper for something approaching a minute. His expression did not change, except perhaps to become a little sadder and more distant. When he looked up he avoided Keogh's gaze and said to the young man, "Farouk, you can go. I will lock up." He reversed the wheelchair, its tires squeaking on the linoleum, and propelled himself past the leather curtain. Keogh followed.

The office was small, tidy and functional: a couple of box files open on the old partridge-wood desk, a hallmark chart, and a harmless airline calendar on one wall. A potted fern and a jeweller's scale in a glass case stood on top of the safe, and on a chair in the corner rested a red fez with a black tassel, the entitlement of a Muslim who had made a pilgrimage to Mecca.

Mayat manoeuvred himself behind the desk. Like many people whose legs have become useless he had developed powerful arms which filled out the sleeves of his check sports jacket. For a minute he said nothing. He unlocked the desk and the safe and carried out what must have been his nightly routine, transferring a bank bag full of money and several trays of rings into safe keeping. But he was alarmed, Keogh had no doubt about that. He was trying to straighten out his thoughts. Through the curtain they heard the assistant tidying up, and at last he called good night and slammed the front door behind him. Mayat locked the safe, hung the key on a leather thong round his neck, tucking it under his shirt collar, and swung round to face Keogh. His expression was as hostile as the bland features could make it.

"Whoever you are," he said, "whatever you know, let me make one thing clear. I cannot be blackmailed. You can threaten as much as you like."

Keogh could not help laughing. Perversely enjoying the suspense he had created, he went to the corner, removed the fez from the hard chair, drew it up to the desk, and sat down. "No, Mr. Mayat, it's not like that at all."

"What do you want then? Who are you?"

"I'll be brief. My name is Keogh. I'm wanted by the police. I happened to meet Shack in Cape Town. No doubt you know that he escaped from Robben Island ten or eleven days ago. I drove him up here. He's waiting outside, in the car."

Mayat stared at him. "You expect me to believe that?" he said finally.

"Come and see for yourself."

"What does it mean? Why should I listen to you? Do you think you're frightening me?"

"Yes," Keogh said. "But I didn't come here for that. He needs help, Mayat. We both need help. He's sick; he must have a doctor."

"Help?" Mayat, looking helpless himself, searched the room as if for a way of escape. "What help does he expect? Why have you come to me?"

"It'll save time if we understand each other. Shack has told me about you. I know about him and you and the Congress at the time of Sharpeville. I know it was you who arranged for Wilby Xaba to leave the country and that Shack was caught taking him across the border. He went to jail; he went there for both of you. It was Shack who saved you from going to Robben Island yourself. He's depending on you to return the favour."

"You don't know what you're asking."

"Don't I? I know the Congress still operates, and I know

your brother Yusuf works for them in Botswana. You've got to arrange with him to get Shack out by the old refugee escape route. I want to go along."

"I've told you I cannot be blackmailed."

"Blackmail doesn't come into it. We struck a bargain in Cape Town. I've kept my part of it by getting him this far."

"I still don't know who you are," Mayat said. "You're English, aren't you? You could be anybody."

"I'm a mining engineer and I live in Zambia. I have no way of proving who I am, and of course I can't blame you for suspecting a trap. Just reason it out. The police have never known about your connection with the Congress or Shack. They never suspected you had a part in Wilby's escape, did they? When they'd broken up the Congress all the ends tied neatly together, and you simply weren't among them. But there's always been the danger that they might find out, that circumstances might arise in which Shack could make it easier for himself by telling them. If you don't help him, why should he carry on protecting you? And why should I?"

"You don't understand," Mayat muttered. "You don't understand at all. You say he's sick?"

"He's got some kind of fever. His wrists are injured and they've become infected."

"Shack Twala. Poor Shack Twala." Mayat tried out the name on his tongue like a forgotten but suddenly familiar taste. Then he recollected himself and noticed, lying on the desk, the slip of paper Keogh had given him. He picked it up. "Do you have a match?"

Keogh gave him his lighter. Mayat held it to the edge of the paper, watched it blacken and curl, and dropped it into a waste bin at his feet. Keogh took back the lighter and lit a cigarette. He could sense the old man's hostility going, but in its place was a heavy impassivity.

Mayat swung his wheelchair round to face the small barred window behind the desk. It looked across three feet of darkening alleyway to a brick wall. "Yes, I've been expecting him," he said. "I've been waiting for a knock on my door ever since he escaped. There's no one else left, you see. I didn't want him. Let me be honest; I still don't want him. You're right, I owe him a great deal. And that makes it all the more difficult to explain that there's nothing I can do for him."

"What do you mean, nothing?"

"A lot has changed, Mr. Keogh. I have changed, to begin with. Rheumatoid arthritis has seen to that. I used crutches for as long as I could, until I could no longer manage." He turned to look at Keogh. "I suppose that's neither here nor there. How did you and Shack come to meet?"

"That can wait, can't it? I want to know where we stand."

"I'll try to explain that. It's only that you seem to know a good deal about me, while I know nothing about you."

Irritably, and as briefly as possible, Keogh told him about the incident in Auntie Dora's the night before—God, had it only been last night?—and what had happened since. He made two omissions from the story: he did not mention Rina or the two men from the Buick who had robbed him. There was no sense in making Mayat any more nervous or in dragging Rina in.

"So you hurt a policeman," the Indian said reflectively.

"Of course you must leave the country. But you seem to think it's simple. Shack has misled you. I knew he would mislead himself." He raised his arm and consulted a gold wristwatch. "I should have closed the shop already. Please turn off the light. If the police see it they may come to investigate."

Keogh stood up, went to the light switch next to the leather curtain, and snapped it off. He turned to the other man, now squatly silhouetted against the dim grey light that filtered through from the alley.

"Inside the country the Congress does not exist," Mayat said. "It's finished. It died the night Wilby left the country."

"But it's alive and kicking outside South Africa. There's Wilby in Lusaka; there's your brother in Botswana."

"Exactly. There's my brother in Botswana. Let me explain this to you. In the old days almost anyone could cross the border claiming to be a political refugee. All that has been tightened up. The authorities insist on bona fides being produced; understandably they don't wish to harbour—you'll forgive me—common criminals."

"Well?" Keogh said.

"Well, this puts Yusuf as the Congress representative there in a position of unique power. He provides the bona fides. The police depend on him; in a small way he's almost like an ambassador. He can give his approval to refugees or withhold it, as it suits him."

A dryness in Mayat's tone prompted Keogh to say, "Would money help?"

"If I know Yusuf, it probably would. You're going across as a criminal fugitive and asking for protection as a political refugee. You can't do without his co-operation. But the point is that I'm not the one to elicit that co-operation. Yusuf and

I have had nothing to do with each other since that very night."

Keogh stared in amazement. He could not see Mayat's face, but he sensed something like a rueful smile creeping into it.

"We quarrelled. We fought, I should say. I can't go into the reasons. We've been enemies ever since."

"And you won't declare a truce?" Keogh asked bitterly. "Not even for your old friend Shack?"

"I'm afraid we Muslims are known for our passionate enmities. But it's not from my side, you see; it's not from my side at all. I am indifferent. If I sent you to Yusuf he would refuse to help simply to spite me. He's a sullen, stubborn sort of man. My name is poison to him. He'll say he owes nothing to Shack either. You'll have to find another way."

"It's the only way out, and you know it."

"Go across, then. Approach Yusuf yourself. Take the chance of persuading him to help."

"It's too big a chance," Keogh said. "I have to be certain before I put myself in his hands. Surely there's some intermediary, someone else on this side who knows him?"

"No. Money might well be your best argument."

"Suppose I tell you I haven't got any?" Keogh turned away, an uncertain anger flickering in him.

Mayat said, "Whatever happens, you'll do best to leave me out of it. I've had my back turned on all this a long time. Are you convinced now that I can't help?"

"I'm convinced that you won't help," Keogh said, "and I want to know why. This story about a quarrel isn't good enough. No quarrel needs to last that long."

"I won't discuss that, Mr. Keogh." His voice, disembodied in the darkness, remained calm. He absorbed provocation like a sponge. "I've told you the facts as far as they affect you. They are quite true. I'm not trying to be obstructive."

"Then get a doctor," said Keogh abruptly, remembering the most urgent need. "Shack must be seen by a doctor tonight. Find one who won't give him away." He turned in time to catch the shake of Mayat's head.

"That will be difficult."

"Why is everything difficult, Mayat? Are you just a pessimist, or are you hoping I'll give up and go away? Because I won't, you know. Maybe it's true that you can't do anything about the escape route. You still claim to be grateful to Shack. Now's your chance to prove it. He may die unless he gets medical attention, and that's not a responsibility I'm prepared to accept. You find him a doctor or I'll dump him outside a hospital. He'll end up back on Robben Island once he's repaired. I can't see him being pleased with you, continuing to shield you."

"Mr. Keogh. . . ." Mayat's shoulders slumped a little and he sighed. "All right. There's a woman doctor I can trust. She may be agreeable as long as she deals with me alone. She must not meet you, and you will not know her name. Now let me state some conditions of my own. Shack will come to my house. I'm unmarried, I live alone, he will be quiet safe, but once he is well enough to leave he will go. I take no further responsibility. There's nothing I can do, and you must believe that. And you, you must fend for yourself."

"I have a place to go."

"I don't want to know anything more. As it is, you took a great risk coming here. Things are not the same any more. There are spies and informers everywhere. For both our sakes, we must not meet again."

It was quite dark outside now and, surrounded by distant traffic noises, the inside of the shop was like a small black vacuum of silence. Keogh said, "What are you really afraid of?"

"Involvement, that's all. The opening of old wounds. At my age, in my state"—he gestured down at his legs—"there is not much else to fear. You come here dragging the past with you. I would rather forget it."

9

Through the smoky darkness at the shabby end
of Market Street, past the scaly old mine dumps and across
a little depression called the Fordsburg Dip, Keogh in the
Valiant followed Mayat's car. The old Morris had been
modified; a lever on the steering column allowed Mayat to
control the accelerator, clutch, and brakes by hand, and a
sticker on the back window warned other motorists that he
was a disabled driver. Whether for that reason or not, he
was also a slow and hesitant driver who stopped laboriously
at every intersection, peering left and right a dozen times
before he ventured across. Keogh followed with dazed impatience; it had not occurred to him until he was about to
leave the jeweller's shop that he would have to carry Shack
into Mayat's house. With his handicap the old man could
not have managed.

Waiting outside while Mayat phoned the doctor, he
had discovered how thoroughly his mind was numbed by
fatigue. He could not even summon up much concern and
thought only that a suspicion he had been forming all day
had now been confirmed: none of this was as easy as Shack

had made out. The two of them were in a trap that had been camouflaged by false assumptions, baited by forgotten loyalties. But he was not annoyed with Shack. He hardly even wondered how much the black man had failed to tell him. He wanted only to get off the streets into the safety of his own hiding place where he could rest and think.

Shack lay on the floor behind the front seats, where Keogh had found him again, moaning and muttering incomprehensibly in Zulu. His eyes sometimes opened but they were unseeing eyes, glazed over, with the brown of the irises seeming to have melted into the whites. There was festering among the patches of broken skin on his wrists and, more ominously, a kind of dark subcutaneous stain. He could only hope the doctor, whoever she was, would be able to treat the infection on her own. She had agreed to be at Mayat's house in an hour's time, at eight o'clock.

Fordsburg—gloomy old streets, creaky hotels with wrought-iron balconies, cramped little one-storeyed houses —was one of those districts that street sweepers and lamp repairmen never seem to get round to. It had once been populated by white miners but was already sliding into decay at the time of the 1922 uprising and general strike, so the shellfire directed at strikers behind the Fordsburg barricades only hurried a process which had already begun. The miners' cause had been a strange synthesis of revolution and racialism. They feared, on the one hand, competition from cheap black and indentured Asian labour; on the other, exploitation by capitalist mine-owners. Proclaiming the brotherhood of man and white supremacy in the same breath, with an armoury of shotguns, pistols, and dynamite, they tried to take on Smuts' artillery. What had happened to Fordsburg since then seemed to complete the paradox. The whites had trickled away; Indians, coloureds, and Chinese had moved in.

Mayat made a turn and soon stopped outside a house at the end of a mean terrace. Keogh parked behind the Morris. The street was deserted. He watched Mayat leave the car as he had entered it, lifting his wheelchair from the back onto the pavement, unfolding it, and manoeuvring himself onto it from the driving seat. He pushed himself through the gateway and up a low ramp built onto the stoep of the house. He unlocked the door, turned, and signalled.

Keogh looked quickly round before stepping from the car. All the lamps in the street were out. He opened the back door, gripped Shack under the armpits, and dragged him out. The black man spluttered and clawed at him. Keogh took him in a fireman's hold over his right shoulder—he was light, all skin and bones—and trotted with him up the ramp and into the house.

Mayat left the lights off until they were all inside and he had drawn the curtains. "There's a bed here," he said, and led the way across a small living room to a door opening onto a narrow room at the back of the house. It was a kind of storeroom. The single bed, covered with a dusty counterpane, shared the space with cardboard boxes, an old radio set, and several coils of rope. Keogh picked a way between them and lowered Shack onto the bed. He lay there staring at the ceiling, breathing hard.

"Keep him warm," Keogh said. "Cover him with blankets. You may have to stay at home tomorrow and nurse him."

Mayat sat in the doorway for a few moments, looking at Shack's face. "They age badly in prison, don't they?" he said, and then abruptly reversed the wheelchair through the lounge and disappeared into an adjoining room. The house was tiny; it was almost possible to believe it had been built for a single occupant. Keogh looked around the lounge, a comfortable bachelor's room panelled in stripped pine and furnished with bulbous armchairs, perhaps just a little too tidy and with the faintly forbidding air of a place that receives no visitors. He glanced at the contents of a small bookcase below the mesh-screened front window. Nothing there to throw any light on Mayat's personality: some paperback crime tending to favour the Californian genre, a leather-bound English edition of the Koran, and a few reference books—Pears' *Cyclopaedia* for 1967, *Collecting Antique Jewellery,* and, for no conceivable reason, Philips' *Modern School Atlas.* He pulled out the atlas and exposed three slender softbound books that had been concealed behind it. They were more interesting: *Strategic Problems of the Anti-Japanese Guerilla War* and *Yu Chi Chan Guerilla Warfare,* both by Mao Tse-tung, published by the Foreign Languages Press in Peking before red plastic covers had become standard. The other was *I Am Prepared to Die,* a transcript of Nelson Mandela's speech at his trial in 1964.

He heard the squeak of tires on the floor and pushed the books back, keeping out the atlas. Mayat came through with blankets piled on his knees and went into Shack's room. When he returned Keogh said, "I want you to explain something."

"You agreed not to linger here."

"I want to know what the setup is in Botswana, that's all."

Mayat hesitated. "All right," he said, and then added, almost diffidently, "I thought of having supper now. Do you want something to eat?"

Keogh remembered he had not eaten for nearly twelve hours. He followed Mayat into the miniature kitchen. The housekeeping was done by a neighbour who came in every afternoon, and she had left a chicken korma simmering on the stove. Together with saffron rice it stretched easily to two helpings.

Mayat produced a bottle of Natal cane spirit and poured a cautious tot for Keogh. He took none himself. "There's nothing else," he said. "I don't usually entertain."

"That's all right." The spirit, strong and tasteless, spread a glow through his chest. He opened the school atlas to a map of southern and central Africa. The scale was small but that helped to give the problem some perspective: to the north-east of the Transvaal the great empty wilderness of Botswana, all of it bush, desert, and swamp, most of it uninhabited apart from a narrow strip in the east, close to the South African border. Here, all the communities that had any claim to being towns were spaced out along the parallel road and railway line that ran north until they entered Rhodesia. Much further north, beyond the salt pans and the Okovanggo Swamp, was the tiny frontier with Zambia, a strip of Zambezi riverbank less than half a mile long.

Mayat examined the map, chewing with mechanical deliberation. "In Shack's day," he said, "the border was virtually unguarded. It was possible to drive to a point close by and then walk across. Now there are patrols there, men with dogs, helicopters—"

"But it's a hell of a long border," Keogh said.

"If you're travelling overland the only practical area for crossing is this strip of about sixty miles at the southern end, between Lobatsi and Gaberones. Further north there are no adequate roads on either side. Naturally, this little strip is the most thoroughly guarded."

"What exactly is to stop me from crossing there, sometime in the next day or two?"

"Several things. Firstly, you should have someone to meet you with transport on the other side. It's not essential, but even the closest point is ten or twenty miles from the nearest town. It's easy to get lost in that much bush. It's easy to die of thirst, or even to walk back into the Transvaal without knowing it.

"Secondly, you'll have to deal with the Botswana police. There's no hope of escaping their attention. They're in a delicate position; they tolerate refugees but they don't welcome them. There used to be streams of people crossing the border to demand asylum. Some were genuine; others were spies and informers trying to penetrate here"—he stabbed at the map with his fork—"into Zambia, into the headquarters of the Congress. Now there's a Refugee Tribunal which considers each case on its merits. The police have an informal system of selection: they will accept only those who are vouched for by one of the political movements who have representatives there. As far as the Congress is concerned, that means my brother. If he refuses to supply an affidavit in support of the request for asylum, the refugee will almost certainly be taken back to the border. He might be handed over to the South Africans—especially, you'll forgive me, if he turns out to be a criminal fugitive who has injured a policeman."

Keogh had finished his meal and sat staring at the empty plate. His tiredness was still there, like a dull ache, but now he understood the full and forbidding scope of what he had heard. Or did he understand it? "Mayat, you've convinced me that I must have Yusuf's help, yet you insist that you can't procure it for me. You say there's nobody else who can act as a go-between either. What sort of riddle is this? What are you holding back?"

"It's no riddle. I don't want to be involved, that's all. The doctor will be here soon; it's time you left."

Keogh glared at him. "That little black bastard stayed in jail twelve years and saved your skin in the process. Is that all you can say, that you don't want to be involved?"

"You'll find it's a common attitude," Mayat said, looking a little pained. "There's a third problem I didn't mention. It's perhaps more difficult to get out of Botswana than to get in. There is only one way, by truck up the Palapye road"— he ran a finger over the map, along the line of the parallel road and railway—"and then over several hundred miles of rough tracks to the Zambezi. It's a long, hard journey. You'll get very little help, precisely because people are afraid to be involved. The Congress will help, though. I believe Yusuf normally phones their headquarters in Lusaka and asks for a truck to be sent down."

"Thanks," said Keogh heavily. "You know a hell of a lot for someone who's out of touch."

"I hear things from other people."

"What sort of man is he, your brother?"

Mayat propelled himself around the small kitchen table and through to the living room, talking as he went. "He is fifteen years younger; we were never close. A difficult man. His ambition always outran his talent, that was Yusuf's trouble. It made him self-important, sensitive to criticism. He wanted to be a lawyer but had to settle for accountancy; he was a good accountant, never a brilliant one. He married a clever woman who eventually came to despise him. His political interests came from our mother; she was a Punjabi Muslim who went to jail as a young woman with Gandhi and his followers. My father, a Malay, a descendant of slaves, believed in letting well enough alone. Do I seem like him, Mr. Keogh?"

"Go on," said Keogh. He was struck by an inference in what Mayat had said.

"Well, Yusuf joined the Congress almost as soon as it began. Eventually he became its full-time treasurer. The inspiration of the movement was African nationalist, of course, but people of all races were welcome. I suspect Yusuf resented living in Wilby Xaba's shadow. Wilby is a creative thinker, a born leader, a very impressive figure; unfortunately these are all talents that Yusuf lacks, and he came off badly by comparison. I've followed Wilby's career with interest."

They had stopped by the front door. Keogh, sensing an opportune moment, said casually, "Why did you fight, you and your brother?"

Mayat gave him a look that was specially thoughtful. "I accused him of betraying Wilby," he said. "Oh, it wasn't quite that bald. He accused me of exactly the same thing, and there was nothing either of us could prove. You see, Shack had driven Wilby to the border, and when several hours had gone by it was clear that he wasn't coming back for Yusuf. We were both afraid. It's hard for you to understand the panic that was everywhere; we could feel the Congress breaking up around us. I suppose we were like a pair of castaways going mad on a sinking boat; all we could think of was getting at each other's throat. We both lost our tempers. We parted. The next night he managed to slip out of the country on his own."

"Leaving his wife?"

"And two children. He hadn't told them he was going. Luckily Fatima was a professional woman, and independent, not like most Muslim wives. Anyway, by then she had lost all patience with him and the Congress.

"The arrests had begun. All our friends gradually left the country or went to jail. The things we'd worked for all those years, they'd suddenly slipped out of our grasp. I was getting old; it all seemed to matter that much less. I've been minding my own business since then, and I don't intend changing that."

Keogh nodded. He understood Mayat better, recognizing in him the equability of disillusionment. He was not afraid of much because he had little to lose. But Keogh felt obscurely threatened in his presence.

"Wilby *was* betrayed, wasn't he?"

"Nobody has ever known whether he was or not."

"He walked into an ambush on the southern part of the border, the area you were talking about. Any of three people could have tipped off the police—you, your brother, or Shack."

"If any of us had wanted to betray Wilby, there had been many other opportunities." He turned off the light and reached for the door latch. "I won't speculate, Mr. Keogh. I shouldn't speculate if I were you either. You'd only waste more time than you have already."

"That's your final word then? You won't help?"

"You'll be better without my help. You're a resourceful man, Mr. Keogh. Good luck." To Keogh's surprise Mayat took his hand in a powerful grip. "I'll look after Shack until he's able to leave. By then I hope you'll be away safely."

Keogh let himself out. Mayat closed the door behind him and he stood on the stoep in the cold, vaguely hostile darkness of Fordsburg with a feeling of unreality. A sharp wind had sprung up. After a few seconds he walked down the ramp and peered cautiously along the street in either direction. Nothing moved; people did not walk out at night here unless they had to. He slipped out to the Valiant and sat in it for a minute, lighting a cigarette.

Mayat. What to make of him? A nature so devious it was impossible to be sure whether he was very clever or rather stupid. Did he, for instance, expect Keogh to give up now that he knew his only real hope of escape was through the machinery of the Congress? To abandon Shack when the black man was his only possible surety? It was almost as if he were stalling, trying to gain time—for what? Keogh was still confused by what he had learnt, but two things had become clear: he had to find some way of making contact with Yusuf Mayat in Botswana, and he had to raise whatever money would be demanded for a safe passage. Plain blackmail; what would the incorruptible Wilby Xaba think of his ex-treasurer's avarice? Again Keogh cursed the two Afrikaners who had robbed him. He needed rest. But tired and afraid and dispirited as he was, he had to find out whether the guess he had made about the woman doctor was right.

He started the car, made a three-point turn, and drove a hundred yards to the next corner. There was a phone box here, and a service lane full of overflowing dustbins behind a row of shops. He backed the Valiant into the deep shadow of the lane, switched off the lights and the engine, and went out to the phone box. Its light was smashed, the telephone and coin box had been ripped out, and the cubicle smelt of urine, but it would do for his purpose. Opposite was a shuttered greengrocer's shop; the wind chased newspapers, packing straw, and cabbage leaves in circles across the street. Keogh stood in the dark and waited.

In the next twenty minutes only two cars went past. The first was a Volkswagen with one of those radio-telephone pylons on the roof. It gave him a jolt until he remembered that telephones in cars had become quite common; they were the kind of gadget that fascinated well-heeled South Africans with nothing better to spend their money on. The second was a pale Cortina. He watched till he could see only its red tail lights and then, at a point roughly opposite Mayat's house, they went out.

His tiredness had receded. He was keyed up. He waited another two minutes to be quite sure the doctor had entered the house before walking back along the pavement. Treading carefully, he went through the gateway, off the concrete ramp into the tiny rose garden, and stationed himself beneath the front window, which was open just as far as the mesh burglar screen would allow.

For about five minutes nothing was said inside the room, but he could hear Mayat wheeling himself restlessly about. The doctor must have been examining Shack in the storeroom at the back. When she returned her voice reached Keogh clearly. It was sharp and nasal, with a marked Indian accent, and she had the trivializing, matter-of-fact manner of many doctors.

"A touch of septic fever. Keep him warm, that's all you can do. The worst of it will be over in a day or two."

"The wrists?" Mayat said.

"There's a suppurative inflammation there. The fever is caused by the sepsis, of course. The blood vessels had been severely constricted. He's lucky; if it had gone on much longer there'd have been a danger of dry gangrene. He's had a good shot of penicillin."

"I'm grateful to you."

"You'll have to stay at home tomorrow. I'll phone and you'll let me know how he is. If necessary I'll give him another injection. No names on the phone, of course, even these days you can never tell."

There was a short silence. Then Mayat said, "I'm in terrible difficulty over this."

"It's a problem of your own making, Hassim. You know what he wants."

"It's a moral dilemma. At my age I should be past moral dilemmas."

"Nothing has ever been moral about it," the woman said. Her tone was brusque. Keogh, with the wind gnawing at him, crouched by the window, straining his ears and trying to keep himself from shivering.

"There's some self-interest, of course," Mayat said. "I want no trouble. If they get Shack who knows what he may tell them? Even this Englishman could cause trouble. But believe me, I have a humanitarian debt as well."

"And you expect him to do something on humanitarian grounds? No, Hassim. He always said you two were lined up against him. Don't ask me to be interested, but there's only one answer to your problem."

Mayat had been sitting somewhere close to the window. Now he moved away and Keogh missed what he said next. There was just one intelligible phrase: "physical impossibility."

"He's only got your word for that," the doctor retorted sharply. "So have I, but it doesn't matter to me. What did you tell the Englishman you would do?"

"Nothing."

"Does he believe you?"

"I have a feeling he may be back. He's stubborn. Rather an intimidating man physically. He's an engineer."

"What's that to do with it?"

"Nothing."

"Were you afraid I might tell him something?" she asked with slight mockery.

Again the reply was lost but then Mayat said, "Could you send a message for me? One that won't be intercepted?"

"There is a way. I communicate with him when it's necessary."

"In a day or two then, perhaps."

"On the other hand he writes lengthy, drivelling letters to me. He's talking seriously about coming back."

"Coming back?" Mayat sounded incredulous.

"That place is driving him crazy," she said unsympathetically. "He's put yet another application in to the Minister of the Interior. This time he seems to think it will work."

"A Congress man? He *must* be crazy."

"He won't set foot in my house, anyway. I'm used to my own life now, thank you. I must be going."

"Thank you, Fatima. . . ."

Keogh slipped away from the window and then walked into the biting wind towards the car. He had a lot more to think about now. It was rather a pity, though, that he had not caught a glimpse of Yusuf Mayat's wife.

10

Avoiding the main roads wherever he could, he drove to Killarney. He knew the general direction and was there in half an hour. Among the white wealthy suburbs north of the city, Killarney was one of the whitest and wealthiest. Apartment blocks, built low and wide as if the price of land had hardly mattered, were set back among acres of floodlit lawns and swimming pools. Close to the shopping centre—expensive little gift shops and boutiques spaced out between the delicatessen, the bottle store, and the posher sort of supermarket—he found Mont Salève, the four-storey building where Paul Blane lived. The French name amused him; it seemed designed to add a touch of class to what was basically a vulgar display of wealth.

There was an entrance at the rear leading to the basement garage. Deciding to brazen it out, he drove straight in and a sleepy Zulu watchman with rings in his ears saluted the car automatically. He found the Valiant's private bay, with its number stencilled above, next to one in which a gleaming olive-green Range Rover was parked. He took out his suitcase and rode up to the fourth floor in a silent lift with stainless steel doors.

Blane's flat, number 43, was at the end of a long enclosed veranda. It had a service entrance that must have led into the kitchen, and at right angles to this was the main door, heavy teak with panels of coloured glass set into it. He peered cautiously through the glass before opening the door. Everything was in darkness. He stepped into a wide entrance hall, hunted for a light switch, and found one that lit up an enormous room ahead of him. He went forward. It was the main living room, perhaps sixty feet long, furnished with expensive modern severity in black, white, and beige. In the far corner, uncurling herself from a patent-leather chair, was Rina.

He let his suitcase fall noiselessly into the thick pile of the carpet. She came towards him, pale and tense, her big green eyes luminous with . . . what? Disbelief, fear?

"Keogh, thank God!"

He took her in his arms, feeling the trembling tension of her body. "Thank God, thank God you're safe. I've been worried out of my mind."

"Why have you come?"

"I caught the first plane this morning. I was almost sure you'd been arrested, but just in case you hadn't I had to reach you at the first possible moment. This place isn't safe. You've got to leave, Keogh."

"What happened?"

"Everything is a mess, an awful mess that I can't begin to understand." There was an hysterical catch in her voice; he knew she was going to cry and he always found this capacity in her slightly shocking. "I had to do *something*.

126

I'm sorry, I've got into such a state." She began to weep against his shoulder, shaking with convulsive sobs.

For a minute he held her close, feeling through his surprise and uncertain fear the same warm protective urge he had had when he first saw her, crying in a cinema queue. This was the vulnerable Rina, the one who needed him.

He gave her his handkerchief and she blew her nose, turning her damp cheek away from him. "This isn't helping. I'm sorry I startled you. If I'd switched on the lights they'd have frightened you off. I've been here six hours, not knowing whether you or they would come through the door first. I can't understand why they haven't been."

He took her firmly by the shoulders and made her look at him. "Tell me what happened."

"It's quite simple. They knew about the car. They knew I had a car in Cape Town, they had the number, and they wanted to know where it was. I tried to bluff my way out but it was pretty clear that they guessed what had happened. It had never occurred to me that BOSS might have a file on me."

"BOSS." Numbly he repeated the silly-sounding acronym. The Bureau of State Security, the powerful and faceless organization that controlled intelligence and secret police work.

"They claimed to be policemen but I knew better. They must have started keeping an eye on me when I got a job with the Race Relations Council. They're interested in anyone who's too friendly with non-whites." More composed now, she dabbed at the mascara that had run down her cheeks. "There were two of them. They gave me the creeps, especially the one who did all the talking. Little man called

Horn, stinks of cigarettes and never looks you straight in the eye. Ugh. But all this can wait. I've got an idea, a way of getting you—"

Something in Keogh's chest seemed to have fallen heavily to the pit of his stomach. "What does he look like? Horn—is that his name? Describe him to me."

"Small. Slender build. Curly brown hair and a moustache. And those eyes, small and brown, and they never settle on you. You can't have seen him, Keogh?"

"The other one?" he said carefully.

"His name is Van Heerden. He's much bigger, with short fair hair. He didn't say a word, just sat grinning like an ape. What are you getting at? You can't have seen them."

"Yes, I've seen them."

"But you'd already left for Johannesburg."

Stunned, feeling his tired brain swimming in incomprehension, he sat down on the arm of a chair. Yes, he'd left for Johannesburg and they'd come right after him. They'd caught up with the Valiant at Kimberley and then . . . then nothing. They'd done nothing but follow until he made the inconvenient discovery that they were watching him. And then the robbery—just a means of diverting his suspicions, though the way they'd stripped him clean had been pretty convincing.

Rina was becoming agitated again. "We've got to get out of here. They could walk in at any minute."

"I don't think they will," he said flatly.

"What do you mean?"

"They don't want me, that's what I mean. They don't want me yet, anyway. Is that hard for you to understand? It's bloody impossible for me, but I still think it's true. Do you realize they've had that car number for twenty-four hours, that they could have picked me up whenever they wanted? They haven't even taken the elementary step of staking out this flat. The car is registered here, isn't it?"

"You've had a lot of Irish luck, that's all. Don't push it."

"I'm going to push it far enough to pour the two stiffest drinks you ever saw."

"Keogh, you're mad!" She crossed her arms sulkily over her breasts and looked away. "Why do I bother?"

"You have a better suggestion?"

"I just happen to know a way of getting you out of the country in a day or two's time, that's all. But let's forget it."

"In a day or two? What do I do in the meantime, walk round the block? Just give me five minutes to think."

She said nothing. Next to the French windows which opened onto a wide veranda was a bar counter, the shelves behind it stocked with cognacs of the highest pedigree and malt whiskies from eccentric little Highland distilleries. He chose one of these, Macdonald's Glencoe, eight years old and one hundred proof, and half filled two crystal tumblers, adding ice from the small built-in refrigerator. He took his time, from behind the counter deliberately absorbing details of the room for the first time. The furniture was all long and low, black patent-leather chairs with tables and bookshelves in contrasting polished ebony and white Swedish oak. The stereo system was a connoisseur's model. The only traditional design, neatly offsetting the rest from a shelf above the big Jetmaster open fireplace, was a row of three Zulu heads sculptured in clay with the unmistakably delicate touch of Anton von Wouw. Keogh detected Rina's taste in all this; he also began to realize how Paul Blane had managed to overrun an allowance of ten thousand pounds a year.

He handed Rina her drink. "There was something in the

Star tonight about the policeman you injured," she said. "He's still in a critical condition. Where is Shack, anyway?"

"In a safe place. At least I hope it's safe. Did your visitors mention him?"

"Tell me what happened."

She sipped her drink, made a face at the strength of it, and sat down. Some of Keogh's fatalistic calm had passed over to her.

They had said they were detectives, investigating an "occurrence" involving an adult European male who might be a friend of hers. Just routine, *mevrou*. They'd been polite, but with an implied familiarity towards her as an Afrikaner that she found loathsome. And the big one, Van Heerden, had undressed her with his piggish little eyes.

It was only an hour after Keogh had left, and they had an accurate description of him. She'd had to admit, of course, that she knew him; she thought it best to be frank about their relationship. She was expecting him for dinner but he hadn't turned up. He'd promised to bring a couple of bottles of wine—that was a detail that pleased her, the kind of thing that would tie in and add conviction to her story. Of course she'd got the table laid, the steak and salad ready, and she noticed them observing these facts. She professed to have no idea where Keogh could have got to.

"They wanted to know a lot about you—your job, background, habits, personality, temperament. I tried to be vague without sounding unhelpful. I implied that we'd gone cool on each other, that perhaps I wasn't all that put out because you hadn't arrived."

Keogh laughed without quite knowing why, searched for his cigarettes, and lit two.

"I thought I had them eating out of my hand," she

said. "Then came the business about the car. If I happened to remember anything else, Horn said, maybe I'd drop around and see him? I had a car, of course? I walked right into it. I said no. Then what had happened to the Valiant, he said, the Valiant that I'd been using around the coloured townships? I tried to talk my way out of it, said it belonged to my husband and he'd taken it back. They knew I was lying. And I knew by then that they weren't ordinary policemen. Perhaps the strangest thing is that they didn't press the point. They knew I was lying but I got the impression that they really didn't care. Can you understand that? They seemed to have got what they came for and they left. If I heard anything from my friend Keogh, they said, would I let them know? And all of us understood perfectly well that I would do no such thing."

He studied the remains of his drink, finished it, and poured another before speaking. "You shouldn't have come," he said. "Didn't it occur to you that they hoped you would lead them here, to me?"

"Of course," she said calmly. "I had a legitimate reason for flying to Johannesburg. The divorce hearing is next week. I've arranged a meeting with my attorney to discuss it tomorrow. And I'm staying at the Langham Hotel, all above-board. I'll have to be getting back there soon."

"Oh," he said.

"And I made very sure I wasn't followed here. As a former resident I know a cunning way in and out of this building."

"Now listen to what I've been thinking," he said, sitting down again. "There is exactly one reason why Shack and I weren't arrested today, and that's because Horn and Van Heerden didn't want us arrested. No, listen. They sat and watched me sawing the handcuffs off him. What do you make of that?"

She had gone paler than before and she shook her head numbly. "You must have the wrong men."

"There's no mistaking those two." He told her very quickly what had happened at the garage in Kimberley and later by the roadside. "Why BOSS, anyway? There's no conceivable reason why they should be interested in me. Who *are* they interested in then? Shack. Congress man, old political campaigner, even if he is a dead-beat now.

"Just consider this possibility: Shack gets off Robben Island, and to suit some peculiar purpose of their own the people from BOSS want him to stay free. They want him to reach Jo'burg, perhaps, or even to leave the country. It happens that I came blundering in and they have to keep their hands off me as well, just so that their precious little apple-cart won't be upset. They probably have to use their power over the uniformed police, who are eager to speak to me about their fat friend Oosthuizen."

"Are you suggesting," Rina said slowly, "that Shack is not exactly what he's pretending to be?"

"When Horn and Van Heerden were watching him in Kimberley he was shit-scared, and that was no act. But who can be sure? What I do know is that he hasn't told me everything about the Congress setup. Nor has Hassim Mayat, and he's anxious that I shouldn't find out any more."

"It sounds quite fantastic," she said.

"Give me a better explanation then."

"Horn's behaviour still doesn't make sense. He caught up with you at Kimberley, followed you for a while, and then abandoned you?"

"No. He must have some way of shadowing us." Keogh

paused, wondering in dismay for a moment whether he might have led Horn all the way to Mayat's shop and the house in Fordsburg. Then the realization hit him like a clenched fist. "Jesus," he muttered. "Oh, Jesus, why didn't I think of it? Those pylons—the radio telephones."

He stood up and went to the door. Rina followed him out in bewilderment, along the corridor, and into the silent lift. He cursed himself all the way down to the basement, knowing with a curious certainty what he would find there.

It took only a minute of crawling round beneath the Valiant to locate it, a flat box of moulded black plastic, about two inches by three, one face covered by a sheet of strongly magnetized steel that had held it firmly clamped under the rear left mudguard. That was where Horn had crawled when he dropped his cigarettes at the garage.

Keogh held it in his palm and turned it over. There was nothing to indicate its function, its identity; it had an oddly purposeless appearance. His first angry instinct was to destroy it, but after a minute he replaced it carefully under the mudguard.

Rina squatted beside him on the concrete floor. "It's a transmitter," he said. "No wonder they didn't need to come near us. We've been sending out our own call sign all the way from Kimberley."

"Something like radar?" she said.

"Not really, but it's just as effective for their purpose. That gear in the Buick reminded me of something, and now I know what it was. In the army they use a field landing-guidance system to steer helicopters down exactly where they want them. The pilot lines himself up between two fixed-beam radio signals from the ground, and when he's getting both together he knows he's in the right place: two lights on his dashboard come on. I reckon this works in reverse. That transmitter sends out a continuous signal on a fixed UHF or VHF wavelength. It's picked up in their car and plotted with a direction-finder. With two cars, say, both carrying receivers, comparing notes on the telephone, they could pinpoint us to within a couple of hundred yards."

"In other words they already know you're here."

"They've followed every move I've made since this morning. They know where I am now, and they know where Shack is. We're not fugitives any more; we're being kept on ice."

"For what?"

Keogh rubbed his painfully tired eyes. "You shouldn't have come," he said.

11

Back in the flat he lay in a scented bubble bath trying to relax, soaking away the nervous exhaustion and feeling in its place a heavy tiredness creep over him that was almost pleasant. Suddenly he had wanted nothing more than a warm bath. It was usually a woman's notion of escape, the mindless, womb-like immersion. Rina had been outraged until he pointed out that there was nothing else for him to do.

The bathroom was mock-Edwardian, the walls lined with grey marble, the bath a great iron thing on claw feet. Hour-glass bottles full of pink and green and yellow shampoo and bath salts paraded on the dresser. It had been her bathroom, adjoining the main bedroom, and Paul Blane had done nothing to change it. He still wanted her back; it was almost as if he refused to acknowledge her absence.

When Keogh was beginning to fall asleep among the bubbles she came, stirring ice with her finger into a fresh drink, set it down in the porcelain soap tray at his elbow, and perched on a stool. She had repaired her make-up and there was an air of brittle self-possession about her.

"What will they do, Keogh?"

He took a sip of his drink and replaced it between the soap and the sponge, leaving a skirt of yellow foam around the glass. "Nothing, I dare say. They know I'm here; they're probably watching the building; they'll act when it suits them. What's the point of going anywhere else? But you'll go back to Cape Town while you've got the chance. In the morning."

"No," she said quickly. "I came here to help."

"I appreciate it. But I've got myself involved in something too big, something I haven't even started to fathom out. There's nothing you can do. The only alternative is to disengage yourself."

"You don't understand," she said. "I've sent for Paul."

He sat up in the bath. "You've done what?"

"I want him to fly you out of the country. I know he will, too, if it's put to him the right way. I was trying to tell you earlier but you wouldn't listen. He's in Mozambique, out in the bush. I've left a message at Beira airport where his plane is parked."

"Let me get this straight," he said carefully. "You're going to ask your husband to fly your lover out of the country. Illegally."

She looked quite serious. "To Botswana," she said. "I had a feeling this Congress thing would cause problems. It's even more important now, with Horn thinking he's got you in a corner to be dealt with at his leisure. Get out when he least expects it. Paul is always dashing in and out of the country on hunting trips; I'm damned sure he knows a way of doing it. You don't know him, Keogh—yes, he's immature and erratic and at times he's a downright bastard. He's still in love with me, you know, and he'll see you as a threat. All

136

right, there's a danger in that, but if he's made to believe that he can remove the threat by getting it away from me, leaving the field clear for himself . . . he sees things in simple physical terms like that. I know he'll do it, Keogh. We'll have to play it carefully, that's all, and not make him too jealous." Restlessly she stood up and stared at her reflection in the etched mirror above the washbasin. "He's a daredevil anyway, a gambler. Once he gets used to the idea he'll probably enjoy it."

Practical objections sprang to Keogh's mind, but he disliked the idea instinctively as well. Paul Blane was unstable, unpredictable. Apart from that, Keogh wondered how far Rina had disentangled herself and whether sometimes she looked for ways of excusing him. All that crying, after a whole year, could not be healthy. But maybe it was just a case of jealousy. He was thinking of Blane in much the same way Blane would regard him, as a threat. He pulled out the bath plug and then stood up and took the big towel she had given him, warm from the drying rail. "What will he expect in return?" he said.

"Nothing, necessarily. But I do have a stick to beat him with. He's due back to defend the divorce action on Tuesday. I'm suing on the grounds of constructive desertion, keeping it as formal and technical as possible. If I want to I can make it very messy, though. I can tell the court exactly how intolerable life became. I can tell them about his crazy bouts, his persecution complex. I can tell them how he left coins lying about the flat to tempt the Zulu cleaner, and nearly blew the poor man's brains out when he did finally pinch one. I can tell them how he used to slap me. How I had to lock myself in the bedroom once and listen to him smashing every plate in the house against the door. How he tied me up one day and stripped me and lashed me with the tip of a fibre-glass fishing rod. I can tell them about that bitch of a nightclub singer in Durban." She looked at Keogh with a satirical twist to her mouth. "There were others, of course, but she's the only one I've any proof of. I can hand in as an exhibit the letter she wrote him that I opened by accident. It's a very explicit letter. It teases him about his moods and his perversions."

"The newspapers will love it," he said.

"And the Johannesburg Sunday papers aren't noted for their restraint. What could be better? Sex, sadism, and a millionaire's son. Blane senior will have apoplexy. His own father was a cardsharp from Glasgow, a convicted thief who made a fortune swindling poor burghers out of their land and using it to buy his way into the gold-mining companies. The family has been carefully building up its respectability for two generations. I can set them right back to square one. The old man has already had about all he can take. If this comes out, Paul knows there's a good chance of being completely disowned and losing his allowance."

"And you'd do that to him?"

"I don't want to. I don't think it'll be necessary. If he refuses to help, then I will."

Keogh wondered. He did not think she had enough vindictiveness in her. As he dried his back he was conscious of her studying his body the way she often had, with a curiosity that was sensually aware and yet detached, like a sculptor's. She said he had a peasant's build, heavy and thick in all the wrong places. In contrast she was slim in all the right ones, huddling on the stool again in an arrangement of sharp angles.

"So let's say Paul agrees to fly me to Botswana," he said.

"I'd want him to take Shack as well. But it's no good unless we can be sure of Yusuf Mayat's help across the border. I don't know how he can be safely approached; his brother refuses to co-operate because the two of them have been having a mortal Muslim blood feud for the past twelve years. Yusuf's wife is the doctor who's treating Shack, but she seems to despise her husband as well. Hassim tried to hide her identity from me; I can't work out why. All I *can* figure out is that there are a number of things that a number of people are anxious I shouldn't know about. I don't even want to know about them. All I want is out. The whole Congress setup seems to have gone sour and corrupt, and it all goes back to the night a few days after Sharpeville when Wilby was betrayed."

"And somewhere in the middle of it Horn has an interest," Rina said. "You can't just wait around to find out what it is. Is Yusuf's help absolutely essential?"

"As far as I can see, yes. Without it, we could be sent back by express delivery to the South African police. Officially he vouches for genuine members of the Congress as political refugees. Unofficially anyone can be a member for a price."

"Then why don't I go and see his wife?"

He stopped drying himself and held the towel suspended across his shoulders. The last of the water gurgled in the plug hole.

"Why not?" she demanded. "If I can win her confidence she may approach her husband on your behalf. At least she could find out what the price is."

"Now that you mention it," he said slowly, "she did tell Hassim that they had a way of getting in touch."

"Better and better," Rina said, standing up, fidgety

with excitement again. "A woman may succeed where a man wouldn't. We don't know where she lives or practices, but doctors are easy to find. I'll go in the morning. You see, Horn probably thinks he's got you here safely, watching your every move. But I can be your eyes and ears. I can set things up for you to vanish suddenly from under his nose."

"Rina—" He did not know quite how to formulate his objection. "Look, I hope you're not getting this situation wrong. There's no part here for a spirited heroine sticking by her man. The man is a rough bastard who thumped a policeman and may very well get what he deserves for it. It may be tough for him and for anybody who helps him. I don't want you any more involved, that's all."

"I'm already involved about as far as I can get, Keogh."

"But I'm giving you the chance to cut your losses and get out."

She looked at him closely in that thoughtful way she had. "What if I don't take the chance? Did you mean what you said last night?"

"I said I loved you." He wrapped the towel firmly round his waist and stepped from the bath. "That was last night. Things were different."

"It hasn't occurred to you that I might love you as well?"

He stared uncertainly down at her face. Yes, he told himself, yes, it had occurred to him. Wasn't it what he'd wanted, and yet was now almost afraid to hear? "Why decide that now?" he muttered.

"I started to decide last night."

"God damn, what good will it do us?"

"The first thing I want—the only thing for now—is to see you safe, Keogh, even if it means being separated from you. That's the kind of thing love means to me."

He kissed her, smelling through her light perfume the familiar sun-warmed fragrance of her skin. Her hands moved around him and clasped his bare, damp back and her small breasts were thrust against his chest. He felt, like a tiny electric shock, the flicker of desire that went through them both, through the layers of tiredness, strain, and fear that had deadened his senses. But it was only momentary. People talked of fear stimulating desire, forgetting that it caused physical exhaustion as well. They both knew they would not make love tonight. She drew back from him and poked a finger into the mat of black hair on his chest.

"I'd better go now."

"I suppose so."

"I must be seen to be staying at the hotel, in case anyone's interested. I'll find the doctor tomorrow morning and come back here in the afternoon. We mustn't use the phone. Don't stir from the flat, either. There's everything you can possibly need here: I checked."

"Why don't I just leave you to do all the thinking?" he said, leading her to the front door. "See you tomorrow—if Horn hasn't called in the meantime."

"Try not to think about that," she said. "Sleep well."

Then she was gone, her footsteps echoing along the veranda to a fire-escape that led to the basement. Originally this and a neighbouring block of flats had been planned as a complementary pair with a single heating system. Before they reached ground level the company financing the project went bankrupt, as Johannesburg companies did remarkably frequently; the creditors re-designed the buildings separately but they continued to share a boiler room, a fact which would not suggest itself to an outsider and was not even known to many residents. It was handy, though, for anyone who wished to slip into or out of either building unseen.

Immediately Keogh switched off the lights in the living room, drew back the edge of one of the heavy beige curtains, and looked out. He had not wanted to alarm Rina any more than necessary. The Volkswagen was there, the one he had seen in Fordsburg with the pylon on its roof. It was parked across the street in front of the shopping centre and diagonally opposite the entrance to the basement garage.

What did they want? What did the secret police ever want? To protect the interests of the state, to eliminate or disable whoever was currently considered its enemy. They had wanted to know where Shack would go; that was the central fact, that was why the transmitter had been placed under the Valiant. Shack was the key to it all, perhaps in some way he did not understand himself. He was being used. Innocently? It seemed probable. Certainly the black man had not told him the whole truth, but on the other hand he did not seem capable of an elaborate and sustained deception. And now he was in a coma, inaccessible. By tomorrow—tomorrow night, anyway—he might be well enough to answer a few questions. Tomorrow? Keogh gave a sceptical snort. If either of them stayed free that long. He went down the passage off the entrance hall, into the first bedroom he found, lay down in the dark, and fell asleep with thoughts of Rina chasing each other through his head.

He woke with a start, shielding his eyes against the sunshine that streamed through a gap between the curtains and feeling a light film of sweat on his brow. Then he knew what it was that had woken him: the snap of a key in a lock.

Now a shuffling noise came from the direction of the living room. Someone was moving about the flat.

He rolled out of bed and seized the nearest heavy object, an alabaster reading lamp that stood on the bedside table. He ripped out the flex with one sharp tug and, still naked, padded across the parquet flooring to the bedroom door. The intruder was approaching down the corridor, in a foot-dragging walk on squeaky rubber soles. Keogh pressed himself against the wall, raising the lamp. The man turned as he was framed in the doorway, eyes white and wide with astonishment in his mahogany face. Keogh sagged with relief and lowered the weapon. The man was a middle-aged Zulu cleaner with a handlebar moustache, wearing a uniform of white canvas blouse and shorts, and sandals made from strips of a car tire. He carried a dustpan and a brush.

"Hau!" he said, a single word of surprise, before averting his eyes from the sight of a naked white man.

"I'm sorry," Keogh said foolishly. "You gave me a fright."

"I don't knock because I think sometime Master Paul is away, seh."

"What's your name?"

"September, seh. I'm coming to clean every day this time, seh."

"What is the time?"

"Something to one."

So he'd slept round the clock, and he was beginning to realize how much better he felt for it. September had the black man's highly developed instinct for minding his own business, and he did not question the presence of a stranger in the flat. Keogh offered no explanation, letting it be assumed he was Blane's guest. While September went about his work singing a repetitive lament, he slipped on some clothes, went to the living room, and parted the curtains. The Volkswagen had been replaced by a fawn Toyota, again with a radio pylon, and this time he could see that there were two men in it. Neither of them was Horn or Van Heerden; the nearer one was reading what looked like a photo-story romance. No doubt there were others at the back, ready to follow if he left the building and working on the quite valid assumption that he would have to use the Valiant again. Nowhere in Africa is it possible to move fast or stealthily on foot or by public transport.

Otherwise it was probably a typical busy Friday in Killarney—children in expensive pushchairs being wheeled in the sunshine by dawdling black nannies, Jewish ladies in American cars arriving at the shopping centre for appointments with the hairdresser and lunch with their friends. Keogh went through to the Edwardian bathroom and washed and shaved, noticing in the mirror how pale his face had become. He still had a faint headache too. With nothing better to do, he explored the rest of the flat.

It was quite enormous, one room opening into another like a Chinese puzzle box. He counted four bedrooms, a study, and a billiard room with a three-quarter-size table. Adjoining this was a small trophy room hung with heads—a kudu, a leopard, and a really big buffalo—a pair of elephant tusks, a tiger fish from Lake Kariba, and a rack of rifles and shotguns with enough firepower for a platoon of infantry. They were locked behind sliding glass doors, with a wire sensor taped inside the glass that must have been connected to a burglar alarm. There was also a framed photograph of Blane, squatting with a rifle next to the dead buffalo whose head was now on his wall. He was a brutally handsome man, big and blond with a prominent jaw and heavy-lidded eyes. There was a certain mean satisfaction for Keogh in knowing that this man, with the money and the freedom to pursue his pleasures relentlessly, had not been able to hold on to Rina. But would she want Keogh instead? How afraid was she of being hurt again?

He did not have much appetite but he went to the kitchen, halved a grapefruit from the refrigerator, and made two slices of toast and some strong coffee. Next to the wall plug for the percolator was a key rack, and on the bottom row, under the heading CARS, each of three hooks had a label identifying the keys that were meant to hang there: Corvette, Range Rover, Valiant. It seemed typical enough for Blane to own three cars, although the keys to the Valiant were missing, of course, and so were those to the Corvette; Blane must have driven it to the airport before flying to Mozambique. The Range Rover parked in the basement would be his, then. Its keys were on the rack.

With amazing simplicity Keogh suddenly knew how he would get away from Horn's men.

He went down the corridor to where September, on all fours with a pair of rubber knee pads on, was vigorously polishing the slate floor. He smelt of sweat and coarse tobacco.

"Can you drive a car?" Keogh asked.

"A little bit, seh. Sometime I drove my brother's van, he lives in Durban. I got no licence, seh."

"That's all right. You can do me a small favour."

The Zulu's eyes widened again as all the money Keogh had left, four rands and some change, was thrust into his pink palm. It was probably more than he earned in a week.

12

Lenasia, set down on a bleak patch of veld fifteen miles from Johannesburg, was neither a suburb nor a town. It could only be called a kind of rural ghetto for Indians and Malays—not that it didn't have its posher parts —created for them as they were gradually moved out of areas of the city which had been designed for whites. Their livelihood still lay in the bazaars and cut-price emporiums of Newtown and Fordsburg; their interests and habits and social patterns were urban and collectivized. Among the monotonous, neatly spaced little houses that stared out across miles of grey surrounding veld, their culture seemed to have lost its vividness. Lenasia was an artificial community, and it still wore the look of a transit camp: streets without lights, gardens without lawns. The municipal clinic where Dr. Fatima Mayat was to be found on Fridays fitted the pattern, a faceless prefab, a row of pregnant women in saris waiting on backless benches in the reception hall, an officious clerk who thumbed continuously through a tray of grubby filing cards.

The taxi driver who had brought Rina was reluctant to

wait, and she had jumped the queue. This was a privilege of being white which she normally made a point of refusing; now, she knew, both she and the patients would be uneasy until the visit was over. It was not the natural way of things for a white woman to visit an Indian doctor. Even the officious clerk had seemed to find her arrival disturbing enough to lead her straight into the surgery.

At first she had been nervous, of course. The doctor, a blue sari under her white coat, was a small, sinewy woman with a brisk manner. She wore her glossy black hair drawn severely back into a bun. At one time she had probably been attractive, but the flesh seemed to have fallen away from her face and left it thin and knobby, with bright eyes which had first been suspicious and then hostile. But finally Rina had broken through the armour of pretence and denial. Dr. Mayat gave a reflective smile and a shrug—a curiously masculine gesture, without flourish.

"What do you know about my husband?" she asked.

"Very little."

"Too little, probably. I ask nothing of him; above all, I ask no favours. We'd been married four years when he left me with two children and hardly a penny, before I was even qualified. It's been twelve years since then, and he's done nothing for me but write letters from Botswana—sometimes aggressive, sometimes snivelling. He hates it there, but he's stuck with it. The black government won't let him into Zambia; the white government won't let him back here. He wields his own kind of power there, of course, but he still wants to come back. I don't need him. Everything I have now I have done for myself, and that's no good for his kind of ego. You may not understand this."

"On the contrary," Rina said. "My own position is quite similar."

"I should have known," the doctor said, "that there would be complications when I agreed to look at Shack last night. It was only because I knew from the symptoms that the fever could be fatal. Common humanity, is that what you'd call it? The Congress never did anything for me—quite the opposite. Old times mean nothing to me. What is it that you want to know, exactly? I haven't much time."

Rina knew by now that they were on common ground, and she had begun to like the other woman's directness. "It's simple enough. Shack and Keogh—he's the man I mentioned to you—must leave the country—"

"Your lover?"

"Yes. However they travel, they will need Yusuf's help sooner or later on the other side. They must be certain of it before they set off. You can approach him, ask him if he'll do it. If he wants money, find out how much. If he's reluctant you can persuade him—that's what I'm asking."

A guardedness returned to the doctor's manner. "Perhaps you still misunderstand the relationship," she said, turning to a small basin at the foot of the couch and beginning to wash her hands. "Yusuf and Hassim hate each other. I do my best to ignore both of them."

"Hassim doesn't come into it," Rina said.

"Inevitably he does. Your friend Keogh has spoken to him, of course."

"He says he can do nothing. Why does he refuse? What did they quarrel over?"

"I have never known whether to trust Hassim, but then I've never needed to. It's a pity Shack and your friend must suffer for this kind of intransigence. I'm not unwilling to help, but I am probably unable. You deserve an answer. Why should I be the custodian of their secrets?" She dried her hands carefully on a paper towel, screwed it up, and dropped it in a waste bin beneath the basin. Then she gave Rina an ironic look. "Yes, I can approach Yusuf. We have dealings from time to time. One can't be inhuman; he wants to know how the children are. Nothing direct, of course; the police still keep a check on me and I don't wish to lose my job. So I can ask him what you want, but I know already what the answer will be. It all comes back to Hassim."

"How?"

"You'll have to go back and ask him to explain. Ask him what happened to the Congress money."

Rina felt confused, almost silly, as if there was some discrepancy she should have noticed earlier.

"I don't know much about it," Dr. Mayat said. "Neither of them has ever really talked, which is curious, especially for Yusuf. He was never one to stay silent if he'd been wronged. But I caught a glimpse of it on the night they all rendezvoused at my house before leaving for the border: fourteen thousand pounds, all in cash, in an attaché case that Yusuf had brought with him. He told me the amount later. They said nothing at the time, but I realized even then it could only have belonged to the Congress. They must have cleared their bank accounts to stop the police setting their hands on it, and they intended taking it across the border with them."

"What happened?"

"They left—the three of them, Yusuf, Hassim, and Wilby Xaba—to meet Shack, who was to take Yusuf and Wilby to the frontier. They were due to meet somewhere on the Far West Rand. All I know is that the money did not get to Bechuanaland. Wilby did not have it when he arrived, and Yusuf certainly didn't. Does it seem curious that I know so little? Both of them have always been strangely reticent about it. I had no patience with politics, you see—I had no patience with Yusuf, really. I knew by then that the Congress was really an outlet for his self-indulgence, his fantasies of power—what shall I call them? I simply refused to be interested."

"At some stage of the night Hassim stole the money," Rina said. "Is that what Yusuf believes?"

"More than that. He thinks Hassim and Shack were in collusion to betray Wilby and keep the money for themselves. The plan went wrong when Shack was caught instead of Wilby, of course, but the money remained in Hassim's hands. From outside the country there was nothing the Congress could do about it. So now you see why Yusuf will not co-operate—with Hassim, with Shack, with anyone associated with them."

Rina nodded slowly. "And I see why Hassim was reluctant to tell Keogh about it."

"Hassim is in a curious dilemma. He's morally obliged to help his old friend Shack. The only way he can do that is through Yusuf, and the only way Yusuf will be appeased is by getting that money back. Even trapped in Botswana his life might have been very different with the help of fourteen thousand pounds."

"But it belonged to the Congress, surely?"

"At this distance the difference must be academic. Besides, the Congress had already ceased to exist." Dr. Mayat glanced swiftly at her wristwatch, again with the sort of gesture a man would make. "Now I really must see my patients. Please understand that none of this has ever meant anything to me. If it had, you would never have heard it. May I depend on your discretion?"

"Of course. The police have never known?"

"No. Yusuf must have been hoping all this time to get the money back."

"But he has no proof that Hassim took it?"

"Both of them *know* exactly what happened that night. Getting either of them to explain it is the difficult part. It's as if they were ashamed."

"If we can find a way around this," Rina said, "can I rely on you to help Keogh?"

"I will do what I can. You love him."

It came out like a statement, not a question, and made Rina bridle for a second. But she had set out to make the woman her friend, and what was friendship without frankness? "I don't really know," she said. "Not yet."

"It occurred to me," said the doctor drily, "that all this was a way of finding out."

Rina thought about this remark for most of the journey back to the city. She was involved with Keogh in a way that was almost self-defeating. He must escape—yes, she was determined that it was still possible—but by helping him get away she evaded the responsibility of loving him. As with Paul, it had all happened too quickly for her cautious nature. Perhaps she was a coward at heart. Perhaps, more to the point, everything in her upbringing rebelled against impetuosity and sudden change. Those eighteen years on a farm in the rolling veld of the eastern Free State were not that easily discarded: the continuity of seasons, harvests and droughts, week nights spent in the hostel of the local high school, weekends at home among piano lessons and dressmaking and baking, the skills and graces learnt on the assumption that one day she, too, would be a farmer's wife. On Saturday nights—strictly till midnight—the less strait-laced parents might allow their daughters to dance to an accordion band with the thick-fingered boys of the district, whose lust was constantly at war with their bashfulness. Those were her roots; what would she be without them? But she remembered those weekends best for feeling, through the immense boredom of one Calvinist Sunday after another, a growing alienation. Choosing the university in Durban had been a conscious rebellion; choosing to marry Paul had been another. It was difficult, even now as a woman of twenty-six, not to see Keogh in something of the same light, and to be a little afraid.

Switching from the taxi to a bus and then carefully ensuring she was not seen when she entered the building in Killarney through the boiler room, she reached the flat a little before five o'clock. Keogh seemed to have spent the day moving restlessly about like an animal installed in a new cage. He led her to a chair next to the French windows. "I've had nothing to do but think all day. Have a drink? No, it's not too early. I've worked out how to get out of this place without them knowing. Whisky all right?"

She sat down, facing through the windows the blood-red glow of a sinking Highveld sun. Keogh squatted on the carpet in front of her, staring at the whisky in his glass and nodding once in a while as she repeated what Dr. Mayat had told her. When she had finished he stood up, went to the window, and looked down at the waiting Toyota.

"They don't seem to care whether I know they're here," he said.

"You can see Horn's men?"

He nodded. "I've thought quite a lot today about them, wondering what they were waiting for. Now maybe we've got the answer. The money."

"The Congress funds?"

"Fourteen thousand pounds, she said. What if Horn knows about it? If it was cleaned out of the Congress bank accounts at the time of Sharpeville, then the Security Police would certainly have found out at some stage. What if he knows that Shack knows about it too? He could have been waiting for Shack to lead him to it. He practically has already, if this story is to be believed."

"But why wait so long? It's been missing twelve years, and it's not a fortune anyway."

"It could still be used for lots of interesting purposes if it managed to reach the wrong hands. Wilby's hands, for instance. It fits what I was saying last night, you see: I wandered into this by accident and they've got to keep their mitts off me—at least until their game has worked itself out. If they bust me Mayat will take fright."

"You're suggesting that they *know* Mayat has the money?"

"Why not? If they know the stuff is still in the country, that it never got across the border for whatever reason, they can only have found out from one of the people directly involved. The Mayat brothers, Wilby, and Shack"—he counted them off on his fingers—"and let's add Yusuf's wife for good measure. Knowing who took the money, even arresting him, solves less than half the problem; it could be so carefully salted away that it's irrecoverable. But this way, if Hassim does the decent thing by Shack, he has to hand the lot over to Yusuf. Which means assembling it all in one place, doesn't it?"

"It still seems a pretty complicated way of doing it," Rina said.

He had no answer to that, and he walked back to the bar counter. "All this is assuming we believe Dr. Mayat," he said.

"I thought she was telling the truth, basically. Perhaps she knows more about the Congress than she lets on, but she made it clear she despised the lot of them. Perhaps she wouldn't be above betraying them herself."

"Hassim told me that he and his brother fought, that night after Sharpeville. He accused Yusuf of betraying Wilby. Now we've got Yusuf accusing Hassim and Shack of exactly the same thing, and of stealing all the Congress's money. Wow! The fact that we mustn't lose sight of is that Wilby *was* betrayed by someone."

"It sounds as if the only person who could clear it up is Wilby himself," Rina said.

"And he's eight hundred miles away and very inaccessible. Lives in a villa like a fortress outside Lusaka, surrounded by armed guards, and has a resident bomb-disposal expert to open every parcel that arrives for him. No, the only way I'm going to get anywhere is by leaning on Hassim and Shack. I'll get the truth out of them if I have to crack their skulls together. This time I've got facts to confront Hassim with. I'm going there soon after dark."

"How will you do that, pray?"

He gestured through the window towards the Toyota. "Dead simple. As long as they haven't seen me leave, and as long as the Valiant hasn't moved, they assume I'm in the building. They don't know that I also have access to your husband's Range Rover. No, I tried it out. I took old September, the flat cleaner, down and showed him how to drive it. I got him to take it out of the basement and watched them for a reaction. Didn't bat an eyelid. It's parked two blocks behind the building, and I get out the same way as you. I can come and go without their knowing I've stirred. Another drink?"

"A small one."

She held out her glass. Impulsively he took her wrist, leaned over, and kissed her. She stood up and they embraced in the last of the sun's mellow evening warmth, feeling desire start up, spread languidly through them, and grow. Eventually he did pour her a drink and took it through to the bedroom he had been using. He found her already undressed—sometimes she liked to surprise him with her boldness—and waiting with an opaque look in her eyes that seemed to want him and mock him at once. The sight of her body still gave him a shock of pleasure: long torso with the deep-seated tan that came of a childhood spent in the sun, slightly jutting stomach, small pert breasts with a spray of freckles above them. There were moments when he wondered how he would ever be attracted to another woman.

Their lovemaking was different this time, better than it had ever been. Perhaps fear and uncertainty had brought a new need of each other, a new level of passion. When it was spent they lay looking into each other's eyes for a long time. Keogh brushed with his finger at the line of sweat on her upper lip, and then from nowhere two bright tears had appeared and were sliding down her cheeks.

"What are you thinking?" he said.

"Oh, something about Paul, that's all." Then suddenly she sat up, drawing the bedclothes protectively round her breasts. "My God, I've just realized he could walk in here!"

"You've heard from him?"

"No, that's just it. I left a message at Beira for him to phone me at the Langham, but I haven't been there all day. If he gets no reply he'll probably fly straight back anyway."

"What were you going to tell me?" Keogh said casually, but the moment had been lost. Rina was up and searching for her clothes.

"It really doesn't matter," she said.

"What if he did find you here? You're not ashamed?"

"It's not that. He's jealous, Keogh, insanely jealous, and I'm afraid of him in that kind of mood. We're depending on him; we can't afford to antagonize him. Have you seen my other earring?"

"Look, he's got to get used to it sometime, Rina. For the last year you've been no more than technically married. Within a week even that will be over. He has no claim on you."

"Oh, damn, I haven't time to look. Let's just not be provocative, all right?" She wriggled into her clothes with the speed only a woman can achieve, unclipped the partnerless earring, and slipped it into a pocket of her suede slacks. She kissed him quickly; she'd become businesslike and rather remote. "I must get back to the hotel and see if there's a message. I ought to be seen there anyway. If I come back about lunchtime tomorrow we should have some news for each other."

13

With a quickened heartbeat Keogh made his way to the basement, through the boiler room, and up, by a dark concrete staircase, to the ground floor of the adjacent block of flats. He could not be sure that Horn's men didn't already know of this exit, but he thought it unlikely that they would have come exploring; it would only have caused talk among the cleaners and washerwomen who were virtually the only visitors to these parts of the building. The sight of a liquor still beneath the stairs, reeking pungently of illegal skokiaan, was reassuring; it would have vanished at any hint of white men poking about the basements.

No, they were content to watch the front and rear doors of Mont Salève. They believed he was too afraid to leave, and they thought they could follow if he did choose to go. After a day of brooding inactivity he found himself taking a curious pleasure in this deception. He felt alert, his senses sharpened by the danger that he had begun to understand more clearly. He stepped into the empty lobby of the building, all mosaic walls, lily ponds, and concealed lighting. Its name was Mont de Lure—he might have known. He hurried to the glass doors, which were opened by an electric eye, and out into the breath-catching cold. The quiet residential street seemed deserted. He walked briskly for two hundred yards to the turning where September had parked the Range Rover. The keys were under the driver's seat.

Like everyone who did outdoor work in Africa, Keogh had a trusting familiarity with Land Rovers. On the Copperbelt they considered the new Range Rover a bit effete, a utility vehicle trying to double as a superior sort of saloon. But after settling into a seat that seemed indecently comfortable and starting the engine, he recognized its powerful throb, the chunky controls, the feel of inner toughness in the gear action and low-ratio steering. The tank was full and there were only four thousand miles on the clock. Paul Blane had bought it last year for hunting trips but had a way of discarding his old toys as new ones appeared. Now he went everywhere by plane.

Friday night. The town was out seeking fast, painless relief from the neurotic pace of its working week. To Keogh this city did not seem part of Africa; it was a colony of aliens from some bustling and acquisitive planet who had landed quite at random on the continent's ancient plateau. The rest of it—inefficient, friendly, relaxed, fallible with the constantly redeeming ability to laugh at itself—hardly penetrated the consciousness of the white people who thronged the pavements of Hillbrow, crowding into bars and cinemas and discotheques. There were not even many blacks on the streets; those not required for work had to be out of the city by ten o'clock. One sat on the kerb, vainly trying to straighten the bent wheel of a bicycle; elsewhere a small crowd stood staring down at a man who lay unconscious in the gutter, but magically they melted back into the dark as the police van swept round the corner. The Range Rover was caught in a traffic jam; the van's headlights held Keogh's face in their glare for half a minute. But it was no longer the police that he feared.

Down in the central city it was quieter. A few seedy tea-rooms were open in Fordsburg, but in the quiet street where Mayat lived Friday night might never have been heard of. Keogh saw at once that the house was in darkness. He parked some distance beyond it and sat waiting a full ten minutes in the Range Rover before walking back. He was sure that his strategy had succeeded; he had not been followed.

Quietly he unlatched the gate, went up the ramp, and peered through the front window. The curtains were open; the room was in darkness. He moved round the side of the house to where he knew there was a back door. Suddenly, as he approached it, a light came on in the kitchen. He ducked below the window sill, blinking away from the brightness. Then he heard the sounds of cupboards and drawers being opened and closed, and through the frosted glass he saw a figure moving around the small room. It was moving slowly, but it was not a figure in a wheelchair. Anyway, Mayat would hardly carry out a thorough search of his own kitchen. Keogh waited another two minutes to be sure he recognized the jerky movements of the silhouette in the window, and to be sure he was alone. He went softly to the door, tried the handle. It was unlocked. He stepped inside.

Shack stood by the sink with Mayat's bottle of cane spirit held to his lips, and for a moment, rigid with fright, he kept it there. Then he spluttered, lowered the bottle, wiped his mouth on a sleeve of the shabby grey dressing gown he wore, and gave a weak grin.

"All right, Jimmy. I deserved a scare."

"I see you're much better," Keogh observed, locking the door behind him.

"I think I'm O.K. Pretty weak, and a lot of aches. Here's the medicine I needed; trust Hassim to hide it. Drink?"

"No," said Keogh. They stood looking at each other, not unlike old friends in new circumstances, expecting to find changes. Shack seemed drained by the fever, thinner and peakier, if that were possible, but his eyes were clear and relatively bright, and some of the dark leathery lustre had returned to his skin. There were clean bandages around his wrists. He recognized Keogh's tone as businesslike.

"The doctor was here an hour ago. Yusuf's wife."

"You know Mayat tried to keep me away from her?"

"She told me about it."

"Where is he?"

"Back at his shop. Says he has to pay his assistant on Friday nights, see to some other things. I'm fit enough to look after myself. The shivering stopped around midday. I don't remember much except the shivering since you cut those bracelets off me. I owe you for that, Jimmy. I won't forget that." He raised the bottle in a salute to Keogh, put it to his mouth, and swallowed. "Couple of days, we'll be across that border, Jimmy; I'll buy you enough drinks to drown in."

"What'll you use for money?" Keogh said sharply.

The black man smiled, shrugged, and drank some more. Keogh, watching the Adam's apple bob up and down in his scrawny throat, wondered exactly how much had been withheld from him. Then Shack gasped and clutched at the edge of the sink in a moment of dizziness.

Keogh helped him to a chair at the tiny kitchen table

and waited for him to recover. "Listen," he said, sitting down opposite. "It's not that simple, and you know it. When you told me the story about what happened on the Friday night after Sharpeville, you left part of it out. You knew about the money, didn't you?"

"Jimmy, baby, I wasn't trying to do you down. I swear it."

"Then what were you doing?"

"Money makes people greedy. It's not the kind of thing you just tell to somebody as soon as you meet them."

"Tell me now."

Shack spread his hands with the resignation that prison had taught him. "Not much to tell. Only what I heard from Wilby that night. They were doing some kind of deal with the Chinaman and he was pretty pleased about it. He'd had a few drinks too; he was talkative—"

"Just a minute. What Chinaman?"

"No, I didn't tell you about him. The Chinaman that owned the store."

"The place where you met them all?"

"Wilby and Yusuf and Hassim had all met at Yusuf's house earlier, and they went together to the Chinaman's store out on the Far West Rand. That's where Hassim told me to be at eleven o'clock. When I got there they were talking to this Chinaman in a room at the back. Little old man with half a dozen gold rings on his fingers. They didn't explain what was going on; it was none of my business; I didn't want to know. I took Wilby and we got to talking on the way to the border. I asked him what would happen to the Congress now and he said not to worry, they'd be O.K. Across the border, he said, the Congress would be richer than it had ever been. It would have money to wage a real war against the Boers. They'd done some deal with the Chinaman that would make the Congress rich, he said."

"That was all?" Keogh demanded.

"That's all he told me. Then we got busted. Later when they had me in the Truth Room they kept asking me where was the money. *Waar's die geld, waar's die geld?* They knew about it, Jimmy."

Keogh's stomach tightened. "What did you tell them?" he said softly.

"In the Truth Room nobody lies. I couldn't tell them much; I didn't know much. After a while the questions stopped."

"And you managed to keep Hassim out of it?"

"They didn't ask. On the Island, later, I got round to thinking a bit. If they had a lot of money, they must have been planning to take it out that night. Wilby wasn't carrying it, and obviously Yusuf didn't have it when he got through. That left the Chinaman and Hassim."

"And you thought Hassim might still have it." Keogh nodded at the bottle of cane spirit. "That wasn't all you were searching for when I arrived, then."

"I thought there was no harm in looking. I mean, if there was something here that really belonged to the Congress, then I got just as much right to it as he has, maybe more. Just personal, Jimmy, no odds to you. I won't let you down."

"Did you find anything?"

"Jimmy, you ask so many questions you should work in the Truth Room."

"Come on, what is it?"

"Not what I expected." Shack grinned and took from the pocket of his dressing gown a manila envelope folded into quarters. It was old and brittle and tore slightly as he opened it out, carefully shaking three objects like tiny sugar lumps into his long palm. In the hard light of the kitchen they had a dull bluish-white gleam. They were roughly cubical in shape, the largest the size of an average pea, the others about half that. Keogh recognized them at once, even before taking the biggest between his thumb and forefinger to feel its weight and its soapy texture.

"Where did you find them?" For no clear reason he felt a flutter of excitement.

"Back of his wardrobe," said Shack. "There's a panel of plywood comes away there. So he does a bit of IDB on the side. So what? He's a jeweller."

"But jewellers don't deal in rough diamonds. Only a registered cutter or dealer can buy them—which doesn't mean Hassim hasn't got contacts. These have been there a long time, though." Keogh returned the stones to their envelope, folded it, and placed it in his own pocket. "He and I will have to have a little heart-to-heart."

"Wait a bit, Jimmy. I don't want him knowing I scratched around here."

"He probably expects it." Keogh stood up, looking down into the black man's gaunt face. "You trust him?"

"I don't know."

"But you had enough faith to put yourself in his hands."

"There was nobody else," Shack said, shrugging again.

If anything ever surprised Mayat, he never showed it. Without a word he unbolted the door of his shop when Keogh rang the bell, wheeled himself back to the office, and sat behind the desk looking at his visitor with a plump, expressionless face. A sapphire brooch and a few rings that he had been tinkering with lay in front of him, together with a row of small tools. The tired fern, the jeweller's scale, and the fez sat glumly on their perches round the room. Keogh was struck by a thought that seemed oddly relevant: Mayat did not *look* like a man who had ever had fourteen thousand pounds in his hands. But nor did he look as if he would dabble in illicit diamond buying. He seemed too untouched by greed, too afraid of involvement.

"I thought you were never here on your own," Keogh said.

"I have been waiting for you."

"Am I that predictable?"

"You're not easily put off. When I heard that you had approached my sister-in-law I knew you would be back. You're an engineer, Mr. Keogh. You're used to mathematical problems which have a solution built into them, if only you can find it. Apply the right formula and the answer must emerge. If it doesn't, that can only be because your calculations went wrong somewhere, so you go back to the beginning and search for the mistake. To that extent you are predictable, yes."

"In this case it seems my figures are right," Keogh said.

"But life isn't an exact science, is it? People behave in ways which defy logic. It would be nice to think that important things always happened for significant reasons. No. A man marries a girl he doesn't love because he is too nice to disappoint her. Another blows his brains out because he enjoys the feeling of danger in holding a gun to his head. It takes an old man like me to recognize all the banality in life. I'm expecting you now to say you didn't come here to philosophize. No? Very well. You have questions, and you've left me no choice but to answer them. That's why I thought we should meet alone."

Keogh sat down slowly on the chair facing the desk. Mayat had clearly set out to take the wind from his sails. He said, "I think I know at least one of the answers."

"Fatima told me a lady had been to see her. Too many people are being drawn in. You and Shack want Yusuf's assistance, and in return he requires something impossible from me. I want to convince you that it's impossible, Mr. Keogh, that's all."

You had the opportunity to do that last night, Keogh thought, but he kept quiet.

The Indian pushed his wheelchair back a few inches, joined the tips of his strong brown fingers, and stared at them reflectively. "You know when it happened. Nineteen-sixty. The twenty-fifth of March. Sharpeville had been on the Monday. On Wednesday evening I had a phone call from my brother, asking me to meet him on a street corner in Germiston, a few miles away. He and the other Congress leaders were already in hiding. I met him and we spoke in my car for a few minutes. He wanted me to arrange the escape of Wilby and himself on the Friday night. He also wanted something else.

"By Friday, he said, he and Wilby would have a large sum of money between them, in cash. To take it with them in the form of five-pound notes would have been useless. South African currency is not freely convertible, and foreign money could only be bought under strict control, in small amounts—"

"Not fourteen thousand pounds' worth, anyway," Keogh interrupted.

"His estimate then was twelve thousand pounds. In the event it was fourteen thousand one hundred and forty. He did not tell me where it had come from and I didn't ask. It was, of course, understood between us. It could have been confiscated if it had stayed where it was. It was no good leaving it in safe keeping either; the currency was due to be decimalized, pounds would be replaced by rands, and those notes would be called in almost immediately. The only solution was to convert that cash, to invest it in something secure that could be re-sold anywhere. Something that would even increase in value with time. It would have to be an illegal investment, of course."

Keogh had already taken out the envelope containing the three diamonds, and he slid it across the desk. Mayat's brow puckered but he allowed himself no other sign of surprise. He turned the wheelchair, propelled himself towards the safe, and fetched back the finely balanced scale in its glass case. Then he found his spectacles and put them on.

"Uncut diamonds. It was Wilby's idea, though Yusuf tried to make it sound like his own. It isn't everyone who can lay his hands on uncut diamonds, even with fourteen thousand pounds to spend. And it isn't everyone who can assess the quality—or even the authenticity—of what is being offered. This is why I was needed, to find them a seller and to make sure what he sold them wasn't crushed glass.

"The notice was very short. But I made discreet inquiries among people in the less reputable parts of the trade. On Friday morning I was visited by Mr. Lee Ah Young, a storekeeper from the Far West Rand. He brought these with him."

Mayat tipped the three stones into his palm. He took

the glass dust-cover off the balance, placed the diamonds in one of the pans, unlocked the beam of the scales, and used a pair of calipers to fiddle some tiny bronze weights out of their slots into the other pan.

"Eighteen carats," he said. "These are fairly good gem stones from the blue ground at Kimberley—I'm not an expert but I can tell a good diamond from a bad one. On the controlled world market these would be worth between six and eight hundred pounds today, before they were cut. Lee Ah Young brought them as samples of his collection. He said at home he had another five thousand carats of similar stuff. Do you know how much that is, Mr. Keogh? More than two pounds, by weight, of gem diamonds."

He sat back for a moment to let the fact settle. Keogh said, "Where does one old storekeeper get a hoard like that?"

"With patience, it's not as difficult as you might think. A diamond that's marketed legally, by the Central Selling Organization, is valued by a more or less constant scale of size and quality. An illegal one has to find its own level at a given time and place. Black miners are almost the only source of stolen dimonds; they smuggle them out a few at a time and they take whatever they can get for them. They haven't the contacts higher up the chain. From there on a stone goes through a series of middlemen, roughly doubling its value each time, usually until it reaches one of the big syndicates that can get it out to an underground clearing house in the Middle East. Beirut is the world capital of the illicit diamond trade. There, a stone might fetch half of what it would sell for on the controlled market. It will reach a dealer and, finally, a cutter in Europe who is an expert at disguising its origin. It might even come back to South Africa quite openly and legally, set in an engagement ring.

"So the nearer you are to the source, the cheaper they come. Lee Ah Young had had a store in Kimberley for many years. He was a hoarder, like a lot of the older Chinese who grew up with no faith in paper money. He hoarded gold and jewellery; he wore gold rings on his hands. For twenty years or more he'd been buying rough diamonds direct from the miners. The security there is phenomenal but the stones do get out: they're swallowed, they're fired across the fences with catapults, there's a constant battle of wits between the thieves and the security people. Lee was always careful, never greedy. He took only good-quality gem stones from three and four carats upwards—and nothing too big, either. He had never sold a single one. He'd bought his hoard at ridiculous prices too, by giving the miners credit at his store. He paid them off with cheap blankets and cowboy hats and concertinas that they'd take back to the reserves."

An edge of bitterness had crept into Mayat's voice, but now he parted his fingers and looked up abruptly, changing his tone.

"I'd say that over the years those stones cost him no more than three thousand pounds. Today their world market price would be close enough to a quarter of a million. Yes, I'm serious. With that number, and that quality, you could fly to Beirut with them tomorrow and get at least a hundred thousand—at once, in cash, in any currency you chose, no questions asked."

Keogh's mouth had gone quite dry. "This is what Yusuf wants from you?" he said.

"Yes. And he simply won't believe that I haven't got them to give."

"What happened?"

The old man removed his glasses and his mild dark

168

eyes searched Keogh's. Keogh found himself, as he had been before, faintly startled at the suggestion of a smile on Mayat's face. It seemed full of wisdom, or cunning, or perhaps simply the amusement of total and genuine indifference. "They became inaccessible. Physically inaccessible. One of life's banalities, I suppose. They're at the bottom of a hole."

Mayat waited for a reaction, but by now Keogh was unshockable. "What sort of a hole?" he said carefully.

"Quite a deep one. Why don't you come and see it? It's an hour's drive away."

Part IV

PIT

14

They drove westwards among the skeletal shadows of old mine workings and factories, and then along a road skirting the edge of Soweto, the enormous self-contained complex of African townships outside the city. Beneath the infrequent street lamps, tiny identical houses in squared and symmetrical rows lay silent and smoke-shrouded like the Greek tents at the walls of Troy, housing an army of one million people—the million most advanced and urbanized and best-educated and best-housed and best-paid and most cynical and frustrated black people in Africa. There was great potential here, either as a bridge of common aspirations that could cross the racial gulf or as the power base for revolution. Hope was a scarce commodity; Wilby Xaba had foreseen the choice a long time ago. If upheaval came, it would come to Soweto first.

The road finally crossed open veld between the small mining towns of the Far West Rand. They had come in the Range Rover at Keogh's insistence; he said it would be much faster than Mayat's old car, but the real reason was that he feared the Morris had been bugged, like the Valiant, with a radio transmitter. The old man had had to be helped onto the high front passenger seat; his wheelchair lay folded on the luggage deck at the back.

Mayat gave directions and Keogh followed them automatically, grateful for the chance to do some thinking. He had almost no doubt now that what Horn wanted was to retrieve the missing Congress funds. Rina had found it puzzling that he should take so much trouble over fourteen thousand pounds. A quarter of a million in uncut diamonds was quite another matter, but if Horn knew about the diamonds he could only have found out from one of the four people involved in the transaction twelve years ago: Wilby, the Mayat brothers, and the Chinaman, Lee Ah Young. Keogh found Hassim Mayat more and more puzzling. Why had he decided to tell the whole story? What had happened in the past twenty-four hours to make him appear co-operative? Only one thing seemed certain: Horn wanted the Congress funds in whatever form they existed; Mayat was the only one who knew where they were. Shack had been meant, unknowingly, to provide the essential link—but now it was Keogh who was caught between the two sides, who could only survive as long as he kept them apart, each ignorant of what the other was doing. Until he knew more about their motives this was his only hope. He kept a careful check in his mirror; as far as it was possible to tell, they were not being followed.

Mayat told him more about Lee Ah Young. The old man had been planning for some time to retire to his birthplace, Singapore, from which he had emigrated illegally forty years before. He wanted an income-earning investment, and the slump in property prices that was bound to

174

accompany the Sharpeville crisis was an ideal opportunity. Whatever his misgivings about paper money, to buy cheap housing he needed cash. He was willing to part with all or most of his hoard as long as it could be done in a single sale.

Wilby, Yusuf, and Hassim rendezvoused after dark that night at Yusuf's house and went on to Lee's store. In his living quarters at the back, once he had seen the money they had brought and was assured of their honest intentions, the Chinaman produced the diamonds from a safe beneath his bed and a bottle of whisky from a cupboard. Two hours of bargaining followed.

Both sides recognized that they were in a weak position; they needed each other too badly. For Yusuf and Wilby it was a question of how many diamonds they could get for their money; Lee's object was to part with as few as possible. His asking price was five pounds a carat. Hassim, who had examined the stones and knew they were good, suggested offering two pounds. Yusuf, in a particularly stubborn mood, refused for a long time to go above this figure. When Shack turned up at eleven o'clock there was still no agreement. He could not afford to delay if he was to get both his passengers to the border that night. Wilby left with him; Yusuf would follow with the diamonds once a price had been agreed.

"What happened then?" Keogh said.

"Finally Yusuf and the Chinaman settled on just over three pounds a carat. In exchange for the money, Yusuf got four and a half thousand carats of gem diamonds in a little canvas tobacco bag. We were all pleased with the outcome, I think. I was only there as an adviser, of course."

"You didn't get a commission?"

"Lee said I should have the three stones he had brought

to me as samples. I've kept them ever since. From Wilby and Yusuf I took only the one hundred pounds that Shack would be paid."

"And then?"

"Watch out for a gravel road on the right. It's easy to miss."

The road was a mile further on. Mayat wanted to tell the story at his own pace, and for now Keogh was prepared to let him. It was enough to know that the Mayat brothers and Lee Ah Young had been left alone with fourteen thousand pounds in cash and diamonds worth six or seven times that much, and to remember that people had been betrayed for much less. The police had been tipped off about Wilby and Shack driving to the border. Any one of the people involved could have had a motive: Hassim or Yusuf, for the sake of the money or even for obscurer reasons; Fatima Mayat to spite her husband and the Congress; perhaps even Lee Ah Young.

The Range Rover bumped off the tar onto an unsurfaced road running between wide mealie fields, their stubble reflecting pale moonlight back to the sky. In the distance to their left were the lights of a mine headgear. Mayat told him to douse the headlights.

"Where is this?"

"The last town we went through was Westonaria. A lot of this is farming country, but the gold mines are much more important now."

Mayat knew the road well. It was taking them in a semicircle towards the shaft head, but well before they reached it he told Keogh to slow down. On the right was an old burnt-brick building with a porch along the front and thick pillars supporting the roof—or not supporting it, rather, because the corrugated-iron sheeting had caved in at the centre. It was in darkness. Keogh parked in a dusty little clearing beside the building, got stiffly down, and looked at it more closely. Khaki weeds were well established in the cracks of the porch, and there were wide black openings at the front where sheet glass had once been fitted to display cheap blankets, belts, guitars, gaudy city clothes, and a lot of other junk to the migrant black miners and farm workers. Nothing had been sold here for a long time. A bat flew out of one window and flitted across the face of the moon. Keogh shivered. The paint had blistered and flaked from a wooden sign above the guttering, but no tags of identity were needed. This had been Lee Ah Young's concession store.

"Why have we come here?"

"It's just a short walk away," Mayat said.

Keogh took the wheelchair from the back of the vehicle and helped him down. Once in the chair he had no difficulty moving across the gravel onto the hummocky dried grass behind the building. There was a barbed-wire fence here, but its rusted strands hung loose. Keogh parted them. Mayat had brought a torch from his shop; carrying it, he pushed himself through the fence and they moved across the bare veld on a winding, scarcely visible footpath that ran directly away from the store. Mayat seemed to know with fair certainty where he was going.

"The land belongs to one of the mines," he said. "There's no need to worry about trespassing; they're only interested in what goes on ten thousand feet underground."

The grass crunched beneath Keogh's feet and under the

tires of the wheelchair. Here and there were black charred patches where the veld had been burnt during the autumn. Around them the wind whispered coldly.

They walked for five minutes before Mayat said, "Careful." He switched on the torch, keeping its beam low to the ground, and pushed a way through a tangle of rusty wire from a fence that had been broken down. Just ahead was another black patch, better defined than the rest. This was not burnt grass; it was a hole—a neatly circular, neatly vertical hole that might have been punched into the ground by a giant pile-driver. It looked about twenty feet across.

Mayat had stopped and put the brake on his wheelchair. Keogh took the torch from him, stepped forward cautiously to within a few feet of the edge, and flicked the beam round the circumference. The hole had been there a good few years; its edges were rounded by rainwater and erosion. He shone the light downwards and the beam bounced off water-runnelled red soil, a few clumps of grass, and dissolved in the darkness further down.

"It's a sinkhole," Mayat said behind him. "Do you know about them? One minute there was just flat veld here; the next this had appeared."

"Yes," Keogh said. He was still a little astonished. Sinkholes had become something of an object-lesson in the mining engineer's handbook, though he had never seen one before. This part of the Transvaal was notorious for them; great, almost literally bottomless pits that opened without warning. The water that collects at the bottom of every deep mine must be constantly pumped out, and often it is cheap and convenient to pump it into an existing natural drainage system of underground streams. The rock in these parts was dolomitic; the lime it contained dissolved in water. When the mines opened up on the Far West Rand after the war, the suddenly increased flow of water ate away the rock substrata much more rapidly than anyone had anticipated, forming vast underground caverns. From time to time the roof of a cavern became too weak to support the weight of rock and soil above, and it all vanished down the hole in a great vertical rush. Some of the openings were enormous; they had swallowed whole houses with their occupants. This one was narrow and was probably considered too remote to need filling in. A fence had been put around it that had subsequently fallen down. There was some kind of warning notice on the other side.

Keogh looked at Mayat. "Well?"

"That's where they are, Mr. Keogh. Down at the bottom, two hundred and thirty feet. Quite inaccessible."

"You've plumbed it?"

"Several times. The readings were always within a few feet of two hundred and thirty."

"I thought you weren't interested."

Mayat, silhouetted squatly against the sky, said nothing. Keogh moved round the hole, picking up pebbles and tossing them in. Their sound was muffled by soft soil they loosened from the sides, and it was impossible to hear them strike the bottom. He was worried by a half-formed thought and by the artificiality of Mayat's excuse for leading him here.

"Where your plumb-line fell isn't really the bottom," he said. "It's just a point where enough debris has fallen to block up the hole. It's like putting a plug in the neck of an hour-glass: a slight disturbance, an earth tremor, might loosen the plug. Then it's a clear drop to the bottom of the cavern below. How far? That's anybody's guess."

"There's been no disturbance that I could detect since nineteen-sixty. The plug seems quite solid. Still. . . ."

"Still, it's a death trap," Keogh said firmly. "Perhaps a very experienced potholer or mountaineer might be daft enough to risk it, but that's all."

"No." Mayat's voice, disembodied in the dark, had an infuriating calm. "There was a stage when I took some trouble to learn about this sinkhole. To make a completely vertical climb of that distance is almost impossible anyway. But at sixty feet the hole widens out, I have no idea how far, and does not narrow down again until twenty feet from the bottom. So with a rope or rope ladder you would not be able to climb against the sides even if you chose to; you would have to cling to an outward pitch most of the way. The only possibility would be to move vertically."

"Through a void, in the dark," Keogh said. "I see what you mean by inaccessible."

"Quite."

"Totally impossible."

"The sides are so uneven. The hole is essentially vertical, though, so if it were in any way possible to suspend a man over the very centre and lower him by mechanical means of some sort—"

"Like the winding system we use in the mines?" Keogh said, hardly trying to disguise his sarcasm.

"Perhaps something like that."

Keogh lit a cigarette and walked slowly all round the hole, returning to a spot a few feet from Mayat. The moon threw a pale glow across the frosty veld. "I can do it," he said.

Mayat did not stir.

"I can do it, and what's more you know I can do it, and

what's more you brought me out here because you know I can do it. Why? If I'm to believe you, there's a hundred thousand quid's worth of diamonds down there somewhere. And you wanted me to get the idea of recovering them. Doing something that anyone else with the right skill could have done any time in the last twelve years. Why, Mayat? I back-pedalled deliberately to see how far you'd go in trying to convince me to convince myself."

In the dark it was impossible to guess the expression on Mayat's face. He said, "Can you believe, Mr. Keogh—have you the imagination to believe—that I don't care about those stones? That I don't want them? What good can they do me? Yes, you're right; the idea of recovering them has fascinated me in a way. Physically, I'm not capable, but I could have found a method. The promise of money will always attract the expertise."

"In this case it's the promise of escape," Keogh said. "I'm a mining engineer. I happen to specialize in rock mechanics, but it would be easy enough for me to build a rig over this hole with a block and tackle and plenty of rope. The question is, why should I? What do you plan to get out of it?"

"Mr. Keogh, you mistake my motives. You're being mathematical. A moral choice was forced upon me: let Yusuf have the diamonds or let you and Shack be trapped."

"The moral choice was before you twenty-four hours ago."

"I wanted time to think, to see if there was another way. Anyway, how could I know to trust you after so little time? You're the first person I have ever told. Get down there if you can, recover them, take them to Yusuf. You won't steal them because they are your only guarantee of freedom. Deal with him through his wife. There. My conscience is clear. Now it's up to you."

"You've never wanted him to have those stones, have you?"

"I'll admit to having enjoyed his frustration," Mayat said. "I thought that if I made it too easy for you, you might suspect an ulterior motive."

"You'd better tell me the rest of the story," Keogh said quietly.

"There's not a lot to tell. Shack left the store with Wilby. Once Yusuf and Lee had settled their business, the three of us sat around talking of this and that. Lee mentioned the sinkhole that had opened up behind his store a few months earlier, and Yusuf kept wanting to go out and see it. Between them they had finished the bottle of whisky and started on another, and Yusuf was argumentative—"

"Just a minute. How much did Lee know? Did he ask where the money had come from?"

"Nothing was said. He guessed, all the same. He certainly knew Wilby by reputation. Well, the car should have returned by two-thirty. By three-thirty I was seriously worried. I knew Shack was absolutely reliable, and there was only one thing that could have gone wrong. I accused—you must see this in the context of the situation—I accused Yusuf of betraying Wilby. His reaction was violent. He accused me of the same thing. He said Shack and I were in it together."

"Why should he think you'd do it?" Keogh asked casually.

"For the diamonds, of course. He had the same motive. Neither of us could prove anything, but we quarrelled viciously. Many old resentments came out; we were very different in temperament; we had been brothers, never friends. Finally, we came to blows. It was ludicrous, of course—a man on crutches, can you imagine? I tried to attack him. He knocked me down."

"The Chinaman sat watching all this?" Keogh said.

"He wouldn't have interfered. I was unconscious for a few minutes. When I came round the two of them were outside; I could hear them talking behind the building. They'd left the diamonds on the table, and at that moment I'd have done anything to stop Yusuf having them. I hated him. I managed to retrieve my crutches and stand up. I took the bag, went quietly out the front way, and got into my car. I drove off before they could stop me. Yusuf could not follow."

"But you came back?"

"Who knows what I was thinking? There was panic in the air. I had wanted to get the diamonds out of Yusuf's hands because I thought he had betrayed the Congress. I drove home. By dawn I wondered whether I had been wrong, and I was also very frightened. I had those diamonds —the visible proof of my part in the illegal activities of the Congress. I thought of speaking to Yusuf again, perhaps of giving him a chance to prove his innocence. So I came back here at nine in the morning. Yusuf had gone. It was too late. It seemed to me that in one night the Congress and everything it had worked for had shrivelled up and died. I remembered the sinkhole, and I came out here and threw that little bag down there. If the Congress could not have it then nobody should, I thought. It was only later, of course, that I heard Wilby had reached safety. That's all there was to it, Mr. Keogh. The stones are still down there. It's the most unlikely place in the world, isn't it?"

Keogh stared at the hunched, square figure. His story was plausible enough, but was it the whole story? Keogh resisted the impulse to question him and instead flicked his cigarette butt down the hole, watching the blackness suck it down and blot out its glow. A bat flew from the opening and made a startled cartwheel over their heads.

"And Yusuf still wants them," Keogh said. "And Yusuf shall have them, no matter how much it still goes against your grain, is that right?"

The Indian said nothing but turned his wheelchair round and began to move back along the path.

Keogh said, "Wait. Assuming I do take this on, I'll need help. Shack's help—and yours. Is it worth a couple of nights' work to get us off your back?"

"I'll do what I can," Mayat said.

"Good. But supposing the diamonds really are inaccessible? Suppose they've been covered by later subsidences? Suppose there's six feet of water on the bottom? There's a lot of seepage at that depth."

"I've tested it from time to time," Mayat said, "by lowering small receptacles on a rope. Even during the summer rains there is no more than an inch or two on the bottom—"

"What you call the bottom," Keogh interjected, "may be nothing but a thin layer of rock."

"The drainage is good, anyway. Of course a certain amount of silt has collected over the years, but it amounts to no more than a foot or two."

"You've done your homework, haven't you?" Keogh said. It had been obvious from the start that Mayat's interest in the sinkhole was less casual than he pretended. He caught the old man up as he started back towards the store. "It'll take a day or two. Obviously we'd have to work at night. I've got to build a rig over this hole one night and leave it here at least a day before using it. Does it stand a chance of going unnoticed?"

"The place is hardly ever visited," Mayat said. "There's nothing here to interest either trespassers or the mine authorities."

Keogh took a deep breath. "All right. Then I'll do it. But I need plenty of help from you. Shack and I will leave for Botswana the minute I come out of that hole. I'll get Yusuf's wife to explain the situation to him, have him suggest a rendezvous on the border, and we'll drive in the Range Rover. I'll need a whole load of equipment. You'll have to get it for me tomorrow. We can come out here and set it up tomorrow night. On Sunday night I should be able to go down, and I expect to be across the frontier by daybreak."

"Can everything be done that soon?"

"I don't see why not. What I'm going to build is a shear-leg tripod with its vertex right over the centre of the hole. The frame will be made out of mild steel scaffold tubing, and the three legs will be cemented into the ground. We'll attach a pulley block to the vertex and suspend a bo'sun's chair of some sort from it—you know the kind of thing that steeplejacks use to manoeuvre themselves about the sides of buildings? You're going to have to find all this somewhere, and about fifteen hundred feet of rope and a lot more besides. Start with a scaffolding supplier. I'll work out exactly what we need on the way back and give you a shopping list. Think of it all as helping to clear your conscience."

Mayat was silent. They moved across the bare veld till

the concession store came into sight with its broken roof silhouetted against the sky.

Keogh said, "What happened to Lee Ah Young anyway? Did he get to Singapore?"

"I never saw him again," Mayat said remotely.

15

Keogh, cold and tired, got back to Killarney about three in the morning. All but the most determined Friday-night revellers had given up and gone home, leaving the streets to the old watchmen hunched against the wind over their glowing braziers, and to beggars and thieves and milk trucks and occasional prowling police cars. Not many white men cared to walk about at that hour.

The watchman at Mont Salève was nowhere in sight when he slipped in through the boiler room and basement and rode up to the fourth floor. He had a lot to think about, but most of it could wait till daylight. For the past hour he had been sitting with Mayat in the Range Rover, parked three blocks from the house in Fordsburg, drawing up a formidable list of the equipment he needed for tomorrow night. The idea of tomorrow night irritated him, almost like an engagement to which someone else had committed him without asking. The most puzzling question was to what degree Mayat was fooling him and how much he was fooling Mayat. And, of course, how far they were both being deceived together. For the moment he wanted no more than a stiff drink and a good night's sleep.

He reached number 43 at the end of the corridor, opened the door, and groped for the light switch in the entrance hall. Then he smelt cigarette smoke.

For an instant he stood there, frozen. Before he had considered any other move he was backing instinctively for the open door, and then something hit him hard in the small of the back. It knocked him sprawling to the floor and he slid several yards across the polished slate of the hall, cracking his head on the skirting of the opposite wall. Air had been driven from his lungs and he lay gasping for breath. A light came on; he saw Van Heerden chain-bolting the door behind him.

There was a wrenching pain in his back. He sucked in lungfuls of air while the blond Afrikaner came and stood over him and frisked him with quick, expert hands. Keogh looked at a pair of dirty *velskoen* and the cuffs of some cheap fawn slacks. It was the sole of a *velskoen* that had struck him, no doubt; Van Heerden had waited for him diagonally across the corridor, behind the kitchen door.

"Stand," he commanded.

"Is that all you know how to do?" Keogh said.

"Fuck you, stand!"

Van Heerden's eyes, seen for the first time without dark glasses, were small and red-rimmed, painful-looking, and there was liquor on his breath and a purposeful air of viciousness about him. It would do no good to argue. Keogh began to rise, and when he was on one knee Van Heerden smirked and hit him with a fist like a pile-driver between the eyes. He went down again, banging his head on the floor, seeing a white explosive flash inside his skull and still, somehow, managing to be angry with himself for being tricked. The pain twisted and ground through his head and he wanted to vomit but wasn't given time. He felt Van Heerden seize the lapel of his jacket and drag him down the hall. The slate gave onto the soft pile of the sitting-room carpet. Van Heerden uttered a weird, high, schoolboy giggle and dropped him like a sack of mealies to the floor in the presence of Horn.

More lights had come on. Keogh lay on his back looking up at the small man sitting cross-legged in a patent-leather armchair, blowing smoke rings. The air was thick with stale tobacco smoke. He closed his eyes. Something was said; something cold, not water, was poured over his head, something that fizzed in his hair and stung his eyes and ran between his lips with a familiar prickling sweetness. It was Coca-Cola.

He half sat up, trying to wipe the cloying stuff from his eyes. Van Heerden kicked him in the ribs, more gently this time, almost playfully, and both the Afrikaners laughed. The laughter was loud and loose, and he realized with a hideous sense of absurdity that they were both very drunk. On the ebony table in front of Horn, among a dozen or more Coca-Cola cans, stood two opaque green bottles that had contained Courvoisier Napoleon brandy; Keogh recognized them from among Paul Blane's stock. The table and the carpet all around Horn were littered with ash, matchsticks, and crumpled cigarette packets.

Horn blew another smoke ring and destroyed it clumsily with a wave of his hand. His collar was loose and his eyes now seemed completely out of focus. "Well," he said. "Well, well. Stay out so late, started to think you're not coming home at all. I said, He's got some bit of an ass; that's what

I told Van. So true as God, never know where anybody's spending the night in Jo'burg. Know how long we waited? Since nine o'clock. That's five hours—no, six. Stupid, to think you'd be here then. See, couple of farm boys like us, ten o'clock at night everybody's tucked up in bed—their own beds—there on the farm. Different here, altogether different." He nodded slowly, with an air of having hit upon a profound truth. "Never mind. Not as if we didn't enjoy ourselves. Had a bit of a party, me and Van. What else can you do, waiting in the dark? This French brandy, never tried it before. Good stuff, eh? Where's your kaffir friend?"

He slid the question in with casual precision. Keogh knew he must say something—anything—but suddenly nausea clutched at him again and he began to retch. Van Heerden hauled him to his feet, slapped his face three times, and shoved him against the mantelshelf. One of the clay African heads fell to the carpet and broke neatly and noiselessly in two.

"He asked you something," Van Heerden hissed.

Keogh's nose began to bleed. He stood clinging to the mantelshelf and watched the crimson drops falling, speckling his shoes and the carpet. Coca-Cola had run down his neck. His head throbbed terribly, and with each pulsation the whole room rushed at him and receded, moving in and out of focus. He wanted to speak; he still could not.

Horn rose unsteadily from the armchair and sucked on his cigarette. "Simple thing to ask, really. Surprised not to find him here, you being the type that wouldn't mind him using your plates and sheets and that. Still, if you'd rather not say. . . . Why don't you tell us where your girl friend is instead? Mrs. Blane?"

Van Heerden stepped forward and gave him an irritated

kick. Pain shot up from his hip and he bent over double, feeling the blood from his nose running down his chin, wanting to pass out but feeling consciousness cling to him like a misguided benefactor. He would answer if he could, if they gave him the chance . . . but in some vague way he knew these were not the important questions anyway. He was being softened up.

This time they allowed him half a minute to recover, get his breath back, straighten up, wipe the blood off his face with his sleeve. Van Heerden stood back with a faint smile on his face, sweat glistening on the greasy skin.

Horn, standing in front of him, breathing brandy fumes, suddenly thrust an orange-stained finger in his face. "Nice Afrikaans girl, what does she see in you? She flew up here to warn you, eh? What does she want with Bushmen and bolsheviks and a kaffir-loving *soutpiel* like you? Tell me, I'm interested. What makes you so special, that you hit a policeman with a bottle? You know what does *soutpiel* mean? No? That's what we call an Englishman. Saltprick." Van Heerden repeated the word and they both giggled. "So tell me, *soutie*, if she warned you why didn't you get out of this flat? Where did you go tonight? Why did you come back? Why haven't you left the country?"

"Which do I answer first?" Keogh said. He had already sensed the kick that was coming. He grabbed Van Heerden's foot as it swung at his groin, twisted it, threw him off balance, and let him fall to the floor.

Almost before he was down Van Heerden had drawn the long-barrelled Colt from under his rugby blazer and was pointing it, two-handed, at Keogh. He came to his feet in one quick move and stood swaying slightly, his eyes red and vicious, sighting along the barrel at Keogh's head.

"I'll make you sorry," he said.

Keogh's scalp crawled. "Tell him to put it down," he said to Horn.

"*Soutie,* you want to do it rough, they don't come any rougher than old Van here," Horn said, shaking his head. "I wanted to make it easier for you. You want to take a short cut, all right, straight to the point, eh? Old Van can blow a hole in your head and we can walk out and not a bugger will ever point a finger at us, do you know that? Do you get the point now?"

"I find it easier to talk without a gun pointing at me, that's all."

Horn waved his hand carelessly. "Don't be so sure. Be surprised, how it helps a person's memory sometimes. You're no good to me without a memory, *soutie,* in fact you're an embarrassment, walking around like this when you should be locked up for *dondering* policemen. If you knew the trouble I've taken. . . . Now don't let me down; don't make old Van shoot you."

"So you did stop the police looking for me," Keogh said.

Horn lit a fresh cigarette from the butt of the first, then dropped the burning end and trod it, unsteadily but deliberately, into the carpet. He looked up. "The money. Where is it?"

"What money?"

Horn said nothing. The only sound was a metallic snap as Van Heerden thumbed back the hammer of his revolver. Keogh felt the blood roar in his head. He was genuinely confused. If he'd ever imagined himself in this kind of situation he had probably thought he would be cool, dignified, a little defiant, exchanging ripostes across a table. And now the reality, being beaten addle-brained by two drunken sadists, one of them ready to blow out his brains for the sheer hell of it.

"I don't know," he said carefully, "what money you mean."

"Memory still vague, eh? I'll jog it a little. Fourteen thousand one hundred and forty pounds. Belonged to the Congress, all their campaign funds collected over several years. Disappeared in cash the week before they were banned. Cheques all signed by Yusuf Mayat, treasurer, countersigned Wilby Xaba, president. Clever. Stopped us confiscating it. Never seen since. Ring a bell?"

Keogh stared at him. So his assumption had been right— up to a point, anyway. "You want the Congress money," he said noncommittally.

"That's better, man, that's better. The money you were planning to take back to them, in Zambia."

"No!"

He had said it too vehemently, fallen into the trap that Horn had prepared. The little man's moustache twitched with the suggestion of a smile. "You know about the money. You don't deny that."

"I don't admit anything."

"Name, rank, and number, eh? Come on, *soutie*, it only works like that in films. It's all a matter of give and take, really. You're sensible enough, you want to save your skin, and that's why you agreed to take that money to Wilby, isn't it? I don't blame you for that. You don't care what happens to it, how many Russian rifles and rockets and land mines he can buy with it, how many of our boys are killed directly because of it. But it's my job to care. It's also my job to know the provisions of the Terrorism Act, to know that for supplying funds to an enemy organization you could be sentenced to death."

"This is ludicrous!" Keogh heard his voice come out in a hoarse whisper. "Where did you get this idea?"

"Not an idea, boy. I've got it in writing. Hassim Mayat's writing. He's arranging it, isn't he? He ought to know."

Again Keogh was stunned. "You know who's got it!"

"Ah. Knowing who's got it: that's not quite what it seems. No help at all, unless you know what he's done with it too. Let me tell you the story. Nineteen-sixty. A couple of days after the Congress is banned, we got round to checking their assets. Gone—every penny of it. It's easy enough to find out that Wilby and Yusuf had it all together in cash at one stage. Within a few weeks it's also obvious through reports from across the border that they haven't got it any longer. So who has? There are half a dozen possibilities. Hassim, being Yusuf's brother, is one of them. We've got no proof; by this time a clever operator will have either stashed the money somewhere very safe or, better still, converted it to something else, perhaps scattered it around among other assets. We keep a close eye on these suspects, their finances particularly. Nothing happens for six months. We start thinking we must have been wrong, or else the money is so safely stashed we'll never find it. Then Hassim gives it all away by writing to Wilby.

"It's a funny kind of letter. A bit defiant and a bit apologetic. Says very little in the end. Refers with regret to the loss of 'the China,' which is obviously the money, but why the code name I don't know. Wilby is in Lusaka by this time, on the bones of his ass and trying to scratch the remnants of the Congress together. He ignores the letter.

Hassim persists in writing to him. Finally they set up a correspondence, a lot of vague letters written in a simple code that still go on talking about 'the China.' They're very discreet—they exchange letters through a private postbox that the Congress uses in Malawi, except we also happen to be clients of the postbox, and we pay a treble fee to look at all Wilby's mail. This morning Hassim sends a coded telegram telling Wilby that he hopes the China will be crossing the border into Botswana within the next few days, and maybe Wilby would like to make arrangements to collect it. It will be carried by a white man called Keogh and a black man called Twala. Further details will follow. So what do you say about that, *soutie?*"

"I don't know what to believe," Keogh said numbly.

"You'd better believe it, *soutie*. Are you starting to realize where you stand?" Horn watched him carefully, with slight amusement, and then signalled to Van Heerden, who lowered his revolver and eased the hammer forward. Keogh released a breath, felt the congealing blood on his face again and the Coke that was making his shirt stick to his chest.

"I think I'm sobering up," Horn said, with an edge of disappointment. "Listen, I told you it's a question of give and take. All I'm interested in is seeing that that money doesn't get out of the country. If you were to co-operate, I might be willing to overlook the fact that you agreed to take it."

"I never agreed to take it to Wilby or the Congress. It was going to Yusuf, as far as I knew."

"Then Hassim has been lying to you."

"Right."

Horn gave a knowing smile. "We could have arrested

Hassim any time in the last twelve years, worked him over. But that sort of thing gets you nowhere with his type. He needs nothing, doesn't care, would rather curl up and die. As long as we knew that he couldn't or wouldn't pass that money along to the Congress in Exile in Zambia, there was no harm in leaving it there. It could even come in useful, maybe."

"You took a lot of trouble over an amount that size," Keogh said.

"In the last two years the Congress has become hot stuff. Wilby is the kingpin of the kaffirs. It becomes important to choke off every single source of funds we can, and we decide it's time we got that fourteen thousand back. Piddling, you think. Surprising how many kaffirs you can fit out as terrorists for that. Hassim has got the money somewhere but he's turned sour, lost interest in the world. Yet he's an old Marxist, believes in the Congress ideals. We still think he would try to get that cash to Zambia if he could find a safe and easy way. So *we* find him a way. We try to push him into it so we can pick him and the money up together. It begins all right and then a big *soutpiel* gets in the way."

There was now a single dull ache in Keogh's head; he wondered if there were any aspirins in the flat. "It was all planned, from the beginning? Shack didn't escape?"

"He escaped. Only he didn't know I arranged it. He was talked into it by another prisoner."

"Who was then shot, to prevent him talking?"

Horn looked past him, dropped another cigarette butt, and mashed it with his foot.

"That's not my carpet," Keogh said.

"No," Horn said vaguely.

196

"Is it worth killing people for the sake of those diamonds?"

"*Shut up!*" Horn flushed with sudden fury. "I don't want any damn moralizing from you—" He stopped short, a sharp animal wariness crossing his face as he realized that he'd been caught by the same kind of verbal trick he had used himself. He stared hard at Keogh. It was a good reaction, almost too good to be true, like a theatrical doubletake. "Diamonds?"

"The money was converted into uncut diamonds. That's what he means by China. They were bought from a Chinaman on the Far West Rand. I thought you might know."

"How should I know?"

"Only if someone involved had told you. Hassim Mayat threw them down a sinkhole—whether because he was afraid or because he didn't want his brother to have them, I don't know. They're worth a lot more than was ever paid for them. Say a hundred thousand pounds."

"So true as God!" Horn whispered, and paced back and forth in front of the fireplace, staring at the toes of his shabby suede shoes. Keogh told him how he intended to recover the stones; there was no point now in hiding any of this, and inwardly he was relieved. He was quite certain that Horn had known all about the existence of the diamonds; he was still trying to shield whoever had betrayed Wilby, whoever had given the police enough information to interrogate Shack that very night. "*Waar's die geld?*" they had asked him. "Where's the money?"

"So true as God," the Afrikaner muttered again. "Diamonds!"

"Do you mind if I sit down?" Keogh said, aware that the atmosphere had become more relaxed. Horn went to the clutter on the ebony table and sorted out two tumblers. He half-filled them with Courvoisier and added Coke; Keogh had retained enough humour to find the mixture amusing. He sat down in an armchair and Horn handed him a drink. Van Heerden lingered near the door, picking his nose.

"Sensible of you to tell me this, *soutie*. On the road, at Kimberley, I got close because I wanted to know more about you. I got too close, made you suspicious. Later I said to old Van, There's a bloke who knows how to look after himself. A bloke with sense, I said. Now what I think is that you should just go ahead and get those diamonds out of that hole. How does it sound?"

"I have a choice?" Keogh said.

"In a way. If you agree it will suit both of us. We don't like using the Terrorism Act if we can avoid it, specially against a foreigner. But of course there's still a charge of attempted murder. Oosthuizen. Recovering now, luckily. If he'd snuffed it even I wouldn't have had the influence to keep the hounds at bay. You'd go away for a long time, *soutie*. Help me get those diamonds and I'll see you leave the country safely."

"You don't need my help to recover them now."

"But if we go out to that hole and dig them up for ourselves, it shows that we know where they are. That won't do, *soutie*. No, we want to pick up Hassim and the ice together. By chance, you see."

"It's not me you're trying to protect," Keogh said. "Who is it?"

"I want to keep the Bureau right out of it, that's all."

"What will happen to Mayat?"

"The police will decide that. Not much, I expect. You don't achieve anything by sending someone like him to jail.

Your English scruples giving you trouble? Remember he's trying to double-cross you."

Keogh nodded. "He's known all along that it was possible to recover the diamonds, given someone with the right knowledge and equipment. But he still hates Yusuf and has no intention of letting him have them. He was playing me along, playing for enough time to notify Wilby—"

"Who will make very sure *he* finds a way of getting them," Horn said. "They're supposed to belong to the Congress, after all. Yusuf's got a persecution complex. The whole world's against Yusuf. He won't get the diamonds, he'll think you and Shack and Hassim and Wilby have ganged up on him, and you think he'll help you through Botswana? Not a damn. He'll shop you to the police as a bogus refugee." Horn lit another cigarette and tossed the packet to Keogh. "So you think Hassim cares? He's an old believer; the cause comes first. A hundred thousand pounds, enough to finance a small revolution. Against that you and Shack aren't even in the running. You've got a pair of skellum Indians there, man. Don't depend on them. I'll send you home on a scheduled flight from Jan Smuts airport."

"And Shack?"

"We'll let him disappear wherever he wants. But you don't tell him a thing in the meantime."

"How did you find me anyway?" Keogh said.

"I knew where that Valiant you were driving was registered. And then we found a bunch of keys in your pocket after old Van had sent you to sleep by the side of the road. Paper tag attached, same address on it. We took an impression of all the keys. By the way, I still have some effects of yours: money, travellers' cheques. Remind me."

He had not mentioned the bug beneath the Valiant.

Good; he thought it was still undiscovered. He downed his drink, collected his cigarettes from the table, and stood up. Keogh watched in surprise.

"We've said all we can for now. I'm sure you'll see the sense of us working together. Whatever happens, those diamonds won't leave the country. May as well make it easier for everybody. You'll be ready to go down that hole on Sunday night, you say. Hear from me before then."

A smile from Horn, a snigger from Van Heerden, and they were gone, letting themselves out into the grey light of a cold and brittle dawn. For a long time Keogh could not summon up the will to move. He sat feeling his head ache, his muscles stiffen, dried blood blocking his nose, staring at the mess of bottles and cans and fag ends they had left. Finally he recollected himself, went to the window, and parted the curtains.

The Toyota had gone; the Volkswagen was back on duty. Keogh went to bed.

16

In spite of his exhausting night he slept badly, woken several times by sunshine and the sounds of Saturday morning traffic at the shopping centre. Finally, around midday, he heard the front door being opened and remembered that September would want to clean the flat. He gave up the idea of sleep, flung back the covers, and lay staring at the ceiling.

The bedroom door opened. A man stood there, looking at him. It was not September, it was Paul Blane.

Even without having seen the photograph in the trophy room, Keogh would have recognized him from Rina's description: the broad, deeply tanned face, cropped fair hair, lazy blue eyes. He wore a khaki drill shirt and trousers, mosquito boots, and an olive serge battle blouse open at the front and patched with dried blood. And he held a Winchester hunting rifle. Keogh realized with a sinking heart that the muzzle was pointing at him and that Blane's finger was on the trigger.

They stared at each other for several seconds. Keogh

sat up in bed. "It's all right," he said. "I'm a friend of your wife's."

Whatever he'd said would have sounded ridiculous, but he sensed that that remark had been positively the wrong one. Blane had seen something on the floor at the foot of the bed, and keeping the rifle steady he bent down, scooped the thing up, and tossed it onto the bedspread. It was Rina's gold earring, the one she had missed yesterday. There was no surprise, or curiosity, or even embarrassment about Blane; there was nothing in his eyes but a slow burn of jealous fury.

"Get up," he said. "Get out of that bed, you punk."

Keogh slowly swung his legs over the side of the bed and stood up.

"Against the wall," Blane said, and he pressed his back to the wallpaper and stood feeling naked and awfully vulnerable. It seemed very important to say something.

"There's an explanation, if ever you'd listen to it."

"It explains itself," Blane snapped. "I gave her those earrings."

"Didn't you get a message to phone her from Beira?"

"I ignored it. I was flying straight back anyway. Now I understand, of course; it was meant to give you time to clear out."

"It's nothing like that," Keogh said.

"Why not just admit it, you cheap punk? She's too soft, easy to take advantage of. She's shacked you up, in *my* flat. Got an eye for good living, have you? That mess in the sitting room—"

"Rina is at the Langham Hotel. Phone them and check. She let me use your flat because I had nowhere else to stay. That's the truth, Blane. I'm here on my own."

"Then there won't be any witnesses, will there?" Blane

smiled slowly and took a step forward, raising the rifle a fraction.

The wide muzzle was about four feet from Keogh's face; he stood on tiptoe, pressing his back hard against the wall, feeling a sick quiver in his stomach. Blane was jealous enough and crazy enough to kill him without caring for the consequences. But he heard himself say, "You'd better think what you're doing."

"Why? No one will contradict my story. An intruder in my flat tried to attack me. It was his bad luck I happened to be carrying a rifle. I'd like you to know about this rifle, punk. It's the biggest one I own. It takes a four-fifty-eight magnum cartridge with a five-hundred-grain bullet. That's big, in case you didn't know. I hit a bull elephant between the eyes on Tuesday, up in the Zambezi valley; it knocked him over in a backward somersault. Be interesting to see what one of these soft-nosed slugs will do to you."

Keogh felt sweat pouring down his face. Every muscle, every nerve was knotted up. "Rina will know what happened," he said.

"Do you think she'll care? It's me she loves, you know."

Blane's hooded eyes narrowed suddenly; his fingers whitened round the trigger. Keogh, his flesh cringing from the coming violation, saw nothing but a grey blank wall, heard a swelling roar in his head, and, through it, Blane's demented laugh and the hollow click of the hammer on an empty chamber.

His legs began to give. He was trembling, sliding against a patch of his own sweat down the wall. He could see again: Blane looking contemptuously down at him, turning aside, tossing the rifle on the bed.

"Jesus, what a sight! You can thank your guardian angel

that I didn't have any ammo, sport. I swear I would have used it. Only an idiot would travel with a loaded gun. Not that this wasn't satisfying in its own way. Now get out, lover boy, before the joke wears off."

Blane sounded confident that he would be obeyed. Perhaps he mistook healthy fear for cowardice; at any rate he hadn't the imagination to realize that there was nothing the least bit funny about looking down the barrel of a gun. It had happened just once too often for Keogh. He launched himself off the wall and drove his head into Blane's stomach. He was in a cold fury. He winded the blond man and smashed his fist three times into his face before Blane recovered from his surprise and kicked him in the ribs. Keogh bored forward with his head; he had to protect his naked belly and groin, and Blane managed to twist his body aside, letting Keogh's own momentum carry him head first against the door of the wardrobe. Something split open; it might have been the wood or his skull.

He took a kick on the base of the spine, turned, lashed out with both fists, and felt his knuckles graze Blane's teeth. But again one of the mosquito boots found a vulnerable target under his ribs. Pain lanced through him; he bent over, clutching his side for a moment, and Blane seized him by his thick hair, dragged him the full twenty feet across the room, and rammed his head against the opposite wall. He went down to the floor, dragging the bedside table, a pile of books, and the alabaster reading lamp with him. He was dazed, panting. He saw Blane go back across the room and turn for a run. There'd be a mule kick hard enough to break his back unless he did something. He grabbed the thing nearest to him, the heavy lamp base with its cord ripped out, swivelled, and threw it.

It was about the size of a pineapple. It ricocheted off Blane's temple and smashed the dressing-table mirror behind him. He stood swaying for a second and then went down on one knee, glassy-eyed. Keogh staggered up, shoved a bare foot in Blane's face, and pushed him over. He saw Rina standing in the doorway with her hands clasped over her mouth.

"You're too late to introduce us," he said, panting.

Blane lay still on the floor, but his eyes were open and he moaned slightly. The side of his head was already swelling.

"You're both mad!" Rina, pale-faced, was shaking her head mechanically. She seemed confused between embarrassment, shock, and anger. "You're like a pair of animals. Why...?"

"Because you've got a jealous husband with a poor taste in jokes, that's why."

"But you've hurt him, Keogh. What's he doing here anyway? How can you expect him to help you?"

"I don't. It doesn't matter any longer."

Blane moaned more loudly and rolled over, supporting himself on a forearm. Rina squatted by his side with her brow puckered in concern. "Paul? How do you feel?"

Keogh looked at her curiously. Then he remembered he was still naked, seized his slacks from the stool by the dressing table, and put them on. Blane finally sat up, rubbing his head.

"Who is he?" he said to Rina.

"His name is Keogh. Paul, I must talk to you."

"Fights like a wounded buffalo, I'll say that. Won't take any crap. Athletic in bed, I suppose."

"Please, Paul."

"I must say, Rina, I didn't think you had it in you. I would have said you had a Calvinist hang-up about the sanctity of marriage—"

"Your marriage is a legal fiction," Keogh snapped. "Why don't you face up to it?"

"Keogh, please keep out of it," said Rina.

"I need a drink," Blane said. He fingered his front teeth experimentally. "He loosened a tooth. Why don't we all go and have a drink on it?"

"I'll take you through for a drink," Rina said, and looked up at Keogh significantly. "Can you stay out of the way for a bit?"

Blane got to his feet and stood looking dazedly around at the broken wardrobe door, the slivers of glass from the mirror spread about the carpet. "Christ, we smashed the place up a bit, didn't we?"

He spoke almost with admiration, but he avoided Keogh's eye. Keogh, watching him follow Rina from the room, guessed that he had made an enemy.

Forty minutes later, bathed, shaved, and dressed, he went through to the sitting room and found Blane flushed and a little boisterous on his fourth martini. Rina had cleared some of the mess left by Horn and Van Heerden and stood with her husband by the bar. The atmosphere was strenuously cordial. The two halves of the broken clay head lay on the mantelshelf.

"We've had our little talk," Rina said. "We cleared up some misunderstandings."

"And?"

"Paul knows what your situation is. He's willing to fly you to Botswana."

"I don't think we can do that now."

"Piece of piss, sport," Blane assured him. "Have a drink? No, I insist. No hard feelings, no need for embarrassment on any side." He grinned, but still managed not to look at Keogh. "Rina has convinced me that I've been kidding myself. About her and me. I mean, we'll never make it work. This divorce will go through, best for everybody. She's entitled to lead her own life. And I'm a realist at heart. Why should I risk losing Daddy's twenty grand a year for the sake of being spiteful to her—er—friend?" He smiled in Keogh's general direction. "Of course, she's holding a gun to my head, but then you know that feeling, sport."

"Better than you think," Keogh said.

"Well, as it happens I think I know a pretty safe way of *schmokkeling* you across the border."

Keogh accepted a strong martini poured from a silver shaker. He spoke to Rina. "It's no good my crossing the border unless I can present Yusuf Mayat with a hundred thousand quid's worth of uncut diamonds on arrival—payola in return for his sponsorship. Without it, the police will send me right back here. The Congress in Lusaka will want to prevent Yusuf's having those stones, and the secret police here want to prevent them leaving the country." He turned to Blane. "Look out of that window. You'll see a Volkswagen equipped with a radio direction-finder. They're keeping a twenty-four-hour watch on me just to make sure I don't have any fancy ideas like trying to fly out in a hurry. Last night I managed to slip out of the building without being seen; I should think that loophole has been blocked by now."

Blane went to the window. Rina said, "What's this about diamonds?"

"The money that Dr. Mayat told you about, the Congress funds. It was converted to uncut diamonds which could be resold at a huge profit. I won't strain your credibility by telling you the whole story, but they ended up down a sinkhole on the Far West Rand. I'm going down to fetch them. Horn knows all about it." He pointed to the broken clay head. "Yes, he and his gorilla, Van Heerden, did that in the course of persuading me to tell them. I've got to continue working with Hassim, get the stones up so that they can catch him with them. And that isn't all."

He took a sip of his drink and a deep breath. Rina watched him with rapt, slightly shocked attention.

"Horn has known all along about those diamonds, I'm convinced of it. He didn't know what had become of them, perhaps, but he certainly knew they existed. He doesn't want just the diamonds—there's something else, and I'm buggered if I can think what."

"How could he have found out?" Rina asked.

"Only from somebody who was closely involved. I keep reminding myself that Wilby was betrayed by somebody closely involved as well, and it doesn't take a genius to connect the two ideas. Take your pick: Hassim, Yusuf, Yusuf's wife, Lee Ah Young. He's the Chinaman who sold them the stones."

They were silent for a minute. Blane mixed a new batch of drinks, noncommittally. He was typical enough of his class of English-speaking South African, not overtly bigoted but preferring to ignore much of what he saw, suspicious of change, afraid of the unfamiliar. He was unpredictable, of course, but it was still strange that he had agreed so readily to fly two fugitives out of the country. "Where's the coon that's supposed to clean this place?" he muttered, look-

ing at the ash on the carpet. "If you can't take these diamonds with you it's not worth flying out?" he said to Keogh.

"That's about it."

Rina pursed her lips. "Perhaps this sounds silly," she
said, "but what if you could find a way of getting out with
them? I mean, do what Horn wants you to do, recover the
diamonds, and hold onto them for long enough to reach
Botswana by plane."

Keogh stared at her. "You mean double-cross Horn? As
well as Hassim?"

"Hassim has already tried to trick you. Horn will too,
if it suits him. Paul, why don't you show Keogh what you
had in mind? Perhaps it could still work."

Blane left the room and came back with half a dozen
maps. Most were one-inch ordnance survey, but there was
a single 1:1,000,000 map of the whole of Africa south of
the tenth parallel which he spread out on the bar. Here
were the empty wastes of Botswana again, with the strip
of civilization in the east. Blane occasionally flew his twin-
engined Piper to the far north, to Maun on the edge of the
Okovanggo Swamp, where there was good crocodile hunting. A few months back, on his way home, he had flown
off course, run short of fuel, and searched for an emergency
landing site. This was how he had discovered the abandoned Valswater chromium mine and its airstrip.

He could not obtain fuel at the mine. It had ceased
production two years before and nothing was left but a few
derelict buildings and some rusting machinery. But the airstrip, surfaced with pulverized and cemented chromium ore,
was still in good condition. It was south of Thabazimbi,
about fifty miles inside South African territory and isolated
in a sea of thornbush.

But Blane had also discovered the diligence of the authorities. He walked five miles along a rough disused road until he reached a farm where he persuaded the farmer to drive him to the nearest depot for aviation fuel. Returning to the mine in the cab of a tanker, he found an army helicopter parked on the strip next to his plane. Their ground radar had observed him crossing the border, and then he had vanished from the screens; they wanted to know why.

"It struck me then," he said to Keogh, "that it would be a good pick-up point if you wanted to run something illegal out of the country. If you can get round the problem of landing at a designated airfield first—"

"What's that?"

"A compulsory landing point, sport. There are about forty of them dotted round the country, close to the borders. Any private plane flying to Botswana or Lesotho or Swaziland has to land at one of these designated fields first. The pilot has to report his flight plan and identify himself and his passengers before flying on. All this was started precisely to stop political refugees skipping the country. Try flying straight across and they'll have the Mirages up after you. The radar network covers all this foreign territory, and they'd probably intrude; who the hell would ever know, over all that bush and desert?"

"So how does this help me?" Keogh said.

"Like this. Look." He stabbed a finger down on the map. "I hop down on my own to Rustenburg in the western Transvaal. That's a designated field. I file a flight plan that'll take me to Okovanggo as usual, with a fuelling stop at Francistown. Also usual. That course takes me directly over the worked-out mine at Valswater. Right, for argument's sake say they're watching me all the time on the radar. But they don't expect to plot me all the time. It's natural for me to do a bit of skylarking, shoot down to a hundred feet to look at a herd of game, for instance. That gets me under the radar. As long as I stay on course and I'm not off the screen for more than a few minutes at a time, nobody's going to worry. In those few minutes I can land at Valswater, pick up you and your coon, and be off again."

Keogh was intrigued. He pointed to Francistown, at the northern end of the Palapye road that linked Botswana's little communities. "You'd drop us here, then?"

Blane shook his head. "It's a busy field, sport. There'd be gossip that might get back to the Transvaal, and I'd be in the shit. My best alibi is to set off alone and return alone. So if you don't mind a little hike I'll dump you here, at the Palapye field, which is deserted when not in use. You'd walk into Palapye itself, giving me time to get clear, and report to the gendarmes. Tell them you fell out of the sky. Tell them anything except that I brought you."

Rina had been studying the map. "Westonaria, where the diamonds are, is about a hundred and twenty miles from Valswater. Two hours' fast driving, if you use these secondary roads to reach Rustenburg. You could time it to get to the airstrip at exactly the same time as Paul. Then there's the question of getting Yusuf to meet you on the other side. I could ask his wife to tell him to expect you."

"No. It would mean letting two more people in on it, two that we can't necessarily trust. I've already told Hassim we'll drive straight to the border, where Yusuf will meet us. As far as everybody else is concerned, that arrangement will stand. I'd be ready to risk a few hours' delay in contacting Yusuf. Otherwise I can't fault the idea. But all this is assuming I'll be left alone with the diamonds for long enough to reach Valswater, and I don't see that happening. Horn's men are watching me like hawks already."

"I think I'm beginning to enjoy this," Blane said to the room in general.

"What alternative have you got?" Rina asked Keogh.

"Horn hasn't told me his plans. He says if I co-operate I'll be free to leave the country openly."

"Do you believe him?"

Keogh held his glass up to the light, studying the pale yellow dregs of his drink. "No," he said.

17

When he drove in the Range Rover to Hassim Mayat's house at nine that night he was only half expecting to find all the equipment he needed there. But Mayat was propelling himself around his small living room with an unhappy frown, surveying the piles of mild steel scaffolding, cordage, pulleys, clamps, bolts, spikes, and tools that were spread about the carpet. There was nowhere else on the premises to keep it all. What he could not carry himself he had had delivered. Along one wall stood two fifty-pound bags of cement, several more cement bags that had been filled with sand and gravel, and two jerrycans of water, on one of which squatted Shack, back in his old sweater and dustcoat, smoking a cigarette made of brown paper. He gave a broken-toothed grin.

"O.K., Jimmy?"

"We're nearly on our way, Shack."

"It's been a wearing day," Mayat said. "And expensive, all this. I was at a dozen different merchants'. It wasn't easy explaining—"

"Is everything there? Rope?"

"It's half-inch nylon. They assured me the breaking strain is at least four thousand pounds."

"Does it fit the pulley sheaves?"

"Yes. There is only one thing I'm doubtful about."

From among the coils of rope he brought out a thing rather like a swing seat for a young child, a trapeze of tubular steel supporting a plank of wood which was surrounded by safety bars. One end of the rope would be knotted through an eye at the top of the trapeze; the other would pass through a two-way twin-handled ratchet fixed at chest height. It would allow the occupant to move himself up and down the rope while suspended from the pulley system above.

"It's an old one. They say the ratchet is loose, and it may slip a little."

"Couldn't you get a better one?"

"Mr. Keogh, I was lucky to find it. A second-hand saddlery. I tried builders' merchants, ropemakers . . . have you ever shopped for a bo'sun's chair?"

"No," admitted Keogh, who when he needed equipment had never done more than fill in a requisition to the stores. "We'll see if we can fix it. Shall we go?"

They loaded the car, or rather Keogh loaded it; neither Shack, still weak after his fever, nor Mayat was able to help much. It took half an hour. The eight lengths of scaffold tubing, cut to twelve feet so that they would lie on the Range Rover's luggage deck, were still too long, and the rear door had to be half opened and tied down. It was another hour's drive to Westonaria—the three of them squeezed in at the front—and the time was almost eleven when they parked in the shadows next to Lee Ah Young's store and Keogh climbed out.

He hoped they had not been followed. It could make no difference to him, and Horn could certainly gain nothing out of it. But if anything made Mayat suspicious he would certainly take fright and pull out. In the foyer of Mont de Lure, the neighbouring building in Killarney, a young man had loitered as Keogh came up from the basement. The loophole had been plugged.

A box full of new hand tools had been stowed at the back. Keogh collected from it a pair of wire cutters and took the opportunity to bend down and examine the underside of the car. Yes, there it was, clear in the beam of the torch, a radio transmitter attached to the mudguard. Another loophole, another plug. At least he knew about it, and Horn did not know he knew; this was the single card he was holding.

It was a frosty Highveld night; his breath rose in a high white column in the still air. He went to the barbed-wire fence and cut a gap between two posts wide enough to take the vehicle. The Range Rover bumped through and moved over the veld, travelling slowly on side lights as Keogh followed the faint footpath. He stopped twenty yards short of the sinkhole and reversed up to the broken fence surrounding it.

"We'll clear some of this wire," he said, "and get the fence posts out of the way. I'll need elbow room."

Shack helped Mayat out of the car and into his wheelchair. The two of them went cautiously to the edge of the hole and peered down into the blackness while Keogh lit two gas pressure lamps and adjusted their flames. He was indisputably in charge now. He set Mayat to cutting away the wire, sawing off the fence posts at the bottom and dragging it all out of the way. Shack set about clearing khaki weed from the side of the hole where the ground was flattest, the side where Keogh had chosen to erect the rig.

He had decided on a shear-leg tripod, the lop-sided kind with one leg longer than the other two, as the best lifting frame for the job. It would stand on one side of the hole, leaning out—if his calculations were right—with its vertex over the very centre to give a perpendicular descent. It would also provide enough elevation at surface level to lift the bo'sun's chair from the edge of the hole before the descent and return it there afterwards.

His first job was to join the mild steel tubes and trim them to the required lengths. The two front legs of the tripod were to be twenty-two feet, which meant joining two of the twelve-foot lengths with a clamp coupling and cutting two feet off the end. The back leg was much longer, taking three and a half tubes joined by three couplings. He worked fast, suddenly aware of the cold, sawing and tightening the clamps; once he had established where the feet of the tripod would stand, he got Shack started on digging holes for them.

Joining the three members at their vertex, and fitting the block and tackle there, was much more difficult in the half-light of the pressure lamps. He had hoped to use a pivoting three-way ring clamp, suspending the pulley block from a hook bolted through the end of the long member. But he could tell now that this would cause too much bending stress on the back leg; it was the kind of mysterious gap between theory and practice that only experience had taught him to accept. He could only guess at the safety-factor value of the steel tubing, and the weight had to be evenly distributed over the whole frame. He unbolted the hook and decided to hang the block directly from a loop of steel wire rope secured with shackles.

Shack could not work for long without resting; Keogh set him and Mayat to mixing concrete and finished digging the holes himself—a foot deep and a foot square, two of them three feet from the edge of the hole and the third another twenty-three feet back from it. The ground was sandy, but hardened by lack of rain.

The ringing of the pickaxe and shovels echoed back from the sinkhole and drifted across the veld. He was sweating when he had finished. Now the structure lay in a flat Y shape on the ground with a jumble of rope around it, ready to be hoisted into position.

They took a short break, drinking coffee from a vacuum flask. It was after one o'clock. Then Keogh went to the centre of the frame and began to lift. The whole rig weighed about three hundred pounds; he could only take the strain a few seconds at a time while Shack drove wedges in at the foot of the long member to hold it there. The legs gradually took most of the weight. Keogh tied a rope to the structure, took two turns round the towing bar of the Range Rover, and let the rig ease itself out over the opening. Once the rope slipped a turn, and for a moment the whole thing nearly toppled down the hole. But he managed to hold it, feeling it drag his arms almost out of their sockets, until the foot of the long member thumped into the trench that had been dug for it and wedged there. They filled the holes with concrete; once it had set the rig would be ready, a great gaunt praying mantis with its head reared eighteen feet high over the centre of the sinkhole.

But there was still the problem of the ratchet on the bo'sun's chair. Keogh examined it. The rope passed round a wheel ratcheted with two cogs to prevent reversed motion in either direction. One cog was sound and did not yield when he tested it; the other was fairly worn. He would be able to descend quite safely, but there would be a tendency for the rope to slip during the ascent. It was too risky to depend on.

"You're going to have to pull me up," he said to Mayat. "Do you think you can manage it?"

"I imagine, yes."

There was a lot of strength in Mayat's arms and thick torso, and the pulley system would reduce the load to about a quarter its actual weight, say fifty pounds.

"I'll lower myself down there tomorrow night," Keogh said. "That's essential; I must feel my own way slowly. When I'm on the bottom I'll release the hauling rope from the ratchet. You'll have the other end up here. You'll take up the slack and haul away when I give you the signal. We'll communicate by tugging on a separate guideline which will be tied to the chair."

Sorting out the enormous length of rope, reeving it through the pulleys, and securing the bo'sun's chair took half an hour more. It would be the best part of twenty-four hours before the concrete was set firm, but in the meantime, with the rig secured by ropes and stakes, there was no harm in running a test with a light load. Keogh emptied the hand tools from their wooden box and tied the box in place on the chair; it weighed about twenty pounds. He tied the guideline to one of the safety bars, seized the hauling rope, and let the toolbox lurch out over the hole.

The chair swung back and forth. He waited for it to

steady over the centre. Then he began to pay out the line, hand over hand, four feet of rope for every foot of descent. The chair and its load sank into the yawning black mouth and vanished.

Mayat sat tense and silent beside him. The pressure lamps hissed, the pulleys squeaked, and he went on endlessly feeding out rope. Once he felt a shudder as the load scraped the side; this must be where the cavern narrowed down. Then, when he had let out perhaps another hundred feet, the rope went slack in his hands. The chair had come to rest.

Mayat let out a breath. Keogh tautened the rope, raised the load about a foot, and let it drop. There was no sound from down there. He tried it again; the chair would fall no further. "It's on the bottom," he said.

"So we can do it," Mayat said quietly.

"We?" said Keogh. "But you're not really interested, are you?"

"I've spent a long time imagining this, all the same."

I'll bet you have, Keogh thought. Imagining the pleasure of thwarting your brother and of making amends to the Congress, even if it means selling two other people down the river. Keogh was resigned now to the fact that he would betray Mayat. He said, "If the hole widens out as you say, it narrows down again about twenty-five feet from the bottom. There was a slight scrape there. Nothing important. It *is* perpendicular."

He tied an overhand loop in the rope at the point where he held it. Then he measured out a fifty-foot line on the ground with his steel tape and got Shack to lay out the rope, back and forth, along this distance as he hauled it in. In a couple of minutes the chair rose from the hole and he drew it to the edge with the guideline. He went back and counted the number of lengths that had been laid out.

"About nine hundred and ten feet of rope. The hole is a quarter of that, say two hundred and twenty-seven. Your plumbing was pretty accurate."

The bo'sun's chair was dry, apart from some damp sand that clung to the bottom of the seat. Curious, that—he could not understand why more water did not collect at that depth. He would find out tomorrow, no doubt. He packed up the Range Rover and they drove back over the dead dark veld.

Rina had lain for some time watching the curtains in her hotel room take on an edging of grey light. It had grown in strength, filtering slowly through the gloom until she could pick out separately all the neo-Regency furnishings, striped wallpaper, satin-backed chairs, the dressing table which was not a parade ground for her cosmetic bottles. It was a good room, a good hotel, yet tastefully anonymous as such places must be. Rina was in an odd state of suspension, of detachment from life; it was not an uncommon feeling at this time of day, but she had never had it so strongly. This was Sunday morning, she knew; that was why the street outside was so deathly quiet. Yet she felt that if she looked out of the window and found that the city, the universe, had somehow evanesced all around her and disappeared overnight, she would hardly be surprised.

Beside her in the bed, Keogh stirred. The detachment ended; she felt obscurely vexed by the light.

He turned over and peered at his wrist, still forgetting that he had no watch. She kissed his shoulder.

"It's just after six."

"I must go then."

"So soon?"

"There's your husband to think about. I'm his lodger, after all."

But he made no move to get up. This time it had not been just fear that gave a new dimension to their desire. It was an urgent uncertainty that had sent him impetuously to the Langham Hotel at three-thirty in the morning, drawn him into her bed, and made her weep with an ecstasy of passion she had never felt before. But now in the half-light and the not-quite-real silence of dawn there would have to be the clumsy business of talk as well. He wanted a decision from her; the longer she had delayed it the more frightened she had become, the more insistent he was. She liked to be positive, that was the irony; but there was a part of her—an Afrikaans part, carrying the guilt of renegation, the burden of enlightenment?—that could not face reality except obliquely.

"You'll have to choose," he said abruptly. This was his way, blunt, head on. "You'll have to choose between him and me."

She sat up, startled. "That's not the choice, Keogh. He's nothing to me."

"I've seen you with him now, Rina. You're half in love with him still, even if you don't know it. *He* knows it, though. He's confident of getting you back."

"I'm divorcing him this week. He's resigned to it."

"No. He's made a tactical withdrawal, that's all. He wants me off the scene, as you thought he would: out of sight, out of mind. He's prepared to take the risk of flying me out of the country to do it. Then he'll put the pressure on you. . . ."

"Keogh, credit me with having a mind of my own!"

He stood up and groped for his clothes. "I do, my love. And I want you to make it up. I'm leaving the country in twenty-four hours. I want you to promise to follow me, that's all. It's not for my sake; I'm worried about what that mad bastard might do to break your spirit. Once you're committed it will be a lot easier. He saw I had you, and he wanted you back. It's that simple. His jealousy is the destructive kind. The very things he wanted you for, he can't abide in you: independence, intelligence, sexuality— he tried to destroy them, didn't he? And he'll do it again."

She sat, arms crossed over her breasts, watching him begin to dress. "Perhaps you're right," she said. "I'm soft in the wrong places. I'm soft for Paul the way I am for some of the coloured drunkards I deal with in Cape Town. Beat their wives, starve their kids, lie, cheat, steal . . . you can't find a good thing to say about them. I gave love to Paul the way I gave money to a man to take his child to a doctor. I knew it was being spent on cheap wine, yet I gave it again and again, masochistically, as if I were trying to drain all his reserves of guilt into my own, thinking sooner or later it would get to the bursting point when *something* had to happen. . . ." She shrugged and spoke more quietly. "It's not just Paul, it's this country. I've got to get them both out of my system, and you don't do that just by running away. At one point I was . . . almost anxious for you to leave, so that you wouldn't tempt me into running. I wanted time to think everything out on my own. I suppose I still do. Can you believe I love you, listening to this?"

"I think so," Keogh said. "What's wrong with running anyway?"

"You're a wanderer. You English—the world has been

your back garden for centuries. You don't have a place bred into your blood the way I do. And you see, doing the work I do, I know how bad things are in this country. It matters a lot to me. Without people here who can be buffers between the races. . . ."

"To be swept away as soon as they clash?"

"Perhaps," she said, and looked at him steadily. "But I want you as well, Keogh. Obviously I can't have both. I think you're asking too much, forcing a decision out of me. These feelings don't recognize an ultimatum like that—"

"But you must try."

"I will try," she said. "That's all I promise."

18

"It's for you," said Paul Blane, standing in Keogh's bedroom doorway, incongruously holding a white telephone with its lead trailing on the floor. Keogh, three-quarters asleep, had been dimly aware of the phone trilling in some other part of the flat. He struggled awake, blinking against the noonday light. Blane pushed the telephone jack plug into a socket by the bedside and handed Keogh the instrument. He gave him a look—part sarcastic and part wry amusement—and left the room.

Keogh held the receiver and spoke dully into the mouthpiece.

"Yes?"

"Yes, *soutie*."

Horn's voice had a hard nasal quality on the phone. He was businesslike. "Still half asleep? You must have been out late last night."

"I was," Keogh said, knowing that Horn knew perfectly well where he had been.

"And?"

"Everything's all right."

"Meaning? You can get the stuff out?"

"We should do it tonight."

There was something curiously like a sigh of relief from Horn. "Now good. Very good." His tone had softened. "Then we must talk. You'll want your money and that back, that I promised you. Let me see. I'm in Pretoria, you're in Jo'burg. I think we'll meet at the Monument."

"What monument?"

"There's only one in these parts. The Voortrekker Monument. Why don't we say two o'clock?"

"I thought that was *in* Pretoria."

"Two miles for me, thirty-five for you. It's a working day for me, *soutie*. Never mind, it's something you shouldn't miss." A short laugh and he put the phone down. Keogh listened to the dialling tone for another few seconds until he heard a soft click. Blane had been listening on the other extension. Good luck to him; at least there was nothing to hide between *them,* even if they did watch each other like a pair of hungry spiders wondering which would eat the other.

He saw the Voortrekker Monument long before he reached it, a monstrous grey blockhouse commanding the approach to Pretoria. Sunday traffic meandered up the brown hillside towards it, and the car park was three-quarters full. Keogh went up the steps among the grave family groups, through a wall of sculptured ox-wagons that formed a laager around this ultimate shrine of Afrikanerdom. Its architecture was puzzling, suggestive of nothing but massiveness, heavy and brooding like the granite figures of old Boers at the corners who gazed out across the hills.

Inside it was dark and echoed, like a cathedral, with reverential whispers and shuffling. An ox-wagon stood in the

225

lower hall, and a perpetual flame, and a cenotaph in memory of Piet Retief and his followers, massacred by the Zulus. Up some stairs, the Boers took retribution in a series of vivid battle scenes sculpted in marble. The visitors moved silently around the frieze; Keogh found Horn gazing at one tableau of phenomenal carnage.

"Well, *soutie*. You can learn a bit of our history while you're about it, eh? Not that I can talk. I like it ready-made, like this. I'm not really a reader; no time. They say my great-grandfather was stabbed to death by a Venda."

"Oh," said Keogh, wondering whether it was a Venda as well who had imported colour into Horn's family. It may have been lost in antiquity but almost certainly it was there; the soft light had suddenly accentuated the darkness of his skin and the set of his nose and cheekbones. Keogh found himself wondering if Horn recognized it.

The small man gestured at the marble relief. "I know this much. Afrikaans history is all about one thing: us wanting to live our own way, treat the kaffirs our own way, and other people telling us different. Whether it's disguised as Christianity against barbarism or British Imperialism against the old republics, it's all the same thing. No different today. We've heard it all before. We've listened to all the bullshit."

A thin-faced woman standing a few feet away glared at Horn. He lit a cigarette.

"Of course, sometimes it's best to pretend to be agreeing. Make a bow to the conventions, and then go back and carry on what you were doing."

"What about tonight?" Keogh said.

"Have you arranged everything?"

"The idea is that Shack and I will drive to the border straight after recovering the diamonds. I intend to arrange through Yusuf's wife for him to pick us up on the other side."

"Hassim? He's happy with this?"

"So he says."

Horn nodded.

Keogh said, "If I collect him at eleven, we'd be at the sinkhole by midnight—"

"Why so late, *jong?* All you need is darkness."

"We're timing it so that we'll reach the border—supposedly—at dawn. That was Hassim's suggestion. Yusuf will probably tell us the best place to cross."

Keogh stared hard at the panel in front of him, depicting a battle between bearded horsemen and an impi riding on the backs of cattle. A lot depended on Horn accepting this schedule for tonight; it was only at dawn that Paul Blane would be able to make a landing on the unlighted Valswater airstrip.

"So you go down the hole a little after midnight," said Horn. "And then?"

"I'm hoping the diamonds aren't buried too deeply. Anyway, I'll be optimistic and allow two hours to find them and get them out. We drive back to the main road, and then about four miles to a crossroads where we part company. Shack and I are in Blane's Range Rover; we turn right and head for Zeerust and Mafeking. Mayat in his old banger goes left, to Jo'burg."

"So to get the stones we'll have to stop you somewhere between the sinkhole and the crossroads. Preferably on the main road, to make it less obvious. It would be an ordinary patrol car, uniformed police, routine check. . . ."

An attendant came up behind Horn, touched him on the elbow, and said something in Afrikaans, pointing at his cigarette. The little man gave him a look of malevolence that was quite startling in its intensity and then dropped the butt and ground it out on the marble floor. The attendant said nothing and turned away.

"Of course, they'll have to arrest the lot of you."

"Oh?" said Keogh, and felt his heart lurch.

"It's got to look good, *soutie*. You'll be carrying the diamonds yourself. We'll keep you a couple of days for form's sake, then deport you to Zambia. On the quiet. That suit you?"

"I suppose so."

"Then let's do it that way. Why don't we go outside, where there are none of these interfering bastards in uniform?"

They stepped out into daylight; the sunny morning had given way to what was a rarity in the Transvaal winter, a raw, leaden afternoon with a hint of rain in the air. Horn lit a cigarette from his packet of fifty, made a show of remembering something, and produced a foolscap envelope which he handed to Keogh. He tore it open. There was his wristwatch, tucked into a wad of green ten-rand notes which he counted carefully. It was all there—two hundred and twenty rands in cash and a book of American Express cheques worth four hundred and twenty dollars; everything that had been stolen from him—with one exception.

"The passport?" he said.

Horn's strange eyes twinkled. "Later, *soutie*, when you've kept your part of the bargain. You'll get what belongs to you, nothing more or less; you wouldn't like to feel like Judas."

"I don't."

"Good. From a little after midnight there'll be police

cars waiting on that road. Keep rigidly to that route. I know you now, of course; you're not above having thoughts of scooting with the diamonds yourself. Friendly advice, *soutie*, as between old friends: Don't."

"All right." Keogh forced a smile. Horn looked past him, down to the amphitheatre cut from the hillside where the faithful paid homage on national days, up to the threatening sky. When his gaze came back approximately to Keogh's face it had softened, rather as his voice had softened earlier on the phone; it was a look imbued with a curious, incongruous sympathy.

"All right, *soutie*, good-bye," he said brusquely.

Keogh, watching him stride away, did not understand that look. But in any case he could think only of the possibilities of the night ahead. He knew that he could do it, deceive Mayat and Horn at the same time and slip out between them. He *had* to do it, because whatever Horn's ultimate intentions were and in spite of his promises, he did not intend to let Shack or Keogh go.

In the car park Horn opened the door of the black Buick and slid into the passenger seat. Van Heerden gave him one of those slow, crafty smiles of his—engaging at first, they had gradually become irritating—as he turned the ignition key. He had passed the time paging through a thick brown file that Horn had left in the car.

They cruised down the hill toward the main Pretoria road. "Rain coming," Van Heerden said, nodding at the sky.

Horn did not wish to make conversation, and to emphasize the point he picked up the file and flicked through it, staring unseeingly at the pages of typed reports, photocopies of letters, newspaper cuttings, transcripts of speeches.

He knew most of them by heart. There were more formal memorabilia too: copies of a medical report, bank statements, passport application forms, a testimonial from a professor, handwriting specimens, driving licence, even a couple of school reports and a birth certification—the whole rubbish heap of paperwork that accumulated round the life of a single man. And there were photographs, a dozen or more photographs of the face Horn had studied so often that its contours were burned into his mind more clearly than the image of a lover. The name stencilled inside the front cover was XABA, WILBY BUSAKWE.

"Where's that bloody coonboy got to?" Blane demanded when Keogh returned to the flat. Apparently he had fried himself something for lunch; now he stood in the kitchen looking at a growing pile of dirty dishes with a distaste only conceivable in someone who had never washed one in his life. "It's the second day he hasn't been in here."

"September?" said Keogh vaguely. "I haven't seen him since Friday, when he drove the Range Rover out of the basement for me. We can make our plans for tonight now."

"Been on a kaffir-beer binge and vanished, I suppose," Blane muttered.

For no definable reason Keogh felt suddenly uneasy. "Where are his quarters?"

"A *kia* up on the roof. The usual place."

"Let's see if we can find him."

"Hell, it doesn't matter that much. He'll be in tomorrow."

"Come on," Keogh said. Followed reluctantly by Blane, he went down the corridor and found a concrete staircase leading up to a door that opened onto the roof. Beyond a set of washing lines hung with canvas blouses and gaudy shirts stood the cleaners' quarters, a row of six small rooms with an adjoining communal washroom. Inexpertly strumming a guitar beside them sat a Zulu all dressed up—pork-pie hat, grey flannel suit, and Jarman shoes—with literally nowhere to go on a white man's Sunday. Keogh asked him which was September's room, and hesitantly he pointed to the steel door at the far end of the row.

It was unlocked. It swung open with a squeak. A single bluebottle heavy with winter lethargy rose and buzzed about the room, thumping drunkenly into the whitewashed walls. The place smelt of September's harsh tobacco. His sharpest set of clothes, a pair of flared hopsack trousers and an oatmeal jacket with wide lapels, were hung carefully to air in front of the small frosted window. His bed stood at waist height; each of its legs had been propped up on four bricks, by tradition a device to frustrate the *tokoloshe*, a tiny devil who might otherwise clamber up and snatch the soul of a sleeper.

September lay on the bed. His handlebar moustache had gone strangely limp, but his eyes were closed and his face was peaceful and it looked as if he had died very quickly. He had been strangled with a turquoise silk tie— his best, no doubt, laid out ready for another well-dressed and aimless Sunday.

"Kee-rist," Blane said distantly, then glanced at Keogh. "You suspected?"

"It occurred to me that they might have picked him up. I never thought they'd go this far."

"Who?"

"Horn's lot. Van Heerden, probably. They'd have marked him when they realized he'd helped me get away from the building the other night. Must have thought I'd got him on my side, that he knew more than he did. The poor bastard never got a chance to explain that he wasn't even interested."

He felt sick with the gratuitousness of it. Blane stood looking dispassionately down at the body. "They made a pretty neat job of it anyway."

The fat blue fly droned past them and rebounded from the window pane. Keogh said, "If I needed anything to convince me not to trust Horn, this is it. Whatever he's planning to do, he doesn't intend leaving any loose ends lying about. I'll be depending on you, Blane."

"You do that, sport."

"Rina will depend on you keeping your promise too."

Blane gave him an odd smile. Suddenly he shot out his right arm like a chameleon's tongue and snatched the bluebottle in mid-flight. He crushed it in his fist and then opened the hand to stare intently—with the fascination but none of the innocence of a child—at the mess of blood and membrane.

"Sure," he said.

19

The Highveld is reputed to have a dry winter, but when it does rain it is a cold, listless drizzle that may go on intermittently for days. As often as not there is a freezing wind off the Drakensberg mountains as well, and at night in this weather few places seem more forbidding than the canyon-like streets and deserted pavements of Johannesburg.

The rain had begun just after dark; the wind had gathered strength through the evening. At ten-thirty, when Keogh set off for Mayat's house, the drizzle danced in the Range Rover's headlights and the wind lashed it in small spiteful handfuls at the windscreen. It wasn't a night for going anywhere, least of all into the bowels of the earth. But he had not had time yet to be nervous. He, Blane, and Rina had spent the evening correlating three parallel and separate sets of plans: the first as understood by Mayat, the second as arranged with Horn, the third—simple enough really, and that was supposed to be the best kind of plan, but one slip could make it go hideously wrong. It relied heavily on the one thing Horn could not have taken into account: that Keogh knew about the radio transmitters, one of which was riding beneath the Range Rover at this moment. Horn clearly depended on those transmitters, and that dependence was his single weakness.

The three of them all knew exactly what to do. Keogh still had misgivings about relying on Blane, but tonight the man had undoubtedly been enthusiastic—almost too enthusiastic. Earlier in the evening Rina had visited Dr. Mayat and waited while a message was passed through a complicated series of phone calls to her husband in Lobatsi. His response had been immediate and eager: if Keogh and Shack were bringing the diamonds he would be delighted to ensure them a safe passage through Botswana. So Hassim had finally seen the light, had he? He would phone the Congress headquarters in Lusaka and get them to send a truck down. It should arrive sometime tomorrow. There was a reasonably safe crossing place on the border ten miles north of Lobatsi, he said, where a farm track petered out by the side of a prominent hill. He would wait there at dawn tomorrow, but if they were forced by the proximity of border patrols to take another route he would understand, of course. They should phone him as soon as possible in Lobatsi. Yusuf would get his diamonds, but his wait at dawn would be in vain. Keogh's real plan could not be exposed to the risk of phone-tapping—or betrayal. It was a plan based entirely on mutual distrust; not even Shack would find out what was happening until it had all begun.

Mayat and Shack were waiting for him, bundling themselves up in as much waterproof gear as they'd been able to find, a plastic raincoat and an old army groundsheet. Mayat also had the extra equipment that Keogh would need, a boiler suit, a pair of gumboots, a resin-bonded fibre helmet with a slip-on lamp, and a lead acid battery that would be secured to his belt. There were spare gas cylinders for the pressure lamps as well, a flask of coffee, and a bottle of brandy; it would be a long wait on the surface. Mayat seemed preoccupied. Keogh and Shack left in the Range Rover, leaving Mayat to follow at his own pace. For a moment, feeling a stab of remorse, Keogh had been tempted to warn him about the trap that Horn would spring. But no; it would jeopardize the evening's planning. Besides, Mayat was needed at the sinkhole.

They drove, mostly in silence, through Westonaria, turned right at the crossroads and right again onto the mine road that the rain had made slightly muddy. Somewhere in the four or five miles behind them, Horn's men would soon station themselves. Keogh had studied the ground carefully on Blane's one-inch maps; the mine road came to a dead end at the lighted shaft head they could see in front of them. The only other way out was across the veld.

Keogh stopped at Lee Ah Young's store, got out, and walked to the sinkhole to reconnoitre. No one had disturbed the rig; it stood silhouetted against the sky, the pulley block creaking slightly as the ropes were tugged by the wind. Spots of rain stung his cheeks. He shivered and went back to the car, drove through the gap in the fence, and reversed close to the rig.

They lit the lamps. Keogh slipped the boiler suit and boots over his thick sweater and corduroy trousers; it would be damp and cold down there. He put on the helmet, tried out the lamp, and checked the level of acid in the battery. He examined the feet of the tripod: the concrete had set firm around them; the framework would support a couple of tons if necessary. The bo'sun's chair stood on the lip of the hole. He fixed the hauling line through the ratchet and sorted its full length of more than thirteen hundred feet into neat coils so that it would pay out without fouling as he descended. He had just finished when Mayat's Morris came grinding over the veld and parked next to the Range Rover.

Keogh helped him into the wheelchair. "I want you to practice for a minute responding to tugs on the guideline," he said, and pointed off into the dark. "Let Shack go out there and pretend to be me down the hole. He'll pull on the guideline and you'll shout out the right responses. One tug will tell you I've reached the bottom safely and released the hauling rope from my ratchet. Then you'll take up the slack, put two turns round the rear towing bar of the Rover, and wait for the next signal. Two tugs will mean you're to start hauling me up. Slowly."

Mayat sat looking up at him, blinking through the rain.

"That's assuming everything goes as planned," Keogh said. "Shack will be sitting in the driving seat with the engine turning over. Yes, all the time, two hours or more if necessary. If you get the emergency signal you'll throw a hitch round the towing bar and bang on the back of the car. Shack, you'll drive like hell. You say you were a good wheel man. Give it all the gun it's got and don't stop till you see me shooting up out of that hole. Can you handle it?"

"You'll show me the gears, Jimmy, that's all."

"The emergency signal will be three tugs then," said Keogh.

"Forgive me," Mayat said. "What kind of emergency are you thinking of?"

"I've told you these sinkholes are bloody dangerous. There's a layer of earth and rock down there blocking up the entrance to a much larger cavity. I don't know how thick that layer is. I don't know how much it will take to disturb it. I only know that if it decides to cave in I'll go down with it like a fag end being flushed down a lavatory. So will the diamonds. More earth may fall in from above. It'll be no use to me at all being pulled up at the rate of thirty feet a minute. You'll have my life in your hands up here. I mean that."

Mayat and Shack moved away to practise their drill. Keogh took the torch, a pick, and a shovel from the back of the Range Rover, dropped the torch, and let it roll under the car. The light was dim here, but the others were not watching him anyway. He crawled under the rear end of the car and used the shovel blade to prize the radio transmitter off the mudguard. In turn it clung to the shovel. It must have been an extremely strong electro-magnet, probably powered by the same miniature batteries that served the transmitter. It would have clung to the car through the roughest of rides. With some difficulty he detached it from the shovel blade, slipped it into a pocket of his boiler suit, and stood up.

He carried the pick and shovel to the lip of the hole and dropped them down. Both had steel handles and were unlikely to be damaged. A faint clatter echoed up from the bottom, and he felt an answering tremor run through him. He was afraid—it would be foolish not to admit it—deeply afraid, not only of going down there but of what awaited him back here on the surface, the unanswered questions, the sinister hints, the motives he did not understand. The murder of September had given them a new dimension. He was safe until he came back with the diamonds, because the diamonds were needed. After that he could only hope to run, fast enough and far enough in the right direction.

The wind mewled across the veld. Rain pattered on his helmet. Turning back to the cars, he glanced round again and knelt on the wet grass beside the Morris, playing the torchlight all over the underside, into the mudguards and the dark crevices above the springs and behind the petrol tank. There was plenty of rust and dried mud, but the transmitter Keogh had expected to see was not there.

Remarkable. Horn was either more careless than Keogh had thought or cleverer than he knew. He took the transmitter from the Range Rover out of his boiler suit and clamped it to the rear axle. Then he moved round to the front of the Morris, felt for the release cock in the bottom of the radiator, and unscrewed it. Warm, rusty water gushed out over his hand. When he stood up Shack was sauntering over to him.

"Show me those gears now, Jimmy?"

"All right."

They climbed into the front of the Range Rover. Keogh started up, depressed the clutch, and showed him how to engage first gear and slip the hand brake.

"Just keep it in first and drive. Don't worry about where you're going; there's nothing to crash into. Watch the mirror: when you see my helmet light come out of the hole, stand on the brake. You can take it up to forty if you like; remember I'll only be moving at a quarter of your speed."

Shack nodded, looking thoughtfully in the mirror at

the sinkhole. Mayat sat by it, immobile, hunched in his wheelchair like an old vulture in a tree.

"Scared?" said Shack.

"Yes."

"You trust him?" A nod at the mirror.

"I don't trust any of them."

"I know. Don't worry, I'll watch everything. You'll be O.K. down there."

"Nothing can happen while I'm in the hole."

He collected the unlit pressure lamp that he was taking with him, went to the rig, and tied it to the side of the bo'sun's chair. He made a final inspection of the pulleys and ropes, turned on his helmet lamp, and squeezed himself awkwardly into the seat. Everything was damp, the ropes clammy to the touch. He made sure once again that the ratchet was working properly and said to Mayat, "I'm going to winch myself up, just a few inches. You hold the guideline and let me out on it. Slowly."

"Mr. Keogh. . . ."

The Indian sat glistening in his groundsheet, staring at him with an odd intensity.

"What is it?"

"Nothing, only. . . ." Mayat frowned and puckered his lips, searching for words. "We've become quite close," he blurted out finally. "The three of us, I mean, in a couple of days; we've had our differences, but in a peculiar way we've become . . . well, almost like friends. I'm sorry I have been evasive at times. There were reasons. You must continue to trust me."

"Oh, yes?" said Keogh neutrally.

"It's just. . . ." Mayat shrugged. Was it true that he was genuinely embarrassed? "I want you to have no preconceptions, not to take things at their face value. You may learn something down that hole. You may, and you may not. I'll be interested."

Keogh looked at him levelly. "I'm tired of hearing you talk in riddles," he said. "What do you think I'll find down here?"

"The diamonds are there, Mr. Keogh."

"And something else as well?"

"Mr. Keogh, I don't know." He spoke with quiet desperation. "Believe me, I don't know. You'll find out, and it will answer some of my own questions as well as yours. Only when I know . . . only then can we be perfectly frank with each other. Do you understand?"

Keogh felt, as he had before, like seizing Mayat and shaking him. But he contented himself with a single obscenity.

"Hold the guideline tight," he said.

He gave the ratchet half a dozen turns, feeling the ropes and the rig take the strain above him as his seat rose from the ground. Mayat had the guideline looped over the brake handle of his wheelchair.

"Let her go," Keogh said.

The hole seemed to widen like a hungry mouth. His helmet lamp flung down its white beam, and enormous shadows chased each other round the sides of the opening as he swung for a few seconds back and forth. The pendulum motion stopped and he was suspended over the hole, looking down to where the darkness swallowed his lamp beam twenty feet below, the blackest black he had ever seen. He licked his lips. Raindrops still tapped at his helmet. His back was to the other men. He gripped the handles of the ratchet and began to wind himself down.

Mayat and Shack were calling good luck to him. The edge of the hole came up on a level with his eyes, and then it was receding above him. All at once everything around him was silent, everything but the clicking of the ratchet and the comforting squeak of the pulleys. The wind, the rain, and the constant undercurrent of tiny veld noises had gone.

A few feet down, twisted dead roots hung from the sides. Further below there was nothing but red soil furrowed by the rainwater that had flowed down it. And then the hole widened out.

The lamplight dimmed, losing its harsh white intensity as it reached out to the far wall of the cavern. It was impossible to say how wide it was: fifty feet, a hundred? There was nothing to compare it with. The light dissolved in shades of grey against the walls, but he could see that they were steeply vaulted. Mayat had been right; to go down the sides with a rope or rope ladder would be just about impossible. It would mean clinging like a fly to the ceiling.

He stopped winding the ratchet and rested, hanging in the middle of the great empty chamber. From below he'd heard the squeaking of bats, and several of them came fluttering past him towards the entrance. He glanced up at the opening; it looked about the size of a coal hole.

What to make of Mayat? No, it was time he gave up asking that question. The old Indian had left it too late to be frank. The Morris engine would be overheated within a couple of minutes of starting; it would leave Mayat stranded somewhere along the mine road. Horn's men, relying on the radio signals, expected the Range Rover and the Morris to be travelling together. They'd wonder at the delay, but they would be anxious not to give their hand away by coming down the mine road. By the time they did, the trap would have lost its teeth: Keogh, Shack, and the diamonds would have vanished.

Still, he had a lingering sense of guilt. He looked at his watch: a quarter to one. At one o'clock exactly Rina would leave Johannesburg in the Corvette. Horn's men were not interested in either her or the Corvette; this had been established that afternoon by getting her to drive it out of the garage under their noses.

The air in the sinkhole was damp and slightly sour. It was also, he suddenly realized, bone-achingly cold. He seized the ratchet handles and went on lowering himself.

The bump he had felt the night before when the empty toolbox came down was at about two hundred feet. This was where the hole narrowed down again. It was like a hosepipe with an enormous bulge in it, but where the bulge ended there was an overhanging ledge of soil and rock, and the hole continued at a slight angle. He used his feet to push himself off the side. There was water down here, quite a lot of it, seeping through the ground and gleaming on the rocks all around him.

Now he was close to the bottom, or at any rate what he preferred to think of as the bottom. To think of it as a layer of rocks of unknown thickness, loosened by the original subsidence and blocking up the entrance to another cavern, would not be good for his spirits. The fact that those rocks were being slowly dissolved by water just as the strata below had been, and that the size of the cavern into which they would eventually collapse probably made the upper one seem like a small air bubble, did not even bear thinking about.

The lamplight picked out the rocks at the bottom, an untidy dark jumble shining with water. They seemed to be piled high against one side of the hole, forming a downward slope against the opposite wall. He stuck out his feet, guiding himself onto a flattish ledge of rock half way dowr the slope, where he settled the bo'sun's chair and squirmea' out. Then he unhitched the gas pressure lamp, pumped it, held a match to the mantle, adjusted the flame, and looked around.

The walls glistened, throwing back the weird flickering light. Everything was wet. Water dripped onto his helmet, and the rocks were worn smooth by it and splashed with bat dung. Nothing lived down here but bats. At the foot of the rock slope there was a flat layer of silt carried down by rainwater and seepage, and here it was oddly reassuring to see some human debris. Besides his pick and shovel there were plastic cups, a few scraps of newspaper, a car tire, and a rusted iron bedstead, its back broken by the fall. Who in God's name carried a bed out into the veld for the pleasure of chucking it down a hole?

He was quite sure that the diamonds were buried in the silt. It seemed everything that was dropped down here came to rest in the same area, probably by bouncing off the overhanging rock shelf onto the slope, then rolling down beneath the ledge. Well, he could only hope the tobacco bag had not burst on impact or had time to rot before the gradually rising silt covered it. Otherwise, nothing short of a week's work with a sieve would get those stones out.

He took the hauling line out of its ratchet, gave it a sharp tug, and felt Mayat's answering pull. He released the rope and watched it disappear up the shaft, discovering uneasily that he could no longer see the opening at the top.

It was hidden by the overhanging ledge. He took the lamp, collected the pick and shovel, and scrambled down to the silt.

The first thing he noticed was that, while everything else was soaking wet, the sand was not much damper than it would be on a beach at low tide. It was not specially porous soil, this, and yet it was absorbing water very rapidly. Which meant that not far below there was loosely packed rock draining it away. And below the rock, nothing. The cavern opened up probably no more than a few feet underneath him.

He shivered and knew that the cold and damp had much less to do with it than the fact that he was plain bloody scared. He wanted nothing more than to get out into the sweet Highveld air. It was impossible to guess how much it would take to shake this blockage loose; a strong tremor from the nearby mine, perhaps. But he intended to work with extreme care, and that meant taking longer about it.

He began carefully shovelling sand, clearing it first from the edge of the rocks and then digging a shallow trench towards the opposite wall. He hoped to avoid using the pick. The patch of silt was about eight feet by twelve; depending on how deep the diamonds were, there could be a lot of sand to shift.

He cut a trench a foot deep and a foot across, all the way to the wall, throwing the sand up onto the rock slope. He found the remains of a miner's boot and the handset of a telephone. At the end of the trench he struck a small rock and edged the shovel around to avoid disturbing it.

It was already a quarter past one. He had hoped to finish by two.

The rock was small and spherical and grey, and the shovel blade scraped from it a tuft of something that looked like black moss. There was a grotesque familiarity about the texture of the stuff. Wtihout quite knowing why he struck at the exposed part of the rock, and it fell quite lightly out of the loose sand, rolled over, and lay gaping at him from the bottom of the trench. It was a human skull.

20

It was not shock so much as physical revulsion that made him close his eyes and turn away from the thing. For a minute he had to suppress the nausea swelling in his throat.

A skull, even quite an old one, is not necessarily a bare, depersonalized lump of bone. In certain conditions, the skin where it is stretched tight, the tough membranes of the ears and nose, and above all the hair may take years to decompose. It was a tuft of straight black hair that Keogh had scraped off with his shovel. Perhaps the perpetual cold and the calcic water seeping through the sand had helped preserve it. Under the thin grey film that covered it like wet cement, the front of the skull still resembled a face—the face of a badly damaged statue, eyeless, shattered, but with eyebrows and some hair still clinging to give it form.

He managed not to be sick, braced himself, and turned to look at it again. He tried to be analytical. The skull had belonged to a man, to judge by the length of the hair. A man with short black hair, turning grey. And if there was a head, presumably there was a body in the sand as well. He used the shovel blade to turn it on its side, loosening the jawbone and seeing a dull gleam from a couple of gold teeth. A massive jagged fracture, partly hidden by the hair, ran up from the left ear. That had been caused by the impact of falling, no doubt, but the fall did not explain the small, neatly circular hole drilled just behind the same ear. The bullet was probably still embedded in the skull.

He stood in the echoing silence of the sinkhole, watching the white lamplight sparkle on the wet walls. Water dripped on his helmet. So this was what Mayat had thought he would find. Had *known?* In a clumsy way the Indian had tried to prepare him for it. Mayat's story had never rung completely true; it had been too pat, too easy. There was something he had left out, and he had stared down this hole as if he were looking into his past.

Keogh began shovelling sand away from the side of the trench. Sure enough, the rest of the skeleton was there. In a couple of minutes he had uncovered the torso and the upper arms and legs, a shape grotesquely curled up in the foetal position, wearing the torn and rotten remains of an old-fashioned double-breasted suit. It was preserved just enough to be recognizable for what it was. A thick ammoniac smell rose from the body.

Identification, that was what he needed. There might just be something that had survived the decomposition and the damp. Trying to shut the smell from his nose and the horror from his mind, he crouched by the headless skeleton and tugged at the jacket. The cloth came away like strips of sodden paper and fell to pieces in his hands. The grey slime clung to his fingers. And then, tearing the jacket away from the left shoulder, he forgot about the dead man.

The diamonds were there, trapped in a little heap in the sand beside the elbow joint. Some shreds of the canvas bag were with them: it had held together long enough to keep them in one place. He felt his heart pounding. He pushed the bones out of the way and scrabbled with his fingers in the sand, gathering the stones in his left palm and then transferring them to a clean handkerchief that he took from his pocket. It was about ten minutes before he had collected most of them; some were still buried, no doubt, but they could hardly matter. They were just as Mayat had said, good-quality gemstones, about four hundred of them, weighing the best part of two pounds. He squatted there for another minute simply looking at them, dull octahedral shapes, trying to relate them to the fortune they were worth. Then he knotted the corners of the handkerchief carefully together and put the bundle into the top pocket of his boiler suit.

The diamonds and the body had come down here at the same time, if not together, then one immediately after the other.

He noticed that in digging for the stones he had exposed the left arm of the skeleton right down to the knuckles. There was a soft golden gleam there, as there had been among the teeth. He knelt down and scraped sand away from between the fingers. Four rings, thick, heavy, inelegant of design, probably 22-carat, encircled the delicate bones. He exposed the other hand: there were three rings there.

He stood up, lit a cigarette, and examined his own hands. They did not shake too badly. He looked at his watch. It was ten to two.

So the Chinaman had been murdered. Whoever had killed Lee Ah Young had wanted the diamonds for himself. The same person had betrayed Wilby. Was this reasoning too facile? Perhaps. But he was at a point now where his own survival might depend on his suppositions. Two people had been with the Chinaman in his store. One of them had shot him and thrown his body down here. The diamonds had somehow followed him. One of those men was waiting for Keogh and the diamonds on the surface. The other waited across the border, for the same things. Horn waited, in the darkness a few miles away, for God knew what.

He left the skeleton where it was, left the pick and shovel in the trenches. The sand brought down by the spring rains would cover them all soon enough. He climbed into the bo'sun's chair and gave the guideline two sharp tugs. Nothing happened.

The rope felt slack. He tugged again and several yards of it came curling down into the bottom of the pit.

"Imbecile!" he muttered, and heard his voice echo up the walls. Mayat was supposed to be holding the guideline, waiting for his signal. Maybe he'd taken shelter from the rain.

Keogh sighed, got out of the chair, and went back to the silt patch, which was as near as possible to being directly below the opening. He cupped his hands and shouted Mayat's name, listened to it echo from the walls all the way up and out into the night air.

There was a sound, close and startling, from the rock slope. The squeak of the pulley. He jerked his head round. The bo'sun's chair was being pulled up. At the same moment from above came the deep roar of the Range Rover's engine in low gear. In a frenzy of bewilderment he flung himself up the slope, leapt at the disappearing chair. It was already out of reach, spinning lightly round as it was hauled up into the darkness. The madmen! What were they doing?

He watched the chair go up, twenty feet, thirty, but it was losing momentum, slowing down, stopping, falling again. The sound of the car engine had stopped but there was a shout. Mayat's voice? He seized the chair as it fell and pinioned it with his weight like an escaping animal. The fools! For some insane reason Shack had started up the car. The rope hadn't been tied to the towbar, just turned around it. What was going on?

There was a scream—human, certainly, and more horrifying than any sound Keogh had ever heard—and then a noise in the shaft above like that of a small rockfall.

He scrambled, slipping on the wet stones, for the only cover there was, against the wall at the top of the slope.

A single heavy object struck the ledge above with a muffled metallic thump, like a bag of tools being dropped. It broke in two and the separate parts fell, slowly, side by side, as everything else had fallen, onto the slope before rolling down to the silt. One of them brought down a flurry of sand from the side of the hole and had a length of rope attached to it; the other hit the rocks with a clatter, striking off sparks.

Mayat's wheelchair. And Mayat.

They lay still on the sand, the wheelchair crushed and bent, Mayat on his back. Everything was very quiet again: the faint hissing of the pressure lamp, the dripping of water. Keogh went down to him with a strange, numb detachment.

There seemed very little blood. It was soaking into the sand in a widening circle from the back of his head, which was smashed to pulp. The face was undamaged, without expression, the eyes slightly open with the brown irises slid into the corners away from Keogh. His dentures lay next to him, broken like two halves of a grin, and the useless, thin, vulnerable legs were sticking out at awkward angles.

The loop of rope had been clutched in his right hand, but the fingers had released it as he rolled and now it dangled from the darkness above. Keogh gave it a tug: it tautened and the pulleys above the bo'sun's chair squeaked. Yes, it was the hauling line. The old man must have held onto it even as he was pushed down the hole. Compulsively, knowing it was absurd, Keogh knelt by him and felt the pulse.

Mayat was limp and warm. But he was every bit as dead as Lee Ah Young, whose skeleton lay a few feet away.

Suddenly he knew he must get out. Whatever waited for him up there, he could not bear another minute here in the company of these two. Imagine the water year by year depositing its silt over them until finally they were buried and forgotten—the Chinaman forgotten for the second time—alone in this cold tomb. Imagine it happening to him.

He ran, carrying the end of the hauling line up the slope to the chair, struggled into it, fitted the rope into the ratchet, and began to wind himself up.

The gas lamp stayed on the floor of the cavern. Slowly the flickering walls and the two inert figures on the sand receded below him. He refused to think, shied away from wondering what had happened up there because he feared it would destroy his nerve. Everything was shut from his mind as he concentrated on the ascent through the darkness.

Scraping past the ledge of rock, out into the main cavern, he saw the pale circle of the opening far above. Turning the ratchet made his forearms ache fiercely. When he stopped for a rest it slipped several notches. Oh, Jesus, he'd forgotten it was faulty. He went on hauling himself up, feeling his arms weaken, and each time he was forced to stop the ratchet slipped more badly; soon it might not hold at all.

He was about half way up when something fell past him, a small heavy thing that bounced once off the side and once off the ropes above him and rattled down over the ledge to the floor of the sinkhole. It trailed a wisp of smoke with a smell that he recognized.

By Christ, he thought, with a calm and stunning clarity. By Christ, they're killing me too.

A second grenade fell down the hole, and still nothing happened, and Keogh hung suspended in the centre of the empty cavern and found himself ludicrously counting off the seconds the way he'd once been taught to: six, seven, eight. . . .

The first blast rippled through his body like a fist flexing a whip, knocking him sideways, jarring his bones. His head seemed near to bursting with some unbearable pressure from inside. Faintly he heard the flat crash of the explosion, felt the second shock wave lash through him as he swung like a pendulum in the void. The sounds of detonation merged into a single roar, but already it was being swallowed by a greater noise, a deep belly rumble from the earth.

The wedge of rocks, a hundred tons or more, forming the floor of the sinkhole shivered and groaned, subsided a couple of feet, creaked, lay still for a few seconds, and then slid abruptly through the opening into a vast cavern thousands of feet deep, carrying with them the silt that had collected over the years and the bodies of Lee Ah Young and Mayat.

Keogh heard the thunderous noise and felt the earth shudder. For a few seconds there was an enormous downrush of cold air, followed by a spray of sand from the sides of the hole.

Then, nothing. He sat slumped in the bo'sun's chair, his mind floating dreamlike in a dark sea of semiconsciousness, his body too limp and shaken to recognize pain.

There never was precisely a moment when he came round, just as there had never been a moment when he was quite unconscious. All that happened was that his thoughts slowly formed some kind of coherent sequence; bit by bit he took cognizance of himself and his surroundings. His sight and hearing did not seem damaged. Neither did his wristwatch. When he looked at it, without much interest, he learned that it was two-thirty.

He had an appalling headache. He had bled from the nose and ears. There was almost no strength in his limbs. He was freezing cold. So much for his body.

He knew they had tried to kill him, to blow him to pieces even before he could get out with the diamonds. That alone was incomprehensible. Only luck had saved him; he knew that too. Those grenades: practice fuses of ten or eleven seconds, probably. They'd had time to roll, like everything else did, under the overhanging ledge, and this had protected him from the shrapnel and the full force of the blast. In that confined space just one grenade would normally be lethal. And no one hearing from above the sound of the sinkhole floor crashing into the bowels of the earth could possibly believe that anything down there remained alive.

He knew, also, that from somewhere he must find the strength to pull himself up through a hundred feet of empty air. He turned the ratchet, stopped, exhausted, after moving six feet, and slipped back four. Up four, down three. At this rate the bloody thing would soon give up altogether and send him sliding down into the pit. He was almost weary and heartsick enough to find the idea attractive. But a minute later he found a way of passing the slack rope around his back, gripping it in both hands and under the armpits when he was not turning the ratchet, and from then on his progress was quicker and less tiring.

A little after three o'clock he rose past the edge of the hole into air that was unbelievably fresh and sweet. It was still raining lightly but the wind seemed to have died down. He was facing away from the rig and the cars again, and with no one to haul on the guideline he had to reach the edge on his own. He took the chair as high as it would go, right up to the vertex of the tripod, and seized one of the legs with one hand. He managed to get his legs around it, released the ratchet, and hung there for a second with nothing more than his own depleted strength to prevent him from falling into what seemed the very centre of the earth. He slithered down the tubing, feeling his hands burn on the steel.

He landed in thin mud at the foot of the pole, still sitting in the chair with a tangle of ropes around him. For several minutes he waited there before he stood up and looked around.

No one, nothing, moved. Mayat's car stood where he had parked it. The Range Rover had been driven about fifty yards directly away from the hole towards Lee's store; that accounted for the bo'sun's chair being jerked up. There was no sign of Shack.

He spotted one of the pressure lamps standing near the edge of the hole and picked it up. It still worked but had gone out through not being pumped. He lit it, examined the mud behind the rig. There were plenty of footprints, not readily distinguishable from each other, with little pools of water in them. And there were the tracks of Mayat's wheelchair, neat parallel lines except for the final gouges where they had dragged him, with the brake on, to the edge and pushed him over.

"Oh, Christ!" he said aloud. That was all. Perhaps he was immune to shock by now. But where was Shack? He carried the lamp to the Range Rover and began to understand exactly what had taken place.

The car had slithered to a stop, broadside on. There were two bullet holes in the windscreen, blood and chips of glass on the driver's seat and the floor. Both the front doors were open. It didn't matter to them how much evidence they left behind; they would be able to prevent anyone acting on it. But it was not their cynicism that appalled him so much as his own abetment of it. They had let him believe he could fool them, had let him lead Mayat and Shack here so that the three of them could be eliminated together and in secret. He had made the mistake of

thinking they would be safe until the diamonds were recovered. Horn had not wanted the diamonds in the first
place.

The ignition key was still in the Range Rover. He
climbed in and started up and then, realizing he could not
see through the bullet-scarred windscreen, he leaned back
and angrily smashed his boot through it.

The headlights spread their yellow glaze across the
veld. Keogh drove in tight, slowly widening circles round
the spot where the car had stood, and within five minutes
he had found Shack.

He had managed to run a couple of hundred yards,
and he lay on his side with his dustcoat and Mayat's cheap
plastic raincoat spread around him in crumpled folds.
Keogh approached with dread and was startled to see the
fierce brown eyes blinking at him.

"Water," Shack said.

His heart surged with hope. He ran to the back of the
Range Rover, brought water in a jerrycan, and slopped it
into the top of the thermos flask. He propped up the black
man's head, pushing back the collar of the raincoat, and
then saw the terrible wound in his neck.

He felt sick again, not with revulsion but with shame
and rage and helplessness. He put the plastic cup to
Shack's lips and watched him drink, grimacing slightly as
he swallowed. He took three cupfuls. He was in a bad way
but there was a terrible tranquillity about him, his face
composed and his eyes unnaturally bright. "Thanks,
Jimmy," he said, and let his head rest on the wet grass
again.

"I'm going for help," Keogh said quietly.

"Better not, Jimmy."

"I'm going for an ambulance."

"It won't help." His voice was calm and disembodied. "I know it won't help, what can you argue? They shot me up the ass, too. Stay with me a bit, that's all. Give me water if I get thirsty."

Keogh bent over him and folded the raincoat back above his waist. A bullet had hit him high on the left buttock—another soft-nosed .357, no doubt, like the one that had made a mess of his neck. This one must have smashed through the pelvis and torn his lower abdomen to shreds. Shack was right: it was amazing that he had lasted this long.

"How do you feel?" Keogh said.

"Cold." He lay silent for a few moments. The effort of speech was starting to tell. "It was the two Boers, from Kimberley."

"Horn. Van Heerden."

"I thought they got you too."

"They tried."

"What's the time?"

"Quarter past three."

"They came just before two. Saw something from the car, turned the lights on." He closed his eyes and a spasm of shivering ran through him.

Keogh said, "You knew they'd come to kill us. You drove at them, and they shot you through the windscreen?"

"The big one. . . ." Shack said hoarsely.

"He shot you and you ran. He shot you again and you kept running till you fell, out here in the dark where they couldn't find you."

"Nearly like the last time."

"You've got guts, Shack."

"No, Jimmy. I'm a three-time loser, that's all. You'll go in a minute, I won't keep you."

"I won't leave you here."

"Hassim wanted to tell you. . . ." He was convulsed by shivering again and he gripped Keogh's outstretched hand, digging into it with bony fingers.

In a minute Keogh said gently, "What did he say?"

"Wilby . . . you'll see him. . . ."

"Wilby? Across the border?"

Shack nodded. "The diamonds are for him. He promises to see you safely to Zambia."

Shack had begun blinking in a puzzled way, as if he could not bring Keogh's face into focus. He shook his head; he seemed too weak to talk. But after another minute he took the hand again and said quietly, "How do you know their names?"

"Horn and Van Heerden? I happened to find out, that's all."

"Who told them we would be here?"

Keogh hesitated a second. "I don't know," he said. He did not want to see the knowledge of treachery in the glazed and dying eyes. Because it *had* been an ignorant, gullible self-interested kind of treachery that had led Keogh to believe Horn. And now in his rage at himself he could not look into Shack's face. He remembered there was brandy in the car, which would comfort the black man's spirits, if not his body.

"Who told them, Jimmy?"

"I'll get you a drink," Keogh said.

He stood up, went to the rear door, poured half a cupful of liquor with shaking hands, and realized, with horrified shame, that he had begun to cry. Great bloody wet tears of anger and self-loathing burned on his cheeks. He brushed them away and went back.

Shack's eyes were closed. Keogh knelt quickly beside him, felt his pulse. Shack was dead.

Keogh drank the brandy himself, slowly, contemplatively. The shock—if there was any capacity for shock left in him—would come later. He drew the cheap raincoat up over Shack's head; it seemed a pitiful little formality, but there was no time for more. Down the hole . . . no, he could not bring himself to do that. Let the fucking murderous bastards find their own way. He climbed into the Range Rover, engaged the low-transfer gearbox, spun the wheel savagely, and drove due north, straight across the veld.

Part V

ROAD

21

The rain had been dying away, and no more than a few drops spat through the broken windscreen as he guided the car over the rolling grassland. This was how he had planned to get himself, Shack, and the diamonds out of the way—by going in the most unlikely direction while Horn was moving in on Mayat's car. Now there was no Shack, no Mayat, but still he must follow the plan through. He was an hour and a half late and could only hope that neither Rina nor Blane, at their separate stations, had given up waiting. He trusted Rina to stay put; he was still not sure of Blane.

Those one-inch maps had proved useful. They had shown that the mine property on which the sinkhole stood extended northwards for six miles, all the way to the main road that ran between Johannesburg and the western Transvaal. It was bare, uncultivated, almost totally unused, but this was how the big companies went about buying land. A time might come when they needed to sink new shafts, and then they would be saved from paying ten times the market value of a neighbouring farm. Most of it was flat open country relieved by an occasional rock ridge or, more alarming, a sudden deeply eroded donga that would have to be followed to a shallow point where it could be crossed. All this took time, and although he pushed the Range Rover mercilessly it was after four o'clock when he reached the fence beside the main road and climbed out to cut a gap in the wire. Once on the clear ribbon of tar, moving at eighty and sucking in breath against a freezing air-stream, he found a little time to think.

He had gone wrong in underrating Horn, not just his cunning but his ruthlessness. What had happened to poor September should have been enough warning; maybe Keogh had believed subconsciously that a white man would be immune to such treatment. There was a pattern to Horn's behaviour, even in the insanity of tonight. He used people and then disposed of them. It saved awkward questions, no doubt. He had used the prisoner called Jake to help Shack escape from Robben Island. Jake had died. He had used Shack to provoke Mayat into revealing the whereabouts of the diamonds. Shack and Mayat were dead. By rights Keogh himself should have been killed. What next? Horn's object had not been to recover the diamonds. He wanted them out of the way, of course; he couldn't risk letting them reach the Congress, and it wouldn't do for anyone who knew about them to remain alive. But they had been only an element in a scheme whose final goal was impossible to guess. Perhaps if Keogh and Mayat and Shack had trusted each other completely they might between them have found an answer. That chance had gone; Horn had played successfully on their distrust.

Mayat had said he would be frank. Or would it have

264

been yet another riddle? Apparently he had intended to tell Keogh that he'd been communicating with Wilby about the diamonds; possibly he'd been going to advise Keogh to keep them until Wilby in the safety of Botswana or Zambia could claim them on behalf of the Congress. As things stood, they must still go to Yusuf, but Keogh did not much care who took them eventually as long as they paid for his escape. The important questions, still unanswered, were: Who murdered Lee Ah Young? Who betrayed Wilby? Somewhere among the events of that night after Sharpeville lay the clue to what Horn was doing now. Maybe Yusuf Mayat could tell him. But maybe Yusuf Mayat talked in circles as well.

His route took him across the low western ridge of the Witwatersrand, through bare veld soaking up the rain, past darkened farmhouses and small holdings huddled among their clusters of blue gums. When he joined another road winding into the Magaliesburg hills the vegetation became thicker and lower. Black thorn trees sprouted among the rocks. This was the tame fringe of tropical Africa, the start of the bush country, woodland and savanna that reached north all the way to the Congo and Sudan. He sped down from the hills into a fertile valley with nurseries and orange orchards flanking the road. There was hardly any traffic; he tensed up at the approach of every car.

Near Rustenburg he looked for a sign pointing to the Wigwam Hotel; it was one of the weekend resorts favoured by people from Johannesburg. He discovered he had already missed the turning and had to double back, cursing, for two miles. At five minutes to five he went slithering off the tar onto the dirt road. Two hundred yards down it, parked in the deep shadow of an acacia tree, was the Corvette. He swung the Range Rover in behind it and Rina was out of the car and waiting for him, her face pale in the moonlight. She wore a dark sweater and jeans.

"Keogh, I've been frantic!"

"Have you got my clothes?"

"You said half past three. I was going to give you till five o'clock, and then clear out. Isn't Shack with you?"

He seized the airline bag that she was holding and began to unbutton the muddy boiler suit, kicking off the gumboots and slipping into his shoes as he did so. "Shack is dead," he said bluntly.

"No!"

"Shack and Mayat are both dead. Horn and Van Heerden turned up while I was on the bottom of the sinkhole. They tried to fix me too."

The whites of her eyes shone hugely. Then she turned away and leaned against the car with her face pressed to the window. "I feel sick," she said.

"It's nothing to what I felt, believe me."

"But why? Keogh, why?"

He took the knotted handkerchief containing the diamonds from the boiler suit and opened a corner so that she could inspect the stones. He transferred them to a pocket of his suede jacket, which he then slipped on over his sweater. "I thought I was being bloody clever, that's why. I thought I was fooling Horn and Mayat together, and it turned out that Horn was pulling something much bigger on both of us. I want to leave this country behind me as fast as possible. I want you to come after me."

She was silent. He said, "Will Paul have given up waiting?"

"I can only hope."

He slid behind the wheel of the Corvette and started

up. Rina climbed in beside him. The engine thundered under the accelerator and he slowed it to a throb, easing the low-slung car over the bumps and then, once they were on the tar, letting it surge forward so that it pinned them back in their seats.

In a few minutes they were in Rustenburg, driving down the deserted main street. There was a telephone box on the left, facing the square, and he stopped the car beside it, went in, and dialled the Johannesburg code, followed by a seven-figure number. After five rings the receiver at the other end was lifted, held for a few seconds, and then replaced in its cradle. Keogh sagged with relief against the side of the cubicle. Blane was still at his post. It was a call box at Uncle Charlie's, an all-night garage and roadhouse on the south-western fringe of the city, where he had gone after spending most of the night in a poker school. There could be no more natural way for Blane to spend an evening —only now he would slip out of the roadhouse and walk across the veld for ten minutes to the small Baragwanath airfield, where his plane stood fuelled and waiting.

A couple of turns took the Corvette off the tarred streets and out of the town for its seventy-mile drive to the Vals-water chromium mine. The road was quite deserted, and the bush all around it seemed so too. Not much of the Highveld rain had reached this area: white dust boiled up in their wake, the dry thorn trees on either side were coated with it, and somehow it filtered into the car and caught in their throats. In the headlights, slender balancing rocks threw their fantastic shadows across the bush. Once an ostrich ran out in front of them, paced the car for twenty yards in great bounding strides, and leapt back into the dark. For most of the way the railway ran parallel to the road; on these flat, empty tracts of land it had usually been more economical to build both at once. They passed one sleeping village. Dawn was breaking behind it in jagged streaks of grey. They had not spoken for some time.

"You still haven't decided then," Keogh said. "About whether you'll come to Zambia."

"No." She tried to study her fingernails in the gloom. "Don't think I haven't thought about it. It's one of those decisions that will have to make itself."

She was touchy. He did not really want to talk about it either. His eyes felt tired and sore as he searched for the turn-off to the chromium mine. In fact it was easily found, marked by a Tswana kraal with a thorn fence to protect it from leopards and scavengers. There was even a metal sign-post, riddled with holes but still faintly legible: Valswater 5M. It had been used for target practice, probably by miners on their way back from a night's drinking.

The road itself was alarming. Unused for two years, alternately cratered by rainwater and baked and cracked by the sun, encroached upon by savanna grass and thornbush, in places it was hardly a road at all. The car lurched and scraped over hidden bumps. "Christ," Keogh muttered. "Why didn't he say it was like this? We'd have come in the Range Rover."

"Perhaps it wasn't this bad when he saw it."

"He was riding in a fuel tanker with plenty of ground clearance. I'm worried about you coming back over this."

"I can take it slowly," Rina said. "Let's worry about getting you there in time."

By now Blane should have completed the formalities at Rustenburg and taken off for Valswater. He could not risk lingering; Keogh would have to be there to meet him. "Hold tight," he said grimly, and accelerated over a series of pot-holes; even twenty miles an hour was a suicidal speed here.

When they had gone a couple of miles Rina said, "What they did to Shack and Mayat: it's too monstrous to believe."

"Have you suddenly learnt something about your coun-trymen?"

"Perhaps."

"So much for your nice liberal attitudes, your idea of being a buffer. As long as there are people like Horn with that kind of power, as long as they drive people like Wilby Xaba into choosing violence, the nice people like you and me and Shack will be crushed between them. You can go on working for peaceful changes, easing the pinpricks, you and the well-meaning Christians and professors and play-wrights. Horn and Wilby know better. They understand that the reality is naked power."

"And you think I don't?"

"You can't stay in this country."

"Keogh, I've tried to explain how I feel. There's still some good to be done here. . . ."

"Not enough to justify staying. But you feel guilty to-wards Blane. You'd like to think that somehow you could make it work again."

"Don't bully me, for God's sake! I—"

A terrible jarring went through the car. The nose dipped, there was a sound of wrenching metal, and the back slithered round before stopping in a froth of white dust.

They looked at each other in horror before opening their doors and going round to the front. Keogh knew he had not been paying enough attention to the road, but in any case he would hardly have seen the boulder, exposed by rain and then hidden by grass, now rammed firmly into the underbelly of the car behind the radiator. The front of the Corvette sagged; the wheels jutted out at unlikely angles.

"The axle's gone," he said.

"Christ," said Rina hollowly.

"It's another three miles, and he's due to land in fifteen minutes. If he's prepared to risk waiting five or ten minutes, we might just make it on foot. If not. . . ."

"You'd better run."

"You don't understand. This settles it. You'll have to fly with me."

"I can't just do that."

"What else will you do? Wait here for a passer-by to stop? Walk back ten miles and find a policeman?"

"Paul won't take us both. His whole idea is—"

"Look, you can fly to Botswana and then come back with him if you bloody well like. All I'm saying is that the only way out of here is on that plane, and the longer we stand talking about it the less chance we have."

They stared at each other angrily for a moment. Then he turned and went at a trot down the track. Still bewildered, Rina began to follow. Around them the air suddenly seemed alive with birdcalls. A solitary impala ram minced into the open ahead of them, watched them approach, and then leapt away. There was a nightmarish, senseless quality to this, hurrying through the bush in an African dawn, going nowhere that was even recognizable, let alone familiar. But Keogh's fear was real enough. If Blane did not wait they were trapped, unable to leave the country, able to go back, yes—but to what?

And if Blane did not arrive at all?

But this anxiety, at least, was ended soon enough. When they had run and walked alternately about a mile and a half, stumbling into potholes, getting burrs and blackjack thorns stuck in their clothes, they heard the faint far-off buzz of engines. Keogh broke into a sprint, leaving Rina to follow as well as she could; it was vital to stop the plane taking off again. In a minute he saw a single flash of light as it banked ahead of him, catching the first ray of the sun. Then it floated down, a tiny white and blue arrowhead, behind a ridge that looked impossibly distant.

He ran, feeling the sweat pour down his face and prickle beneath his woollen sweater. The fine, choking dust was stirred by a light breeze. Glancing back every minute or two he saw Rina falling behind him; still, she was running steadily. He could feel his strength draining away. But the ridge drew laboriously closer. The airstrip was beyond it; on this side were some straggling remnants of the old open-cast workings, black gouges in the hillside, iron storage bins, a line of rusty cocopans on twisted tracks that led nowhere. The road meandered among them and vanished round the end of the ridge; he could save time by going over the top, where the burnt-brick ruins of the mine office buildings stood. At any moment he expected to hear the plane's engines start up.

He was gasping for breath and his leg muscles were quivering when he reached the foot of the ridge. He looked back: Rina was five hundred yards behind. With a final lunge he went up the slope, his feet slipping in sand blackened by the dust of chromium ore, groping for handholds among the dry tufts of grass. He reached the top, scrambled a few yards over the crest, and then stood very still, trying to suppress the sound of his breathing.

The airstrip, paved with black ore, was clearly visible against the rim of daylight that had crept in from the horizon. The Piper was parked at the end of it, about a hundred yards below. Much nearer, twenty yards down the slope, Paul Blane crouched behind the wall of a ruined building.

His back was to Keogh. He was watching the plane and the area where the road twisted round the ridge. In his hands was the big Winchester rifle, now fitted with a telescopic sight. He took quick, nervous draws at a cigarette. Keogh caught whiffs of the smoke; the breeze that blew it to him had also covered the sound of his approach.

He stayed exactly where he was, not daring to move in any direction, staring at the back of the blond head and willing it not to turn. For perhaps two minutes they remained like this. Blane's only movement was to stub out the cigarette and look at his watch. He too was anxious about the time.

Finally Keogh heard, very faintly, the noise of laboured footfalls from behind the ridge. Rina called out; Blane did not hear it. Another few seconds and she must have reached the top. She shouted, "Keogh, where the hell are you?"

Blane whipped around, bringing the rifle up to chest height. Keogh saw the confusion in his eyes as Rina came trotting down the slope and halted. He lowered the weapon hastily.

"Paul, what are you doing?" Rina asked.

"What are *you* doing, sneaking up from behind?"

Keogh walked down to him.

"Where's the car? Where's the coon?" Blane demanded. "Why'd you creep up on me?"

There was a wild flicker in his eyes, but his questions were nervous and defensive. Now was the only time to tackle him, while he was surprised, distracted by Rina's arrival. He held the rifle loosely, guiltily, and hardly resisted when Keogh stepped up, seized it by the muzzle, and wrenched it away. He slipped off the safety catch and drew back the bolt, revealing in the breech a magnum cartridge the size of a cigar. There were three more in the magazine.

"What are you doing with that?" Rina asked deliberately.

"I'm supposed to be going hunting, right?"

"I thought you never travelled with a loaded gun," Keogh said. Blane said nothing. Keogh could sense the hatred hardening round the guilt, and he snapped the rifle bolt forward. "He was going to kill me. He'd probably have killed Shack as well, to keep everything tidy. It's an ideal spot. Nobody ever comes here. The jackals and vultures would soon get rid of the evidence."

"He'd have to be mad—" Rina whispered.

"He is," said Keogh bluntly. "But he's cunning with it. He can't stand losing, that's his trouble. You had him summed up wrongly because all along you've been too willing to believe in him. He didn't see this as just a way of getting me off the scene. He thought he'd do it permanently. Of course he wouldn't do it in front of you. He expected you to drop Shack and me here and drive away, and then while we were looking round, wondering where he was—"

"Maybe you're wrong," Blane muttered. "Maybe I wouldn't have had the guts. There's a lot of difference between sighting on a man and pulling the trigger."

"Exactly." Keogh raised the rifle and swung it to point at Blane's middle. "I knew you'd have pulled the trigger the first time if this thing had been loaded. I knew it and you knew it, even if we did joke about it afterwards. Do you believe I'm willing to kill you?"

Blane looked up at him with defiant, red-rimmed eyes.

"I'm not sure. I'm not sure if I reached out and took my Winnie back whether you'd be able to bring yourself to do a damn thing about it."

"Don't," Keogh advised him, though there was a tightening in his chest at the thought of shooting Blane. "You're still going to fly us out of here."

"Us?" Blane repeated, his eyes darting to Rina.

"Both of us," she said with sudden determination at Keogh's side. "There's nothing left for me here."

"You're still in love with me, whether you like it or not."

"No, Paul. I've just learnt finally that I'm not."

There was a moment's silence. Then Blane gave a harsh laugh, throwing his head back and narrowing his eyes against the sun's early rays. "So I get the job of flying the lovebirds across the border?" he said. "Well, let me tell you something. Your Happy Honeymooners charter holiday has been cancelled, folks. There will be no refund. I've been under the radar for more than twenty minutes, and that's far too long. They'll be out looking for me. Besides, since I didn't intend crossing the border, I didn't bother getting a clearance at Rustenburg. If they pick up an unidentified plane piddling along in that direction they'll let all hell loose at it. No, folks. What I suggest is you give me my Winchester back and I piss off back to Jo'burg and leave you to make your own arrangements. As they say."

He stood chuckling in front of them, his hands on his hips. Keogh, with the rifle butt squeezed between his ribs and his elbow, praying that his unsighted aim was right, squeezed the trigger.

The Winchester leapt in his hands. The sound of the shot racketed back from the ruined buildings. Rina gasped.

274

Blane fell, lay inert in the black-streaked sand, and then got to his knees.

"Fucking hell!" he said. He was pale, quivering to the ends of his fingers. The bullet had passed within three inches of his right ear.

"How do you like the feeling?" Keogh said. He worked the bolt, pumping out the hot shell and sliding a new cartridge up the spout. "I've got nothing to lose by killing you, Blane, believe me. Now you're going to fly us out."

"You don't understand." Blane still knelt on the ground, his mouth working in a nervous spasm. "It'll take half an hour to reach the border. In that time the Mirages can scramble from Pretoria, shoot us out of the sky, and get home for breakfast."

"But will they? How do they know you're not just a bumbling weekend pilot who's strayed off course? They don't know I've escaped. They don't know I've got the diamonds—not yet, anyway. Maybe they'll try to force us back, but all this is assuming they spot us in the first place. It's half an hour to the border on the course we plotted, but if you head due west from here you can knock about a third off that distance. I've studied the maps too, Blane. And I told you, I've got nothing to lose. Stand up."

Blane rose, glaring wildly at Keogh. "You'll kill us," he muttered, then turned and started down the slope. Keogh went behind him, keeping the rifle trained on his back. He felt Rina squeeze his arm and glanced at her; she wore a smile and a slight flush of surprise at the commitment that had finally been forced upon her.

Keogh made Blane scramble through the Piper's single door and take his place at the controls before climbing into the seat behind him. Rina sat on his right. Blane respected firearms; he wouldn't do anything silly with a rifle muzzle six inches from the back of his head. He was still shaking as he started the engines, released the brakes, and taxied to the end of the airstrip. Keogh said, "I know the trick about landing on this side of the border and pretending to have crossed it. Don't try. I'll be watching your instruments."

They strapped themselves in. Blane said nothing. He lined the plane up, opened the throttles, and let it thrust forward. The black airstrip unravelled beneath them; they lifted against the blinding golden spread of the sun. He banked to the south and they caught a glimpse of the Corvette, stranded like a white ship in a sea of dark bush. As soon as he switched on the VHF receiver a clear Afrikaans voice boomed out at them.

"That's your registration number," Rina said.

"Air Traffic Control at Thabazimbi," Blane said. "They want me to acknowledge."

"Don't answer," Keogh ordered.

Blane levelled out and settled down to concentrate on his contour flying. The sun was directly behind. The altimeter read two hundred feet and soon the air-speed indicator had crept round to nearly a hundred and sixty knots. A minute later, absently re-tuning the R/T set, he had picked up one end of a conversation between the pilots of two spotter helicopters.

"Chopper Two Chopper Two. Delta Bravo four-two, one-two. No sighting. Bearing three-two-zero. . . ."

Their positions were reported by grid references, and there was no way of telling how close they were. But clearly enough they were searching for the Piper. Rina gripped Keogh's free hand; the other held the big rifle. They stared out at the empty, hazy sky while close beneath them the plane's shadow raced across the bush.

"How far to the border?" Keogh demanded.

"Say fifteen minutes. If those choppers are Alouettes we've got an edge on them in speed. But they have low-level radar. They could lock fighters onto us, and there's no guarantee that we won't be followed across."

With that thought to digest they sat silent for a few minutes, listening to the indifferent voice on the radio and the flow of meaningless information read off the navigation computer. Keogh gave up searching for the invisible enemy. His neck and shoulder muscles were knotted with tension. Blane dropped the Piper another hundred feet; he could afford to over this country, very flat and dry, with only small clusters of hills appearing abruptly here and there like brown warts. He kept re-tuning the R/T to see if he could pick up new information on the search. ATC were still telling him to acknowledge their calls, but the plane flew so low that it was moving rapidly beyond range of the signals. Reception broke up and suddenly ceased.

An agony of time went by. With a following wind the Piper was making nearly a hundred and eighty knots but still seemed to be moving too slowly. The engines at full throttle sent a lot of noise and vibration through the cabin. Both the others found themselves watching Blane. He was pale and expressionless, perhaps enjoying their anxiety. Finally he pointed to a dry riverbed a mile or two ahead.

"There it is."

"The border?"

"The Marico River. In one minute you'll be in Botswana."

Keogh wished there were more to show for it. The

frontier was a sliver of sand in the flat sweep of thorn trees, guarded by nothing but its own isolation. He was wondering how soon they could consider themselves safe when his ears felt the pressure of a sharp implosive boom, like the sound of a train entering a tunnel. An enormous shadow crossed the cabin for an instant. The Piper made a stomach-lurching dip in the slipstream of a Mirage interceptor that had dived practically on top of them before arcing away in a steep climb.

For a few seconds the horizon oscillated until Blane regained level flight. He was swearing steadily. They watched the fighter go into a turn above and ahead of them, rolling so that its belly glinted silver in the sun and the pentagonal South African emblem was clearly visible. Rockets nestled beneath the stubby delta wings. A voice on the R/T crackled through the Piper's cabin.

"Z-AGD, this is Cheetah Squadron SAAF. I'm calling on ATC's frequency and I hope to hell you're listening. I'm warning you to turn back now. If you read me, acknowledge."

Blane made a grab for the transmitter microphone. Keogh jammed the rifle muzzle into the back of his neck.

"Don't!"

"You crazy bastard, he'll shoot us down!"

"That's just what he wants you to think. He can't even tell whether you've heard him."

"Jesus Christ, the message is pretty clear, isn't it?"

Keogh glanced desperately down at the ground. They had just crossed the border. "I don't believe he'll do it in foreign air space, that's all. Keep to your course."

Convulsively Blane tightened his grip on the control column. Sweat trickled from the hair at the back of his neck and began to run down the rifle barrel. Below, the moving carpet of grey-brown bush rolled away at dizzying speed. Keogh watched the Mirage, glinting against the steely blue sky, do a high loop to come round behind them again. He glanced back: just visible, just above the horizon, two needle-nosed shapes trailed thin lines of dark vapour. Two more Mirages, closing fast.

"If you're listening, Z-AGD, this is your last chance," said the voice on the radio.

"We'll call his bluff," Keogh said grimly.

"You'll get the lot of us killed—" Blane began.

"Shut up!"

The altimeter needle was shuddering at around a hundred feet. For a full minute Keogh and Rina sat facing the rear and watching the jets move into formation behind them. There was no need for orders on the radio; the drill was well rehearsed. Suddenly Keogh understood what was happening. Two Mirages were positioning themselves one on either side of the Piper, nearly touching its wingtips, their jet engines thundering at a heavy, almost leisurely pace. The leader moved in fifty feet above and a short way behind the quarry. The Piper was boxed in, unable to manoeuvre. It would not be shot down as Blane had thought; it would be herded back to the Transvaal like a wayward calf.

"So you were right," Blane said with a sneer. "So where does it get us?"

"It *was* a bluff," Keogh said. "They weren't prepared to open fire."

"And these boys don't like this kind of manoeuvre any more than I do."

The R/T crackled again. "I've got an idea you *are* listening, Z-AGD. For your own safety maintain your present speed. Don't try to gain height until we do or you'll have me riding piggy-back on you."

"Shit!" said Keogh numbly.

"So you've finally run out of big ideas," Blane muttered. "I could have told you we wouldn't make it. They'll turn us round as soon as we can all pick up height. That stuff about our own safety was balls, of course."

"Why?"

"They're worried about themselves. At a hundred and eighty knots we're at full throttle but they're just about down to stalling speed."

"So they're trying another bluff. What if you lost speed suddenly and let them overshoot?"

"Throttle back at this height? You *are* crazy!"

Keogh glanced at the jet on the starboard side. The white-helmeted pilot, no more than fifty feet away, watched the Piper intently, concentrating on holding his place in the formation. Over the penetrating whine of engines the radio came to life again.

"Looks as if you've decided to be a good boy, Z-AGD. Now we're all going to start climbing as slowly as we possibly can."

Keogh prodded Blane with the rifle. "You're in as much trouble as I am now. You'd better try something."

"Start climbing," said the voice on the radio.

Blane began to ease the stick back. Then he made several swift movements. The plane shuddered. The engine noise died to a whisper and the Piper seemed to drop like a stone, turning Keogh's stomach over. The bush beneath them rose, swayed, and tilted. He caught a glimpse of the parallel vapour trails of the three jets above them. One of the stall warning buzzers went, and Rina drew in breath with a quick squeal. Then they were pinned back in their seats, as the engines regained their full thrust, and wrenched to the left by the motion of banking. Blane had dropped out of the formation and was flying thirty feet above the ground at right angles to the course of the Mirages.

There was a hubbub of voices on the radio. Then they went abruptly silent. Keogh waited tensely for the jets to reappear, knowing it would take time for them to find their target again and to formate, knowing that every extra mile they were drawn into Botswana made it more difficult for them. He lowered the rifle, which was still pointing at the back of Blane's head, and said, "Nice flying."

"I throttled right back and gave it some flap—just for a second. We cleared the treetops by about five feet."

"You may have to do it again."

"I doubt it," Blane said, and nodded ahead through the windscreen. "Too big a chance of sightseers. There's the Palapye road."

22

After seeing the road marked on a map it was impossible to mistake it from the air, a wide furrow of grey-brown dust ploughed straight and flat through the bush with the single-track railway line running beside it. Together they travelled four hundred miles from south to north, parting company only at Francistown where the road forked and meandered off to find its way to Zambia. The plane's course had intersected it well to the south. Blane banked again and settled the Piper above the road for the one-hour flight to Palapye. The tension was draining. Keogh felt like a wrung-out sponge.

The villages that straddled the dusty road and the railway line were all alike: scatterings of iron-roofed bungalows and mud huts whose daily life cycle was governed by the arrival of one passenger train going north and another going south. Palapye itself had a few Indian shops, a hotel, and a police station, in front of which the blue and black flag of Botswana flew stiffly in a south-easterly wind.

Keogh told Blane to buzz the police station and announce their arrival before flying to the airfield a couple of miles away. He complied silently; his mood had become sullen again with the growing knowledge that he would be in trouble back in South Africa. Bad trouble, perhaps, and neither he nor his father would be able to buy his way out of it. But he did not seem to question the necessity of returning.

The airfield was a clearing in the bush with a windsock at one end. Blane bumped the plane down, trundled it to the end, and cut the engines. He clambered out and waited for Keogh and Rina to follow. Keogh still held the rifle.

"You're not giving that back to me?"

"In a place like this? Don't be silly."

"Well, you don't expect me to wish you good luck, do you?"

"You'll need that yourself," Keogh said. "I suppose the score between you and me is about even, Blane. Thanks for the trip, anyway."

"Yeah." Blane let his glance linger on Rina, who stood beside the wing, shading her eyes from the sun. "I *was* taking it a bit far, wasn't I? Don't know what comes over me sometimes."

"Good-bye, Paul."

He nodded once, climbed into the cabin, and stabbed at the self-starters. The propeller blades cut through the warm air, flattening the savanna grass beneath the wings. Rina and Keogh stood together watching the plane turn, bounce to the end of the runway, and take off, skimming over the black line of bush. In a few seconds it had vanished.

They looked at each other, both aware for the first time of how unavoidably they had been thrust together. It was not the way either of them would have chosen; it left too much room for resentment. But perhaps after all it had been the only way, and now they must make the best of it. There had been no regret in Rina's farewell to Blane. And to emphasize it she reached up and kissed Keogh hard on the lips, and they stood embracing in the warm sun in the middle of the airstrip until they were disturbed by a police Land Rover nosing its way into the clearing behind them.

An African corporal was driving. A white man in baggy shorts, leather leggings, and a bush jacket stepped down from the passenger's side and came towards them. He was probably about thirty, but his freckled face and clear, pale blue eyes gave him a boyish look that did not quite match the authority of the two pips shining on his shoulders. He stopped in front of Keogh and they stood appraising each other.

"Am I interrupting?" the policeman asked eventually.

"We're refugees," Keogh said, and began to explain that Yusuf Mayat would have to be approached to vouch for them on behalf of the Congress. But the other man cut him short, pointing at the Winchester rifle that Keogh still held by his side. He spoke with a Yorkshire accent.

"What are you doing with that shooter?"

"I happened to be holding it while we flew here."

"Have you got a permit to bring it in?"

"Of course not. It's not even mine."

"Not yours?" The policeman stared at him incredulously. "You're English, aren't you? Don't you know you can't just carry a shooter like that from one country to another without a permit? You weren't thinking of doing any hunting, I hope? I mean, we've got enough trouble with poachers and all their unlicenced weapons, you know. I'm afraid all I can do is impound it until we get it sorted out."

For a few moments Keogh fought to control a fit of

laughter. Finally he said, "You're welcome," and tossed the rifle to the policeman, who caught it by its stock but went on staring at him with suspicion.

"It's no joke," he said sternly. "If you could see how the game herds are being decimated . . . and a cannon like this, with a scope too. Not even yours, you say."

"Are you at all interested in us?" Keogh asked. "Who we are, where we've come from?"

"We can sort that all out at my office," the inspector said carelessly. "As long as Yusuf Mayat will vouch for you; we all know him. You've got no passports? You'll need temporary ID documents and residence permits then. We're used to this sort of thing." He paused, shook his head, and muttered, "Not even yours—hm!" He led them to the Land Rover.

The corporal, who wore a jauntily tilted bush hat, drove with more bravado than skill along the faintly marked track to town, twisting round acacia and baobab trees and dry *wag-'n-bietjie* bushes with thorns like white fangs two inches long. The inspector was affable, when not on the subject of poachers and firearms permits, and welcomed the chance to talk. His name was Moorcroft, he had been a junior sergeant in the West Yorkshire police until three years before, and now he had his own manor the size of an English county. He complained about the drought and the shortage of police manpower and white girls. Keogh listened with only one ear; he was tired and tense and still full of nameless misgivings.

The wind was worrying wisps of sand across the stretch of sun-baked mud that constituted the centre of Palapye. The corporal parked at the front of the police station. Along the veranda of the building, with a look of infinite, listless patience, a group of Africans sat waiting for something or other. One was a woman suckling a child on her shrivelled breast. Inside, Moorcroft's office was cramped and rather musty, the walls painted regulation cream and brown. An avocado pip was suspended hopefully in a glass of water on the window sill. A stack of dossiers and Time Law Reports above the filing cabinets half hid a portrait of Seretse Khama; next to it was a large-scale map of the country with the police districts outlined in red. Moorcroft looked around a little helplessly for somewhere to lock the impounded rifle and settled on a stationery cupboard from which he took cyclostyled forms, rubber stamps, and an ink pad. He was used enough to refugees, he said, though he hadn't had a white one for nearly two years.

Keogh and Rina sat down and answered his questions: name, date and place of birth, nationality. It was particularly important to establish Rina's status. As a British subject Keogh could at least call in the help of the High Commissioner and was not, strictly speaking, a refugee at all.

"If we decided your bona fides weren't acceptable we'd probably do you for illegal entry and let the HC fight the South Africans over who was to have you," Moorcroft said cheerfully. "But all this is informal. The Refugee Tribunal considers each case on its merits; in fact, most refugees don't intend staying long enough to have their cases heard by the tribunal. As long as we're satisfied with your bona fides and you're able and willing to move on as soon as possible, we're usually accommodating. You weren't actually members of the Congress?"

"No."

"Then what's your case for claiming asylum?"

286

"To start with," Keogh said, "I was wanted for hitting a policeman."

Moorcroft looked thoughtful. "What else?"

"I helped an escaped political prisoner. So did Mrs. Blane. At one stage I was told I was furthering the aims of a banned organization and I'd be liable to the Terrorism Act. That's political legislation by anyone's standards, isn't it?"

Moorcroft got up, walked to the window, and inspected his avocado pip. "It's a mite complicated," he said. "A political refugee is defined as a person who would face the real danger of political persecution if he went back. What if they put through a request for your return on a straight criminal charge—assaulting a copper? It would put our Government in a sticky spot."

Keogh said nothing. Moorcroft walked up and down the cluttered space behind his desk.

"I don't like apartheid any more than you do. I'll help you as far as I can, you can count on that. But our first priority here has got to be to avoid trouble. We've got problems. If we provoke the South Africans they can retaliate in almost any way they choose. Hurt our economy. The railway line, for instance." He gestured towards the village station. "It's one of the daft things about this country that our railway line is run by Rhodesians and staffed by South Africans. Now, if the police over there tell us they want you, we don't want to be in the position of refusing them directly. Legal niceties apart. We'd like to be able to smile and shrug our shoulders and say sorry, too late, he's already left. I'd advise you not to waste any time. There are people around here who won't be at all sympathetic to you. I'm talking with my hat off, of course."

"I appreciate it," Keogh said. "We're just as anxious to leave as you are to get us off your patch."

Moorcroft gave a youthful, freckled grin. "My strength here right now is two black policemen. We can't even keep up with the poachers, let alone handle any real trouble. You say Yusuf Mayat was arranging your transport to Zambia. The first thing is to get onto him and have it expedited. At the same time he can give an endorsement to your request for asylum. Afraid he'll have to come up here from Lobatsi and sign some bumf."

"He won't mind that," Keogh said, thinking of the diamonds in his pocket. "He was expecting us to cross the border further south this morning. The truck from Lusaka may already be down here."

Moorcroft looked at him sceptically. "How long have you been in Africa, Mr. Keogh? Rely on everything to be late; that's the first lesson I learned. That way you're never disappointed and about once a year you might be pleasantly surprised. Leave it to me. I'll phone Yusuf in Lobatsi, tell him you're here, find out exactly what the score is. Security in Gaberones will have to be informed as well—just a formality." He moved round the desk. "Technically you're both in detention. In fact if you want to wash and change I'll get the corporal to run you over to my quarters."

"I wish I had something to change into," Rina said. "But after being up all night what I'd really like to do is lie down for a while."

The suggestion seemed to embarrass Moorcroft slightly. "Yes, yes, help yourself. Both have forty winks if you want. Bachelor establishment, of course, but there's food there if you want it." He shuffled together the forms he had filled in. "I'll send for you, all right?"

Keogh nodded. In the nicest possible manner Moorcroft wanted them out of the way while he made his inquiries. They left the police station and the corporal drove them the few hundred yards to Moorcroft's home, a pleasant, newly built bungalow on the edge of the village.

A houseboy let them in. They showered, breakfasted on toast and tea, and found a bed in the guest room on which Rina lay down and fell asleep almost at once. Exhaustion had kept them from talking too much, though now Keogh knew he would not be able to sleep. His eyes burned with tiredness but he moved restlessly about the house. He was eager for news. He was anxious to meet Yusuf Mayat and talk to him, and at the same time nervous about it. He felt none of the relief that escape from South Africa should have brought him; instead, in an obscure way, it was as if the centre of tension had shifted across the border with him.

At midday, two hours after they had reached the house, there was still no word from Moorcroft. Keogh left the bungalow to walk to the police station, taking care to keep the diamonds with him.

It was a bright, warm day rendered unpleasant by the wind and the fine stinging sand it carried with it. Naked children played among the thorn fences around the mud huts. On the stoep of the police station the same crowd of people still glumly sat. Keogh found Moorcroft's room locked and walked through to the main charge office where the corporal was on duty, filling in a charge sheet with laborious concentration. Moorcroft was in the radio room at the back of the station, he said, and could not be disturbed.

"Tell him I'll be at the hotel across the road, will you?"

"All right, seh."

Outside the hotel bar stood a green and maroon Dodge

truck of the South African Railways, and inside the only customers were two railwaymen, big surly Afrikaners in sweat-stained bush shirts, who watched Keogh as he came in and then continued their conversation in undertones. He sat on a stool at the opposite end of the bar and ordered a Castle lager.

The black barman polished glasses and kept his eyes averted. The air was still and cool, the atmosphere intangibly hostile. A lot of people must have seen the plane arrive, and obviously word had got round that it had carried refugees. Keogh had only the haziest notion of what was disturbing him, but it was not really the idea of trouble from the local whites. He was drinking his second lager when the bar door opened. Moorcroft glanced at the railwaymen and Keogh and then beckoned to him. Keogh followed him into the sharp glare of the sunlight, along the stoep, to a quiet corner facing the village square. The policeman turned, leaning against the wrought-iron railings. There was a purposeful look about him that warned Keogh to be on his guard.

"Tell me again," he said, "what your connection is with the Congress."

"There's no direct connection, as I explained."

"You were never a member?"

"Never."

"Mrs. Blane?"

"Not that I know of."

"So you just happened," said Moorcroft in a tone dangerously near to sarcasm, "to get into trouble and fall in with some people connected with the Congress. They very kindly agreed to slip you out of the country, no bother, free of charge. You—a complete stranger. Is that true?"

Keogh held his gaze with difficulty. The diamonds,

wrapped up in the inside pocket of his jacket, made an awkward lump against his chest. "Are you suggesting it's a lie?"

"I'm suggesting, Keogh, that there's a hell of a lot you
haven't told me about yourself—or about the two of you. I
want to know what's so special about you. And I want to
know now."

"I'm not sure I understand."

"No? Let's reduce it to one question, then. Why is
Wilby Xaba coming to meet you?"

Keogh was astonished. He saw the realness of his own
surprise reflected in the policeman's eyes.

Moorcroft said, "You didn't know?"

"Tell me."

"Yusuf claimed not to know either. Let's say for the
moment I accept both your stories. Obviously it's in Wilby's
interests not to spread it about, but Security began quietly
doing their nut when I told them a few minutes ago—"

"When is he arriving? How?"

"Yusuf told me the Congress in Lusaka had two trucks
standing by for the southward journey. He phoned them last
night as soon as he had news that you were coming across
and told them to get moving. They crossed the Zambezi at
Kazungula early this morning. I phoned the DC in Francistown and asked him to look out for them, and he put a radio
call back to me half an hour ago; at a time like this the
phones have decided to go on the blink.

"The convoy reached Francistown at eleven this morning. One truck stopped there; the other carried on south. It
just happened that there was a rather bright copper staked
out to watch them, and he spotted Wilby riding in the cab
of the one that passed through. He was with two other men.
Bodyguards, probably. It checks out at the border; his pass-

port is quite legally in his tribal name, Busakwe Xaba. It's a common enough surname. Wilby was always just a European nickname anyway. The important thing is he came through without anyone noticing. He'll be here in something like an hour."

Keogh's hands were shaking as he lit a cigarette. Yes, he had known that Wilby would be interested in the diamonds, but suddenly all his fears had crystallized around a single, awful possibility. He said, "I don't know how to begin impressing this on you. It could be bloody dangerous."

"Are you kidding?" said Moorcroft bitterly. "Do you know what the South Africans would give to get him out of the way? Can you guess what might happen if some of the locals got to hear about it? Up in Lusaka he's safe. To come down here, fifty miles from the border, he must be. . . ." The policeman shrugged in exasperation.

"Out of his mind?" suggested Keogh.

"But he's not out of his mind." Moorcroft watched him intently. "He's intelligent, shrewd, careful. You don't get where he's got without those qualities. There's got to be a very good reason for him to take a risk like this. He's coming to meet you, Keogh. I think you know what the reason is."

Keogh stared across the baked sand to where the road from the south entered Palapye. A plume of dust rose behind an approaching car. His brain seethed, and the calmness of his own tone surprised him. "First let me say this. I believe there's more than a casual risk of Wilby being attacked. I believe he's been enticed down here. You've got to guard him, Moorcroft. He must have a police escort; he must be watched every minute."

"You're full of advice, lad. It happens that my orders are to wait for him here and turn him quietly round. No fuss, no curiosity. A minute ago you had no idea he was coming here. Now you're telling me there's a plot to assassinate him."

"Listen to me, Moorcroft. It may already be too late. A whole lot of things are suddenly making sense to me. Other people know that Wilby is coming here—I'll swear that Yusuf knows, however much he denies it. Where is Yusuf now?"

"He was leaving Lobatsi immediately after I called, coming to sign your refugee bumf." Moorcroft glanced at the dust cloud at the edge of the village. "That may be his old banger now. You've been talking a lot, Keogh, but you're not telling me anything. Why is Wilby Xaba coming here?"

"Suppose we do a deal?" Keogh said desperately. "You've got enough influence to help me out of the country without Yusuf's support—"

"No deals," Moorcroft snapped. "You've been reading the wrong sort of book."

Keogh sighed, reached into his pocket, and brought out the packet of diamonds. His trump card, and he was giving it away—but there were the remains of his self-respect to consider. "That's why Wilby is coming," he said. "That's why Yusuf is coming as well. It's worth a hundred thousand pounds, that little bundle. Technically it belongs to the Congress. Both of them want it badly, badly enough for one of them to want to kill the other."

Moorcroft took the packet, opened one corner, and studied the contents for several seconds. Nodding slowly, he stuffed the diamonds into a pocket of his bush jacket. "I think," he said coldly, "that you and I will go across to the nick and have a nice long chat. And, by God, you're not leaving until I get the whole story out of you."

"I'm trying to tell you, Moorcroft. . . ." But it was useless to argue. There was a streak of Yorkshire stubbornness in the policeman which Keogh might have admired at any other time. What could he say, anyway? What did he know, even now, that was not based on intuition and surmise?

Together they walked back along the veranda and stopped, waiting for the car from the south that was now approaching the hotel. But it was not Yusuf, it was another railways vehicle, a Land Rover with several men crowded into it. The other two railwaymen had come out of the bar to meet them.

Moorcroft stepped down and began to walk across the square. Keogh followed. The Land Rover swung in beside the hotel, slowing down just long enough for the driver to lean from the window and shout something to the men on the veranda.

Recognition exploded in Keogh's brain. The driver was Van Heerden. Next to him sat Horn.

"Moorcroft!" he screamed. The policeman turned a startled face. The Land Rover accelerated away from them in a lather of dust. The other two men had leapt into the Dodge truck and it, too, swung off among the mud huts and the tethered donkeys, and in convoy the two vehicles disappeared up the long, lonely road to the north.

23

"Moorcroft, those men. . . ."

He could find no more words, and stood choking on the sudden and certain knowledge that had eluded him for so long.

"The railwaymen?" Moorcroft said. "What about them? What's the matter with you?"

"They're not railwaymen." He tried to pick his words carefully but knew that he was stumbling through them. "They're from BOSS. They're the ones who are going to get Wilby."

"You're mad," said Moorcroft softly. "Those are maintenance vehicles. They're up here from Lobatsi twice a week."

"I don't care what sort of bloody vehicles they are! You've no idea how clever they've been, Moorcroft. Everything that's happened to me has been part of a big filthy con trick. It's had just one purpose, to bring Wilby down here to within striking range. Horn and Van Heerden—they've already killed at least three people to get this far.

They're going to kill or kidnap Wilby Xaba, and you've got to stop them!"

His voice rang across the village and he realized he had been shouting. A couple of waiters stood staring at him from the hotel veranda. There was a hard glint in Moorcroft's blue eyes, but at last an edge of doubt had come into his voice. "They wouldn't dare? Who's Horn? Who's Van Heerden?"

"By the time I explain it'll be too late," Keogh said. "You'll have to take my word for it. You said Wilby was an hour's drive away; that means they'll meet up in half an hour or less. On your patch, Moorcroft. Is that a chance you're prepared to take?"

Moorcroft hesitated for one second more before he turned and strode towards the police compound. Keogh hurried after him. "There's no need to follow them," the policeman said. "I can radio ahead to Seruli, get them to send a car out and check the identities of that lot. For your own sake I hope you're right, Keogh."

"If I know Horn his bona fides will be perfect. Besides, they may have a back-up operation in case anything goes wrong."

"Kindly don't teach me my job," Moorcroft growled. "At this moment I've got only two coppers available; there's nothing we can do from here. Seruli will delay those white men for long enough to get word to Xaba. They can escort him back to Francistown or, better still, put him in the lockup till it's safe for him to go. You realize I'm going directly against the orders of Security? Your story had better be a good one."

They entered the police station. Moorcroft told Keogh to wait in his office and vanished down the corridor to the radio room. Keogh paced up and down, lit a cigarette, and by the time he was crushing out the end the policeman was back. He looked pale and alarmed.

"I can't reach them. I can't raise anyone. There are noises on the set like I've never heard before."

"What's gone wrong?"

"I'm a layman, but if I thought anyone would believe me, I'd say our frequencies were being jammed."

"I'm ready to believe you," Keogh said. "It's the kind of detail Horn wouldn't overlook."

"So it's not just a coincidence that the phone lines are down as well. It's starting to look as if you're right, Keogh."

They stared at each other, letting the realization grow. There was no way of stopping Horn except to go after him. And he had a ten-minute start on a journey of half an hour. Still slightly incredulous, Moorcroft said, "They really hope to get away with it, don't they?"

"They will get away with it, unless you do something. Your chances aren't all that good either. Horn will have an escape route laid on. He must know exactly what Wilby's movements are, and there's only one person who could have told him."

"Yusuf?"

"Yusuf has been working with Horn. There can be no doubt about it. He was an essential part of the trap."

The policeman smiled grimly. "I'll take my two after them then. We're hardly the U.S. Cavalry."

"There are six or seven white men in that convoy," Keogh said. "There may be others too, and they'll all be armed. Be honest with yourself: your two black coppers will be scared out of their wits."

"You have a suggestion?" said Moorcroft with swift sarcasm.

"Take me along. Get that Winchester out and let me have it."

"Out of the question. I can't get a civilian involved."

"Horn won't ask to see my warrant card. He also won't come along quietly and ask if he can phone a lawyer. Apart from that rifle the most valuable thing you can have around is another white face. At this rate you'll be too late anyway."

Moorcroft gave an irritated shrug. He unlocked the stationery cupboard and tossed the loaded rifle to Keogh. "Damn you. I reckon this has cost me my job anyway. Now let's go."

From a drawer of his desk he seized a holster and Sam Browne, a service revolver, and a fistful of .38 ammunition. Trotting through to the charge office he snapped out instructions to the two black policemen, who prepared to follow him. One already had a revolver; the other hastily found an old Lee-Enfield .303 and a few five-round cartridge clips. Moorcroft led the way out into the glaring sunlight, stopped on the veranda, and said, "Oh." Keogh looked past him into the square. Yusuf Mayat had arrived.

He was just getting out of a battered green Vauxhall Velox parked next to the police Land Rover, a very lean, round-shouldered Indian in a black polo-necked sweater and stained corduroy trousers. He saw Keogh and the policemen and waited for them to approach, glancing noncommittally at the weapons they carried. He had sharp eyes and a tight nervous mouth, yellowish skin, and unruly hair that was still thick and black but had lost its natural lustre; it was as if the sun and wind of Botswana had dried him out physically the way enforced exile had eroded him within. At a glance he bore no resemblance to his brother and his manner was quite different too, with all the restless tension that Keogh

298

had expected, and—well, these things were easily seen once you knew they were there—all the potential for treachery in an erratic personality eaten by vanity and unfulfilled ambition.

"I'd forgotten about you," Moorcroft said sharply, going down the steps. "You're not a minute too soon."

"Something is wrong, Mr. Moorcroft?"

"Something's very wrong, Yusuf. This, for a start." He pulled out the package of diamonds and dangled it by one knotted corner in front of the Indian. Yusuf's mouth became a little tighter, and he looked at Keogh.

"You didn't. . . ?"

"Yes, I surrendered them when I realized they'd been used to trick Wilby into coming down here, to draw him into an ambush. Were they meant to be your reward?"

Yusuf Mayat's eyes slid away in a confusion of anger and fear. "Are you sure you know what you're saying?" he muttered.

"We're saying," said Moorcroft, "that you were willing to see Wilby killed for the sake of these." He returned the packet to his bush jacket. "I don't even know whether that's a crime, but in the meantime I'm holding you on suspicion of diamond smuggling. I've no time to lock you up; I reckon you'll come north with us."

"Don't do that!" Yusuf said in sudden alarm.

"Come and see Wilby," said Keogh. "Or come and see what's left of him if Horn has got there first."

Yusuf stood clenching and unclenching his bony fists. Defiance and resignation seemed to conflict in him, but he did not try to challenge the assumption of guilt. Keogh stepped forward impatiently, seized him by the neck of the sweater, and shoved him towards the Land Rover.

"They told me they wouldn't kill Wilby," he said suddenly.

"Did they say the same about your brother?" Keogh retorted.

The harsh question jolted Yusuf. "Hassim?"

Obviously he had not known, and Keogh could take no pleasure in telling him. "They killed Hassim last night. They killed Shack. They tried to kill me and prevent the diamonds from reaching you. None of us mattered once we'd played our parts, Yusuf—not you either. When are you going to learn?"

Moorcroft and the two Africans were in the Land Rover and the engine was running. For a moment Yusuf held his head and looked as if he would faint. Then he let Keogh steer him through the rear doors of the vehicle.

"Must I come?" he asked mechanically.

"Yes."

Keogh scrambled in behind him, laying the rifle down on the floor next to the corporal's Lee-Enfield. Before he had closed the double doors the Land Rover was slithering round the corner onto the main road, scattering a flock of scrawny chickens. In a minute they were out of Palapye, dust foaming behind them as the corporal took the car up to a giddy eighty miles an hour over the treacherous surface.

For a while nobody spoke. The two police troopers did not have a clear idea what was happening, which was probably just as well. Keogh and Moorcroft understood the reckoning exactly and did not need to talk about it. Horn and his men had fifteen minutes' start. Other things being equal, they would meet up with the Congress truck carrying Wilby and his two bodyguards fifteen minutes before the police vehicle could get there. The bodyguards would not stand a chance. Keogh did not care to wonder how he and Moorcroft, with the backing of two black policemen, would prevent seven or more armed and determined white men from doing exactly as they pleased.

The road stretched ahead to a flat horizon shimmering in a haze of dust and heat. Sometimes it ran dead straight and parallel to the railway line, sometimes it looped away for a couple of miles before returning, and occasionally it bumped over an unguarded level crossing to continue northwards on the other side. Yusuf Mayat sat on the shuddering steel floor of the Land Rover with his head between his knees. No one took any notice of him until he said, "Mr. Keogh?"

"Yes?"

"What did they do? To Hassim?"

"They pushed him down the sinkhole while I was down there, collecting the diamonds. They left me for dead. They never intended you to have those stones, Yusuf."

The Indian looked haggard. "They told me no one would be harmed, least of all Hassim. They assured me Wilby would be taken alive, that they only wanted him for questioning."

"And you believed them?" Keogh asked. "I suppose you can believe anything if you want to badly enough." Yet on reflection Keogh too had chosen to believe Horn's promises. Yusuf's behaviour might be contemptible, but it was difficult to despise him. Keogh offered him a cigarette.

"The last time it failed, of course. Wilby escaped and your greed got the better of you. You killed the Chinaman, didn't you?"

Yusuf sucked smoke into his lungs and nodded absently. "It was not meant to happen. When I heard yesterday that the diamonds had been in the same place as the body all this time . . . well, it seemed typical of Hassim, his sense of drama. One secret could not be uncovered without the other."

"He knew about the Chinaman?" Keogh asked.

"No. He guessed, that was all. He guessed as soon as he went back to the store the next morning and found neither of us there. We had been talking during the evening about the sinkhole behind Lee's store. It was the logical place to dispose of a body."

"But why did you do it?"

"It was not intended. I wanted only to salvage something from the disaster of the night. . . ."

"You had told the police when and where Wilby and Shack would be crossing the border?"

"To be precise, I had told Captain Horn, as he then was, of the Special Branch, as *it* then was. I went to him deliberately two days after Sharpeville, once Wilby had gone underground and we had begun to make our plans. I offered him the information in exchange for a promise that I would be allowed to keep the diamonds. He agreed." Yusuf looked at Keogh defensively. "I regarded that money as mine more than Wilby's. I had collected it, found ways to invest it, done all the work while he made speeches and basked in the glory. I thought the Congress was finished, that the money would never find any legitimate use. Wilby had never liked me, really. I believed that once we were safely out of the country he would get rid of me and keep the diamonds for himself."

"You judged him by the wrong standards," Keogh said quietly.

"Perhaps. I was nervous while we waited at the Chinaman's store. I drank a lot of whisky. When Shack didn't come back after taking Wilby away, Hassim guessed what had happened and accused me. My only answer was to accuse him in turn. We fought. Then Hassim sneaked away with the diamonds. I was desperate. I had a gun in my pocket, a small automatic, and I brought it out and told that old Chinaman to open up his safe. I wanted the cash, at least. But he was more afraid of losing his property than his life, and he ran out of the store and across the veld. I fired just one shot; it was meant to be over his head, to warn him. It went low.

"I was horrified. My only thought was to get rid of the body. I remembered the sinkhole we had been talking about and found it in a few minutes. I dragged the body to the edge and threw it in."

"And then opened the safe?" Keogh inquired.

"I couldn't find the key. I remembered too late that Lee had put it in his pocket. It had gone down the hole with him." Yusuf stubbed out his cigarette on the floor of the Land Rover. Failure had followed him everywhere, beyond tragedy into comedy, and still he did not seem to recognize the fact. He said, "I left the store and went to Horn. He told me there was nothing more he could do and advised me to leave the country. He arranged a way out for me—"

"Knowing he could use you again whenever he chose," Keogh said. "Knowing he could use Hassim and the diamonds too, whenever the time was ripe. Hassim was left with nothing but a strong suspicion. If you were capable of killing the Chinaman for the sake of money, you were capable of betraying Wilby for the same reason. Only he couldn't prove that suspicion till someone went down the hole to recover the diamonds, and when that happened the last person on earth that he wanted to have them was you. If he'd just told me what he suspected, he might still be alive."

They had been driving twenty minutes and had seen nothing. A few lean cattle, a few children tending them by the side of the road, were the only signs of life. But near another level crossing a snake with its head crushed by a car wheel writhed in the middle of the road.

"They can't be more than a few minutes ahead," Moorcroft said.

The road, the railway, and the telephone wires that sang in the wind constantly met and criss-crossed like three strands in a tenuous plait of civilization. Moorcroft and the two African policemen ignored Yusuf. He looked at Keogh, his eyes large and a little hysterical in the thin, jaundiced face. He had a compulsive need to talk.

"I suppose it seems very bad? I suppose you think I'd do anything for money? I wasn't given that much choice. Twelve years I've lived in a limbo in this country, trapped between South Africa and Zambia, unable to leave even for a day. Horn told me they'd let me back home if I co-operated. That's all I wanted, to be back with my wife and family in a place that I knew. I grew up in a city, lived there nearly forty years. I couldn't survive much longer in this. . . ." He gestured out at the surrounding bush.

Keogh nodded. He would hardly blunt Yusuf's capacity for self-deception by pointing out that his wife did not want him back.

"All Horn's promises have been lies. I only listened because I was desperate, Mr. Keogh. Believe me, I don't want Wilby killed. Will we be able to stop them? If there's anything I can do. . . ."

304

"You're a bit late offering," Moorcroft muttered.

"I could kill Horn myself," Yusuf said, with a thoughtfulness that suggested it might be true.

"Do you know anything about his plans?" Keogh asked.

"He told me almost nothing. I realize now how clever he has been. It did not really matter whether the diamonds were brought across the border or not. As long as the idea of passing them on to Wilby could be planted in Hassim's head, as long as Wilby thought there was some danger that I might intercept them, he was certain to come down here and try to retrieve them. He would have to do it himself, because it was not the kind of thing he could leave to his lieutenants."

The Land Rover crossed a small rise. On the horizon ahead, perhaps seven or eight miles away, lay a wisp of black smoke.

"The train from Francistown," said Moorcroft. "It's due here about now."

Keogh looked at his watch. It was almost one-fifteen; they'd been travelling for twenty-five minutes and a sick apprehension was growing inside him. Yusuf stared broodily ahead.

"I won't endure this easily," he said.

"You'll have a lot more to worry about soon," Moorcroft snapped. "If they murder Wilby you'll be an accessory before the fact."

"Poor Wilby," Yusuf murmured; there were moments when he seemed quite remote from the reality around him. "A clever man, Wilby, and perhaps he's been beaten by his own cleverness. He has never really known which of us two to trust, you see. He knew quite well that someone had betrayed him on the border that night. When I came across and met him the next day in Lobatsi, I told him Hassim had stolen the diamonds; that shifted the suspicion onto him. Later Hassim wrote to Wilby in Zambia trying to explain what he'd done, accusing me of being the traitor. Everything is complicated by the fact that the three of us have not set eyes on each for more than ten years. The one constant factor in this arrangement of Horn's was Shack, the one man Wilby could trust with absolute certainty. He'd spent many years in jail, after all. Yes, I sent him there; let me say it before you do. If Shack was coming across the border, bringing the diamonds with him, then everything must be all right. Shack was a faithful servant of the Congress, first and last. If Hassim's role was still mysterious, if I was thought to want the stones for myself, then it was even more important that Wilby should come south and claim the rightful property of the Congress for himself. That was all either of us had to do, Mr. Keogh, just be ourselves, just be difficult and unreliable."

He gave a painful parody of a smile. Keogh said, "But you also had to pass on to Horn the place and date and time of our arrival, and give the same information to Congress headquarters in Zambia—knowing that Wilby would act on it and come south. From then on the two sides were on collision course. It didn't matter if we arrived, if the diamonds turned up, if you got your reward. . . ."

Across the bush from the north, against the wind, above the engine noise and the humming of tires on sand, came very distinctly a long metallic shriek, then a single flat crash and a sound as if a gigantic tin can were being slowly buckled and torn apart. It continued for half a minute or more and then abruptly stopped.

"Jesus God," said Moorcroft. "It's the train."

Convulsively the corporal trod on the accelerator, punching the Land Rover's speed up to ninety. They swayed and shuddered along the road, which at this point was running back towards the railway after curving away from it. Ahead was one of those sudden clusters of hills that rose out of the bush every few miles, and soon the column of coal smoke they could see rising above it had thickened into a broad oily band that drifted north-west with the wind.

"If that's not the bush burning I hate to think what it is," Moorcroft said grimly. "Yusuf, do you know anything about this?"

The Indian shook his head numbly. He was staring ahead with wide, wild eyes. Keogh did not dare to begin guessing what had happened. It took an appalling time—in fact, three or four minutes—to reach the scene. It was spread before them suddenly as they topped a small rise.

"Jesus God," said Moorcroft again.

The road slipped down to another level crossing. Once over the railway tracks it made a long leftward curve round the side of a rock-strewn hill. The train had passed over the crossing and stopped; the big black locomotive was blowing steam five hundred yards to the south, and a little way back a bush fire had started which a hundred or so African passengers were attempting—without much enthusiasm—to bring under control. Flames blown by the wind along a widening front ripped through the tinder-dry thorn trees. It was easy enough to see where it had begun, around a black and buckled lump of metal that was still burning fiercely in the charred grass. It had been the petrol tank of a truck—the Congress truck, which lay in a thousand torn and scattered fragments along the line from the crossing where the engine had smashed into it.

24

The corporal drove down to the crossing and spun the Land Rover to the right along the strip of cleared ground beside the low railway embankment. They rode alongside the passenger coaches, with black children staring wide-eyed from the windows, until the way was blocked by the rear axle and twisted driveshaft of the truck. Nearby, a tortured piece of steel was still recognizable as a door painted with the Congress motif, crossed spears over a map of Africa. The wreckage was grotesque: a wheel here, a wing mirror there, and scattered among them strips of cloth and shapeless bits of crimson pulp which everyone's eyes avoided. The occupants had been almost totally obliterated.

Keogh felt only a numbed sense of calm. The five men climbed out. Moorcroft went to inspect the shattered remains of the cab and came back grimacing. "Nothing recognizable there. They made a thorough job of it."

They walked on towards the hissing Garratt locomotive, one of the last generation of great African steam engines. The buffer and cowcatcher at the front of its water tender had been slightly bent, but otherwise it seemed quite unmarked by the impact. Across the narrow-gauge tracks, flames leapt and crackled up the hill and a great sheet of blue-grey smoke was swept up and dispersed by the wind.

"Looks bad, seh," said the corporal.

"It looks worse than it is," Moorcroft said.

A guard from the train had marshalled the men passengers—a party of Bamangwato tribesmen on their way south for work—into a fire-fighting line. They seemed to realize that without water the job was hopeless, and they prodded ineffectually with branches and pieces of damp sacking at flames that reared twenty feet in the air.

"You don't want me to organize them in their own lingo, seh?" asked the corporal anxiously.

"Not worth the bother," Moorcroft said. "The road and the railway between them form a firebreak. As long as the wind doesn't change, it'll burn itself out within a couple of miles."

The train driver came round the front of his engine as they approached, a leathery white Rhodesian in a black cap and waistcoat, wiping sweat from his forehead. He was clearly shaken and glad to see Moorcroft.

"Hell of a do, this, man. There's a curve in the line back there; sight distance to the crossing is about a hundred yards. There's this bloody wagon stopped right across the tracks. I used the emergency brake, but it takes nearly half a mile to stop this animal from full speed. I must have hit them at forty. You got here quick. You can see for yourself, there was nothing I could do."

"Are your passengers all right?"

"A few bruises when I slammed on the anchors. I used the whistle too, of course, but these two munts in the truck didn't even hear it, didn't look at me—"

"Two?" said Moorcroft sharply.

"Two of them." The railwayman nodded and accepted a cigarette from Keogh. "Drunk. They must have been drunk. Stalled on the crossing and fell asleep. Didn't even look up."

"Are you quite sure there were only two?"

"Positive. Ask my fireman; we couldn't take our eyes off them."

Moorcroft turned to Keogh and said quietly, "There were three in the cab when it left Francistown. What do you reckon became of the third one?"

"It couldn't be Wilby?"

A jolt of alarm went through him again. Moorcroft spoke to the driver. "I've an idea those two men were dead, not drunk. That they'd been killed and left on the crossing deliberately. Did you see anything that was suspicious in any way at all?"

The Rhodesian whistled and scratched the back of his head. "Not a thing. Man, you'll have to scrape them off the ground if you want to prove anything. What do you think—"

"Thanks. That's all for now."

Keogh had his arm seized and was marched determinedly back towards the Land Rover. "Arranging this accident starts to make sense," Moorcroft said. "It's the best possible way of preventing positive identification. Let's say they stopped the truck a bit further north, as we expected them to. They pulled Wilby out, killed the two bodyguards, and put his clothes, his documents, on one of them. That's all we would have to go on. We would *have* to assume Wilby was dead."

Keogh shook his head. It was impossible to believe that Horn had come up with yet another red herring.

"Why not?" Moorcroft demanded. "I think for once Horn was telling the truth when he told Yusuf he didn't want Wilby dead. Think about it. Officially, no more Wilby; dead under suspicious circumstances, perhaps, but dead all the same. The unifying force of the guerilla movements gone. Unofficially, alive and living in a cell in Pretoria, a source of top-grade intelligence for years to come. Wilby knows his own successors, their strengths and weaknesses; he can predict the strategy they'll follow; he knows the sources of their funds, their arms, their manpower. And he'll tell it all in time; there's no one who wouldn't. Wilby dead sets back the anti-South African cause by a couple of years; Wilby alive sends it right back to square one. And nobody need ever know. It's beautiful, Keogh."

Perhaps, Keogh thought, he was in a state of mild shock, or perhaps he was simply exhausted. He had realized that Moorcroft's thinking was several jumps ahead of his own. "So what can we do about it now?" he asked dully.

The policeman looked around him in despair, at the hills and the endless bush. "God damn it, they're somewhere within fifteen minutes of here, if only we knew which direction. They're getting away and they're taking Wilby with them, I *know* they are."

They had reached the Land Rover. Keogh glanced in through the rear doors and then in puzzlement turned to look back towards the locomotive. It took only a few seconds to establish that Yusuf Mayat had vanished. So had the Winchester rifle.

Moorcroft shouted a question in Tswana to a little girl who gazed at them from a window of the coach above. Diffidently she pointed to the rear of the train and round to the right; that was across the tracks and up the road to the north.

"That's where he's gone," Moorcroft said. "The bastard knew more than he was telling. Come on!"

They leapt into the Land Rover. Moorcroft made a tight three-point turn, and they bounced over the level crossing and up the road that traversed the hill. The fire was rolling rapidly up the slope, meeting no resistance among the slender, interlaced boughs of the thorn trees. The trunks and thicker branches fell and burst with harsh snapping noises, and sparks and ash were swept high into the air by the updraught. The men felt the intense heat for a moment as they passed within twenty yards of the flames, and then in the lee visibility was halved by grey smoke that tumbled through the bush.

In a minute they saw Yusuf, trotting along the road ahead with the rifle held low by his side. But he heard the Land Rover, glanced round, and went scrambling up the rocky hillside to the right. Moorcroft slid to a stop just below him, jumped out, and began to follow. Keogh shouted at him.

"Wait!"

In a gully formed by erosion between two rock outcrops just ahead he had seen a flash of bright green. He left the Land Rover and walked forward with a thumping heart, to an opening where dry thorn twigs had been snapped off and where there were tire marks on the ground. Inside, abandoned, stood the two railways vehicles in which Horn and his men had travelled north.

"Jesus!" said Moorcroft at his shoulder. "They're over the hill somewhere. Let's get after that man."

"Hold on a minute."

The figure of Yusuf, partly hidden by smoke, was two hundred feet above them and climbing steadily among the rocks.

"Don't you understand?" said Moorcroft. "He knows where they are, what their escape plan is. He'll lead us to them."

"Quite. And when we get there what do we do, the two of us?"

"I'll go alone, then. It's my patch—"

"Shut up about your patch," Keogh said. "Unless I'm mistaken, Yusuf is trying to have a go at Horn. He wants his own personal revenge for being double-crossed, for the murder of Hassim. He may not know it, but he's only got three rounds in that rifle. He's committing suicide. So will we be if we try to stop them on our own—no, listen to me. Between us we can't even frighten them. But we've got to frighten them, make them panic, throw out their plans. It's the only hope there is of rescuing Wilby."

"How do you—" Moorcroft began.

"There are a hundred or more black men back there wasting their time against this fire. Go down and bring them up here. You've got the authority. Get the corporal to dragoon them into it. Tell them Wilby is being kidnapped— they must know who he is. They can bring any weapons they've got, spread out, go through the bush like beaters, make a noise . . . they can get Horn on the run, that's the point."

Moorcroft's caution had vanished. His eyes shone at the utter extravagance of the idea. "You crazy man," he said, and turned and ran to the Land Rover.

"I'll chase Yusuf," Keogh yelled. "Give me the other rifle."

Moorcroft started the engine, reached into the back, and tossed him the corporal's Lee-Enfield. "Watch yourself," he said and drove off scattering dust and woodsmoke.

Keogh began climbing. There was not much bush on the rocky hillside, but in the smoke that seeped across it he could hardly make Yusuf out. He was near the summit now, about four hundred feet up. The acrid smoke burned in Keogh's throat and made him immediately short of breath, but he was grateful for the cover it offered. If Yusuf suddenly decided that he was threatened from the rear, he had no wish to offer a clear and magnified target for the rifle that had blown an elephant off its feet. The .303 was a clumsy antique by comparison.

It was impossible to guess by what Yusuf would feel threatened, or even by what he was motivated except a destructive urge leading logically to self-destruction. When he had first betrayed Wilby he had been trying to destroy something he could not have. Ambition without tenacity, cleverness without talent, these were Yusuf's problems. Now he had been at the receiving end of treachery, he probably saw things in a new perspective. He had killed his brother; in his strange way he saw suicidal revenge as an atonement.

By the time Keogh was half way up the hill, Yusuf had vanished over the crest. Panting and occasionally coughing, Keogh reached the top two minutes later. The view on the other side was not encouraging: a gentler slope shouldering down to flat ground where the bush had taken over again, a great plain of thorn forest stretching as far as he could see. Where in all that space were Horn and Wilby? Where was Yusuf, for that matter? If he expected to find Horn he must know of some landmark, but this small cluster of hills in itself was the only conspicuous feature for miles.

The fire, on a broad front to his right, ate its way up the hillside. As Moorcroft had said, it would burn out against the road some way to the north, where the obverse slope steepened into low cliffs; he must remember that and leave the path of the flames in good time. He went down and plunged into the trees.

No terrain could be more confusing. He found a narrow game trail almost at once and followed it, but among the dense thorn branches and the undergrowth of savanna grass he could see no more than a few yards. His only guide to direction was the thickening smoke that filtered through from his right; he tried to move parallel to the fire while edging constantly ahead of it. Soon he had no idea where he was. The grass all around rustled with lizards and rats fleeing the flames.

Then there was another sound, a powerful whine, a giant shadow flashing across the bush, a downthrust of air that buffeted the creeping smoke for a moment. The helicopter swung away in a slow arc to the north, and Keogh's heart missed a beat. Had they seen him? No, beneath the pall of smoke it must be impossible. Then if Horn and his men were anywhere nearby, they too must be invisible.

He stood clutching the rifle, watching the Alouette circle again. When its jet turbine engine was screaming a hundred feet above him he could see that this time there were no identifying marks at all. Of course, it was quick and simple, and he wondered why it hadn't occurred to him: Wilby and his kidnappers would be in Pretoria in a couple of hours after another violation of airspace that nobody would even have noticed. Except that the pilot, hardly able to see the ground, was moving as uncertainly as Keogh himself; the one thing Horn had not counted on was the possibility of starting a bush fire.

A blast of heat and a thick cloud of smoke reached him on the wind. The fire was drawing closer. He turned to move on, and a man coughed somewhere behind him.

He stood dead still, not daring to turn his head. The sound continued, half obscured by the crackling of the fire and the crash of a falling tree. It might have been twenty or thirty yards away. Yusuf? No, it was a lingering, painful cough, one he had heard before.

His mind strained against the enticement to look round. It was just such a movement that would give him away. He was well screened by the trunk of an umbrella thorn, and unless they actually stumbled upon him. . . .

They came tramping through the bush, behind him but to the right. He had to suppress a cough of his own as smoke tickled his throat. In a minute, in the corner of his eye, he was able to see them move out onto the game trail he had been using. They had been forced back by the fire and now walked away from him in single-file procession: Horn in front, wearing a khaki shirt and shorts and a Robin Hood hat, followed by a man with an olive-green radio strapped to his back. He was talking on a headset microphone to the helicopter pilot. Behind him came the two men who had been in the Palapye bar; between them they were leading another figure that wore shapeless khaki fatigues and had a hood made of sacking over its head. Wilby.

Black hands were the only part of his body that were visible. They were tied together behind his back and he had a rope around his waist by which the man in front drew him along. The other guided him from behind. Both wore pistol holsters. Following them were two more guards carrying shotguns and wearing rucksacks. Van Heerden, in dark glasses, brought up the rear. He held a machine pistol and had spare magazines stuffed into the waistband of his shorts. He turned to glance back along the trail before moving off northwards behind the others.

It was a full minute before Keogh stirred. The first thing he did was slip off the safety catch on the Lee-Enfield and pump a round into the breech. It seemed a clumsier weapon than ever, and he certainly would not use it except in an emergency. The helicopter circled again; obviously the men were looking for a safe landing site. Success for them was as close as the nearest patch of clear ground.

Smoke stung his eyes; the heat was becoming intense. The only way out was the way Wilby and his captors had gone, and he followed carefully, pausing every few yards to peer through the branches ahead. Soon he heard Horn coughing again. Their progress, impeded by the bound and hooded Wilby, was slow; if they felt themselves to be in serious danger they would probably kill him.

In ten minutes they moved perhaps a quarter of a mile north and steadily uphill; they must now have come quite close to the road again. Keogh crept behind, never seeing them but following by the sounds of snapping twigs and the voice of the radio operator relaying information to the helicopter. The fire was advancing at about the same speed.

Finally he sensed that they had stopped. Through the lower branches of the trees ahead he saw an unshaded stretch of ground reflecting the weak sunshine that filtered through the smoke. They had found what they wanted.

Where was Moorcroft now? Where were the Africans he was fetching? To avoid being trapped between the men and the fire, Keogh would have to circle round them. He stepped off the game trail into the thick bush, moving as quietly as possible and still hearing thorny twigs snatch and whip at his suede jacket. He reached the cover of an enormous ant-hill on the north-east side of the clearing and, by lying flat on his stomach, could see through the tree trunks roughly what was happening.

The open space was about twenty yards across; the men, visible only from the waist down, stood around its edges. Two small metal boxes supporting long radio antennae had been set on the ground, one at either side of the clearing. The nearest was thirty yards from Keogh. Their function puzzled him until the helicopter approached again. It moved in a tighter, more positive circle this time and then went into hover above the clearing, the downthrust air from its big rotor blades raising a storm of red dust to mix with the woodsmoke.

Keogh's mouth went dry. In a minute or less the aircraft would be on the ground and Horn would be safe. The two transmitters were part of a guidance system similar to the one that had been used to follow his car. The pilot, relying on a signal from either side, could make a blind landing through the smoke. There was only one way to stop him.

He would have time for one shot only. Without daring to think beyond it he raised the Lee-Enfield, took aim through the peepsight, and squeezed the trigger. It would not budge. Christ, he'd put the safety back on! With a shaking forefinger he released the catch and fired.

The brass heel-plate pounded his shoulder; the bang was deafening. The radio transmitter nearest him somersaulted and snapped its aerial in two. Keogh dropped the rifle, scrambled to his feet, and ran.

Thorns tore at his face and his clothing. In a couple of seconds bullets from Van Heerden's machine pistol spat among the trees around him. He ran in crazy, giant bounds along the game trail, hearing curses and the sounds of blundering pursuit behind him, hearing as well the whine of the Alouette as it arced away like a beetle with a singed wing. The fire had advanced; thick smoke curled and eddied around him, and he tripped over a tree root and fell, piercing his hands with thorns. He came up coughing, his lungs raw and painful, and ran on more weakly. Suddenly the noise of the men crashing through the bush had stopped. Overlaying the raging crackle of the fire came instead a deep rhythmic ululation spaced out by a pounding beat, the sound of a tribal war chant. It was from his right, the east. The fire encroached from the south. He ran on, stumbling and breathless, his mind filled with chaos, and reeled suddenly out into daylight and clean air, onto a steep rocky slope down which he could not stop himself sliding and bumping and rolling until he reached the bottom and sat, faint and bewildered, at the edge of the Palapye road.

Moorcroft's Land Rover approached slowly from the left. The policeman stepped out, helped Keogh to his feet, and propped him up against the side of the vehicle. He could not speak, but stood bathed in sweat and gasping for breath. They were alone on the road. Above them the fire raced towards the clifftops two hundred yards ahead, and from the north, louder now, came the chanting of the Bamangwatos advancing through the bush, invisible and menacing. They carried knobkerries, and they must have been beating time on the trunks of trees as they passed.

"They didn't take much persuading," Moorcroft was saying. "You were right—Wilby's name worked like magic. I just hope they don't get too carried away."

Trapped in a narrowing V between the flames and the tribesmen, Horn and his men had only one way out, onto the road. Yet they were far from helpless; at the very least it was still in their power to kill Wilby. Too tense to speak, the two men stood watching the slope ahead. The fierce wind cooled Keogh's sweat and made him shiver.

In two minutes the white men came spilling down the hillside like termites from a log. The fire had come close behind them, devouring the bush almost at their heels as they ran clear. Wilby, the hood gone from his head but his hands still tied, moved shakily and stumbled. It was Van Heerden now who held in one hand the end of the rope tied around the black man's waist, in the other hand his machine pistol.

"Bastards!" said Moorcroft hoarsely, but he was not watching the men. Three or four hundred yards ahead the helicopter had appeared from the smoke clinging to the edge of the hillside. It hovered above the road and then settled, the rotor blades still spinning slowly. Horn and his men, breaking cover at the foot of the hill, turned onto the road and ran towards the machine.

Moorcroft and Keogh leapt into the Land Rover, knowing suddenly that they were just as powerless to stop Horn as they ever had been. They saw Wilby, exhausted, slip and fall to his knees and Van Heerden drag him to his feet and push him forward. The first of the Bamangwatos were running down the hillside, but they would be too late to stop the white men. The two from the Palapye bar, at the front of the group, were barely a hundred yards from the helicopter.

320

Horn followed fifty yards behind. Only Wilby, at the back, was delaying them.

He fell again, pitching forward to lie full length in the dust. Van Heerden stopped and tried to lift him, but by this time he could not be moved. Coolly the big Afrikaner glanced back, gauging the distance of the police vehicle and the nearest of the pursuing Africans. He bent over Wilby, cocked the machine pistol, and held it to the back of his neck.

Keogh flinched. Moorcroft swore. Then Van Heerden's head blew apart.

In the madness of the moment it seemed to happen spontaneously. The back of his head shattered in a spray of red vapour before he was flung off his feet and went cart-wheeling across the road. The radio operator, running a little way ahead, was kicked several yards sideways into the bush. Moorcroft jerked the Land Rover to a stop and said blankly, "Yusuf!"

Through the roar of the fire on the clifftop Keogh had hardly been able to separate the two sharply defined cracks. Yusuf was up there with the big Winchester, shooting at the white men through a telescopic sight at a range of a hundred yards.

Above all he must have wanted Horn. The small man was still fifty yards from the helicopter, unaware of what had happened behind him and racked with coughing as he ran. The first two of his party were scrambling through the door of the Alouette and the blades were spinning fast, whipping up a screen of dust. Yusuf shot one of the men. His leg crumpled beneath him as a soft .458 bullet smashed the bone. He was dragged aboard. Horn turned a startled face for an instant towards the clifftop, ducked below the whirling blades, and dived into the helicopter. The other two men piled in behind and the machine lifted and backed away into the smoke.

Moorcroft had run forward and helped the dazed Wilby, smothered in dust, spattered with Van Heerden's blood, back to the safety of the Land Rover. Behind it the Bamangwatos stood in a silent staring row. The helicopter appeared for only a few more seconds, well to the north, circling once before it vanished behind the line of hills.

It seemed typical enough of Yusuf that he should have failed to kill Horn simply through neglecting to count the number of rounds in his magazine. But it was impossible to say whether it was also by accident that he had not left himself enough time to get away from the cliff. The fire had encircled him and raced in a final suicidal sprint to the edge. In ten minutes it had burnt itself out, leaving behind it a great black swath of charred ground and smouldering tree stumps. Yusuf had not tried to jump. Moorcroft said he must have suffocated in the smoke before the flames reached him.

25

Wilby went back to the Zambian border the same night, with a strong police escort but without the diamonds he had come to collect. They were contraband, and technically still the property of De Beers; the Botswana Government had no option but to confiscate them. Keogh was indignant but Wilby did not complain. He seemed grateful enough to be alive. The two men had hardly met, and both were glad to keep the acquaintanceship slender. The episode was over, after all; there were too many raw and recent memories.

Keogh and Rina were lodged for three days at the home of a deputy commissioner of police in Gaberones while the legal, diplomatic, and administrative mess was cleared up. In fact it proved easy enough; most of what Moorcroft called the bumf could be quietly buried, as Yusuf had been. A brief telegram had gone to his wife explaining that he had died in a bush fire. She did not ask for further details. It was tacitly understood that there was no point in trying to have Horn extradited for the murder of the two Congress officials who had travelled south with Wilby, just as it was understood that the South Africans would not ask for Keogh to be returned. Improbable excuses were privately offered and accepted by both sides; as the Commissioner of Police himself soothingly pointed out to Keogh, they could not afford a confrontation.

They were driven to Francistown by Moorcroft. He said good-bye and handed them over to another police patrol for the journey north to the Zambezi. For most of the way they sat silent in the back of the truck, absorbed in their own thoughts about each other, wondering how the enforced partnership would work out. Near nightfall, as they approached the river crossing at Kazungula, Keogh looked up and found Rina smiling at him, and they stood up and kissed in the swaying truck, and he guessed it would be all right.

Outside, the acacia trees stood in silhouette against a superb African sunset, flaming bands of orange and mauve and purple stacked on the horizon. Keogh counted up the days and found it was Thursday; he might even get back in time for the presentation of his medal.